LATE
TO
THE
PARTY

KELLY QUINDLEN

LATE
TO
THE
PARTY

ROARING BROOK PRESS · NEW YORK

For my godmother, Patty Kearney Lister.
Thank you for seeing us as we really are.

Praise for

LATE TO THE PARTY

"Perfectly captures the joys and hopes and thrills
of being a real, authentic teenager . . . A fantastic
read for queer teens today."
—KACEN CALLENDER,
Stonewall Award— and Lambda Award—winning
author of *This Is Kind of an Epic Love Story*

"*Late to the Party* is right on time to being your
favorite read. I didn't want my time with
Quindlen's characters to end."
—SARA FARIZAN,
Lambda Award—winning author of *If You Could Be Mine*

"A stunning journey of discovery and friendship."
—MASON DEAVER,
bestselling author of *I Wish You All the Best*

"A heartfelt exploration of self, love, and friendship . . .
Quindlen has written a slow-burning, exquisite
book well worth savoring."
—AMINAH MAE SAFI,
author of *Tell Me How You Really Feel*

"A celebration of late bloomers, queer solidarity,
and friendships both old and new. This book has
a permanent place in my heart."
—DAHLIA ADLER,
author of *Under the Lights*

1

IT WAS THE FIRST DAY OF SUMMER, AND IT WAS RAIN-
ing, but not hard enough to keep people out of the pool. We watched
them from inside Maritza's car, parked at the top of the clubhouse
parking lot, with the windshield wipers dragging and the engine
humming beneath us. JaKory was leaning forward from the back
seat, his arm bumping against mine in the passenger's seat, but I
hardly noticed. I was transfixed by the people swimming in the rain.

"Let's go in, just for a minute," Maritza said. She was trying to
sound bold, but I could hear the strain in her voice.

JaKory inhaled sharply. "No, thanks," he said, shaking his head.
"The rain's gonna pick up, and there could be lightning. They really
shouldn't be in the water."

It was a group of kids our age, maybe seven or eight of them.
They were splashing each other and cannonballing off the diving
board and drifting into the corners to make out. We were parked

right by the gate, only a few yards from the pool, close enough to see their grins. I wondered if we knew them, if we went to school with them. I wondered why they scared me so much.

"Do they live in here?" Maritza asked.

"I don't know," I said, peering harder at their jubilant faces. "I guess they must."

It was something I should have known, given that it was my neighborhood pool we were parked in front of, but there were so many houses in my huge, sprawling subdivision that it was hard to keep track of who lived in them.

"They look like they're having a blast," Maritza said, her expression hungry.

"What if they get in trouble?" JaKory asked. "What if the lifeguard bans them?"

The lifeguard was blowing his whistle so hard that we could hear it from inside the car, but the kids in the pool ignored him. Beyond them, huddled under the canopy that housed the bathrooms, was the usual pool crowd: moms, little kids, swim coaches. They watched the madness with disbelieving frowns on their faces, their towels wrapped tightly around them.

Maritza looked at me. "What do you wanna do, Codi?"

A crack of thunder sounded above us, but the swimmers were oblivious: They had started a chicken fight, the girls squealing on top of the guys' shoulders, the rain hitting them at a slant. My stomach felt like it was reaching outward, yearning to be in the water with them, yearning for that raw recklessness. It was a feeling I'd had more and more lately.

"We could wait it out . . ." I said.

"We've been waiting for ten minutes already. It's time to shit or get off the pot."

Maritza's biting tone grated on my nerves, but I'd learned over the years that she was chastising herself more than us. She had always been her own harshest critic.

"Why don't we just go home and watch a movie?" JaKory suggested. "We can swim tomorrow instead."

Maritza hesitated, her eyes fixed on the pool. Then she turned off the ignition, reached around JaKory, and grabbed a towel from the back seat.

"*Maritza*," JaKory whined.

"What?" she said, her voice high-pitched. "We've been dying to swim for *weeks*. I'm not giving that up just because the weather won't cooperate. Besides, those kids are swimming, so why can't we?"

She meant it rhetorically, but it sounded more like a plea. We were silent for a beat, looking at each other. Then Maritza opened the door, covered her frizzy dark hair with her towel, and dashed out into the rain. JaKory and I looked at each other, already knowing how this would play out, before we grabbed our own towels and followed her.

It was pouring. My feet were instantly soaked, and the towel over my head was useless. In a matter of seconds the rain got worse, pounding down on us. We caught up to Maritza as the wind picked up and the trees started dancing. Another crack of thunder shook the sky.

"Maybe this wasn't my smartest idea!" Maritza shouted.

"You think so?!" JaKory shouted back.

We hovered at the pool gate, gripping the bars. Water was moving across the pool like sea spray, and the guys and girls were howling with delight. One girl was floating on her back with her eyes closed, water hitting her from every direction.

I looked at my two best friends. Their eyes were fixed on the kids in the pool, and they looked as inexplicably scared as I was.

"I'm going back!" JaKory yelled. "Unlock the car!"

Maritza turned with him, her key already pointed toward the car, but I couldn't tear my gaze away from the pool.

"Codi!" Maritza called. "Come on!"

I took one last look and ran after my friends.

It hadn't rained on the first day of summer in years. I knew this because for the last five years in a row, Maritza, JaKory, and I had gone swimming on the first day of summer. It was tradition to meet at my house, pack a cooler full of snacks, and flip-flop our way through the burning late-May sun to the clubhouse at the front of my neighborhood. "Clubhouse" sounds bougie, but all the neighborhoods in the suburbs of Atlanta had clubhouses, and all the clubhouses had pools, and all the pools were filled with toddlers in soggy diapers and kids who'd just finished swim team and brave mothers who'd recently moved down from the Midwest or Northeast and were hoping to make friends in this transient half-southern, half-everything-else place. And then there was us: three teenagers splashing around in the shallow end, totally engrossed in playing a game of Celebrity, or practicing back twists, or guessing what songs JaKory was singing underwater.

We'd started this tradition the day after sixth grade ended. That was the day Maritza and JaKory had shown up at my house with swimsuits, squirt guns, and their summer reading books, and I had been so nervous and excited that I'd painted their portraits as a way of thanking them for coming. Embarrassing, I know, but you have to understand that before that sixth-grade year with Maritza and JaKory, I'd never really had a best friend, at least not the kind who lasted more than a single school year. And I knew it was the same for them, because when I'd gone to their houses a few days later, Maritza had taped her portrait to her mirror and JaKory had tacked his above his favorite bookshelf.

"You made me look so pretty and cool," Maritza had said, beaming at me.

"My mom said you really captured my essence," JaKory had said, trying not to look too pleased.

I'd soaked in their compliments without saying anything, but in that moment, I felt like I'd swallowed the sun.

We'd rediscovered those portraits this past Christmas and nearly died laughing. They looked *nothing* like my friends. Maritza's likeness should have been gawkier, her eyebrows thicker, her nose more beak-like. JaKory's should have captured his knobby elbows, ashy legs, and worrywart expression. I'd painted my friends as I saw them instead of how the world saw them, and now I was starting to recognize the difference.

"You made us look like we were *the shit* in sixth grade," Maritza had said, laughing, as we passed the portraits back and forth.

"Blissful ignorance," JaKory had said, shaking his head in amusement. "Remember when we spent a whole month choreographing dances to that Celine Dion song? We had no idea how uncool we were."

"Oh god," Maritza had muttered, going still. "I think we still don't."

I thought about that conversation for weeks afterward, wondering if it was true, if that was really how other people saw us. Maybe they did. Maybe to them Maritza was just the gawky, outspoken, frizzy-haired dancer, and JaKory was the skinny, neurotic, Tumblr-obsessed black nerd, and I was nothing but the shy, reclusive, practically invisible artist who never raised her hand. Maybe that was why nothing *real* ever happened to us.

With our junior year behind us, things were supposed to feel big and important and, as JaKory described it no matter how much Maritza and I begged him not to, "pregnant with potential." But the thing is, nothing felt big or important or bursting with potential to me. We'd gotten older, and taller, and maybe a *little* less awkward than we'd been the year before, but I'd come to know adolescence as a rolling stretch of hanging out with my friends the same way we always had, without anything new happening.

You know how adults are always talking about teenagers? When I was in fourth grade, my family drove past a house that had been rolled with toilet paper, and my dad shook his head and chuckled *Teenagers* under his breath. My mom griped about Teenagers every June, when dark figures hung over the monkey bars of the club-house playground long after closing hours, but she never actually seemed mad; she seemed wistful. And then there's all those shows and movies, the ones where thirty-year-old actors pretend to be high schoolers, and they go on dates and drive their fast cars and dance at crazy house parties where their fellow Teenagers swing from chandeliers and barf into synthetic tree stands. You grow up with these ideas about Teenagers, about their wild, vibrant, dramatic lives of breaking rules and making out and Being Alive, and you know that it's your destiny to become one of them someday, but suddenly you're seventeen and you're watching people cannonball into a swimming pool in the pouring rain, and you realize you still haven't become a real Teenager, and maybe you never will.

By two thirty that afternoon, we were dried off and well into our second movie, burrowed down in my basement with a feast of soda, Gushers, and Doritos on the coffee table in front of us. Maritza and I were sharing our Gushers packs because she only liked the red ones and I only liked the blue ones, while JaKory didn't like them at all because he had "texture issues."

"Maybe you'll like them better if you eat them on a Dorito," Maritza said, shoving one toward him. "Come on, 'Kory, try it."

"Get behind me, Satan," JaKory said, flicking her away.

"Aww, come on, JaKory," I said, offering him a chip and Gusher of my own. "They're great together. You'll 'ship' them in no time."

I caught Maritza's eye, grinning. There was nothing we loved more than teasing JaKory about his obsessive fandom habits.

"Pretty soon you'll be writing fanfic about them," Maritza said, her expression mischievous. "*Oooh, little Gusher guy, you're so juicy, do that squirty thing for me again.*"

"Shut your filthy mouth," JaKory said as I fell back laughing. "You'd be a terrible fic writer."

Maritza looked genuinely offended. "I'd be a *great* fic writer."

"Shouldn't y'all be focusing on this movie, anyway?" JaKory said. "Or can you finally admit that it's boring?"

"It's not boring," I said, looking at the women on-screen. "Look how beautiful they are."

"That was literally a shot of her bending over a mailbox," JaKory said dryly.

"Women look beautiful from an infinite number of angles, JaKory," Maritza said in her know-it-all voice. "Not that you'd understand."

"I'm perfectly fine with not understanding that," JaKory said. "But lesbians or not, this movie is atrocious. Let's watch something else. How about a gay romance?"

"Ugh," Maritza and I said together.

"Y'all love to outnumber me on this, but I *always* watch your stupid girl-meets-girl movies, even the desperate dramas where one of them gets shot or eaten by a sea monster or whatever."

"This isn't even a drama," Maritza said. "It's a comedy."

"Yeah, and I'm laughing so hard."

"Fine," Maritza said, tossing him the remote. "Pick something else. Give us all the gay."

I guess that was the other part of the equation: the queer thing.

Four months ago, on a bitingly cold January night, we'd been watching Netflix in my basement when Maritza started acting all twitchy and nervous, hardly responding to anything we said.

"What's with you?" I'd finally asked, pausing the movie.

Maritza opened and closed her mouth, seemingly at a loss for words.

"What?" JaKory asked, his brow furrowed. "Did you poop your pants again?"

"Fuck you," Maritza snapped, smacking him with a pillow. "That happened *one* time."

"What is it?" I asked again, pulling the pillow out of JaKory's hand before he could retaliate.

"Well . . . okay," she said in a shaky voice. "So . . . you know how I have that crush on Branson?"

"Yeah?"

"I really like him. Seriously, I think he's so hot—"

"How is this news?" JaKory asked.

"Shut up, ass-wad. The thing is . . . well, I've started having a crush on someone else, too, and . . um . . . it's not a guy."

I'd never seen Maritza look so vulnerable. JaKory and I stared at her for a long moment, and then we glanced at each other to check we'd understood correctly. Then JaKory clutched his hands together and started saying all these dramatic things like *Thank heavens* and *Praise Jesus* and *I'm saved*, and it wasn't until Maritza jabbed him in the stomach that he yelled, "I'm gay, too! Like so gay I can't even handle it!"

"I'm not gay, JaKory, didn't you hear what I just said?! I like them both!"

"Bisexual! Whatever!"

The two of them fell forward into a sloppy hug, laughing with relief. Maritza actually kissed JaKory's forehead in delight, and JaKory couldn't stop wiping his eyes. I could only sit there, stunned, while the two of them calmed down. JaKory wasn't exactly a surprise— Maritza and I had speculated for years that he might be gay—but Maritza liking girls was definitely a shock.

I knew it was my turn to say something, but the words got caught in my throat. I sat there with a weird sense of wanting to freeze time, to remember every little detail of the moment, from the happy tear tracks on JaKory's face to the texture of Maritza's fuzzy orange socks. I could feel my heart banging with the significance of it all.

After a minute, Maritza said, "Well, I guess we can all talk about boys together."

That's when I burst out laughing. Maritza and JaKory stared at me, and I shook my head and the words poured out.

"We can't," I said, "because it turns out I like girls."

The three of us laughed so hard we ended up flat on our backs on my basement floor. Maritza kept squeezing our hands and JaKory kept saying, "What are the odds, though?!" When my mom called us upstairs for dinner, we sat around my family's kitchen table trying to hide our secret smirks until JaKory choked on his water when my dad asked if he wanted a piece of pork sausage.

I guess it was pretty significant that all three of us turned out to be queer. Or maybe it wasn't. Maybe it further explained why we'd always felt a little different from other kids, and why we'd never clicked with anyone the way we clicked with each other. In any case, it made me even more certain that I would never find anyone who understood me like Maritza and JaKory did.

We still hadn't told our parents. Maritza's parents were devout Catholics, and JaKory's mom was burdened with too many nursing shifts, and my own parents thought I was alien enough already, given that I'd inherited none of their perfect, all-American charm. But it went beyond that, too. We hadn't told anyone else simply because it wasn't relevant yet. I'd never kissed anyone, and neither had JaKory. Maritza's only kiss had been last summer in Panama with some boy who hung out with her cousins. In short, we had no experience, so why worry about making an identity claim? Our sexuality—or, as JaKory sometimes called it, our "like-eality"—was something we all knew to be true, but which hadn't really drawn a breath yet.

The thing is, I wasn't sure it ever would.

"God, I want a boyfriend," JaKory said, staring dazedly up at the movie he'd picked. He hugged a pillow to his chest like that would help.

"Me too," Maritza said. "*Or* a girlfriend. Just someone I can send flirty texts to and make out with whenever I want."

"Yeah, and eventually do *more* than make out," JaKory said, wiggling his eyebrows. "But we need to get the first step down before any of that can happen." He took a long breath and sighed. "Damn, I need to kiss someone so bad. Don't y'all wanna kiss someone?"

I nestled further into my blanket. The fact that I was seventeen and had never kissed anyone was *not* something I liked to think about. As much as my friends wanted to talk about it, I never had anything to say. I guess because I knew, somewhere deep down, that simply talking about it would never get me anywhere.

"I've already kissed someone," Maritza said smugly. She liked to remind us of this achievement at least once a week. I caught JaKory's eye and mimed stabbing myself in the face.

"I can see you, asshole," Maritza said, tossing a Gusher at me.

"I know," I said, tossing the Gusher right back. "And by the way, you kissed a *boy*."

"That counts, Codi. I *like* boys."

"Yeah, but don't you want to kiss a girl, too?"

Maritza went silent. She'd gotten more sensitive lately about identifying as bisexual, and for a moment I worried I'd offended her. "Of course I do," she said in a clipped voice. "I actually think it'll be better than kissing a boy."

"How?" I asked.

"I don't know, like . . . more delicate."

"I'd take passionate over delicate," JaKory said, shaking his head. "I want to *feel* something. I want it to be like . . . like the moment you hear a brilliant line of poetry. Like it knocks the breath out of you."

"I think it feels like the top of a roller coaster, just before the drop," Maritza said.

JaKory made a face. "You know I hate roller coasters."

"So? You still know what the top feels like, with butterflies in your stomach and your heart pounding—"

"And like I'm gonna pass out or throw up everywhere—"

"What do you think, Codi?"

I kept my eyes on the TV screen, not looking at them. "I'm not sure," I said, trying to sound uninterested. I didn't want any part of their fantasizing; it embarrassed me almost as much as my lack of experience did.

"You've never thought about it?" Maritza pressed.

I waited a beat. Maritza and JaKory were silent. "I don't know," I said finally. "I guess it's like . . . I don't want to overthink it, because I want it to surprise me when it happens."

They remained silent. Then Maritza said, "Doesn't that take the agency out of it?"

I craned my neck to look at her. "What?"

"I just mean, like . . . you can't just expect to be surprised with your first kiss. Some part of you has to *go* for it. I mean, if I hadn't dropped those hints to E.J., or made an effort to see him, we never would have kissed."

I felt my heart rate pick up. It was typical of Maritza to think she had everything figured out already, but I knew she was right, and I didn't want to admit it. The problem was, I didn't know how to "go for it." I didn't even know where to start.

Maritza's point seemed to suck the energy out of the room. None of us were looking at each other; we were all lost in our own thoughts. Then JaKory said, with his eyes on the floor, "My mom and Philip broke up."

Maritza and I looked up. JaKory's mom had been dating Philip for a full year, and JaKory often gushed that he'd never seen her so happy.

"What?" Maritza gasped. "When?"

"Last week, during finals," JaKory mumbled. "I didn't feel like talking about it. It was easier just to focus on studying."

Maritza and I exchanged looks. JaKory worried about his mom a lot. She'd divorced JaKory's dad years ago, and JaKory was always fretting about her being lonely.

"What happened?" I asked gently.

"She said she and Philip weren't on the same page, that they had the whirlwind but not the calm blue sky."

"Your mom's a fucking poet," Maritza said.

"What if loneliness runs in my genes?" JaKory asked in a low voice. "What if I'll never experience love because I'm just not compatible with anyone else, like my parents?"

"Oh, 'Kory, of course you will," Maritza said.

"You'll definitely find someone," I said, holding his eyes. "You're too wonderful not to."

Even as I said it, I felt a flickering of doubt in the pit of my stomach. If I believed so certainly that JaKory was destined to find someone, didn't that mean I could believe it of myself, too? And yet I couldn't fathom how or when that might happen.

Maritza must have been thinking along the same lines, because she gripped her head in her hands and said, "We'll all find someone. I just need to figure out how."

It sounded more like a wish than a certainty. For the second time that day, I found myself yearning for something that seemed far outside my reach.

Just then, we heard the upstairs door creak open, followed by footsteps pounding down the stairs. I sat up as JaKory pressed pause on our gay movie; luckily, the frame was only showing the interior view of the main character's apartment.

My little brother, Grant, zipped around the corner, sweeping his hair out of his eyes. He looked sweaty the way all fourteen-year-old boys look sweaty, even when they're not. His legs had gotten long but were still so skinny that it almost looked like he was running around on stilts.

"Can you take me to the movies tonight?" he asked breathlessly.

I stared at him for a moment, caught off guard by the request. He hadn't asked me for anything in months, not since he'd hit his growth spurt and started "feeling himself," as my dad put it. Grant and I had been pretty close when we were younger—he'd even danced along to some of the Celine Dion choreography that one time—but over the last year, as he'd started to excel in sports and spend more time with his friends, it had become pretty obvious that he saw me as nothing more than his boring older sister.

"Why can't Mom or Dad take you?" I asked.

"They have that gala to go to for Mom's job," Grant said, rolling his eyes. "They said to ask you. Mom said they give you gas money for a reason. So can you take me?"

"I don't know, maybe. Ask me later."

He dropped his head back like I was impossible. "Come on, Codi, all my friends are gonna be there!"

I hated when Grant mentioned "all" his friends. I always felt like he was doing it on purpose, trying to rub it in that he had a whole crew of people to hang out with while I only had Maritza and JaKory.

"It's only five minutes away," Grant went on. "And it's not like you're doing anything else."

"We're hanging out," I said testily, gesturing between Maritza and JaKory.

"Doing what? Sitting around in the basement like you always do?"

I felt my face go hot. My little brother had recently developed a cruel streak. It didn't come out often, but when it did, I never knew what to say back.

"Grant," Maritza cut in. "If you want us to drop you off, try asking without insulting us."

Maritza often talked to Grant like he was her own little brother. I guess it went back to all those summers she'd spent over here, with Grant following her around trying to impress her with broken bits of Spanish, or maybe it was because she was an only child who'd always wanted siblings. It used to make me proud that she felt so close to him, but lately it had started to dig under my skin. I hated feeling like a wall had gone up between Grant and me, and Maritza's way of talking to him as if *she* was the cool, unruffled big sister only made me feel worse.

Grant took a deep breath through his nose. "If you guys could drop me off tonight," he said evenly, "I'd really appreciate it."

I stared at him. It would have felt so satisfying to tell him no, but Maritza seemed to read my mind.

"Codi," she said.

I ignored her and took a deep breath of my own. "Fine," I told my brother. "Anything else?"

Grant's eyes flicked up to the TV. "What are you watching?"

"Nothing," the three of us said together.

He looked suspicious for a moment, but then he shrugged, dashed out of the room, and thundered up the stairs, shutting the door with a loud snap.

2

WE TOOK GRANT TO HIS MOVIE AROUND SEVEN FIF-
teen. The rain had stopped and the sun was shining meekly as we
wound our way down familiar roads. Maritza drove, mostly because
she liked to be in control, but also because her car was newer than
mine and smelled like her "Summer Rain" air freshener. Grant was
unnaturally quiet on the way there. When he got out of the car, he
looked around at the dozens of people heading into the theater before he turned back to us.

"Can you get me at nine thirty?"

"Sure," Maritza said before I could answer.

Grant seemed distracted. "Thanks," he said, sweeping his hair to
the side. He shut the door and tore off to the ticket window.

Maritza, JaKory, and I went for pizza at our favorite local joint,
Mr. Cheesy. Over the last year, since Maritza and I had gotten our
driver's licenses, we'd come here dozens of times. The guy who owned

the place liked us so much that he usually gave us free sodas, and he'd even tacked a picture of us to the Wall of Fame behind the register. We wolfed down our usual large stuffed-crust Hawaiian while we played MASH on the paper tablecloth, and Maritza and JaKory squealed when they both ended up marrying Michael B. Jordan.

"Let's walk over to Walgreens," JaKory said after we'd paid and stepped outside. "I want to get my mom a card. Or maybe some flowers."

"Your cards are the best," I said, stealing a sip from his to-go cup of Sprite. "What's that thing again? About words being your—"

"Love language," JaKory said automatically. He loved answering questions. "Mine is Words of Affirmation. And yours is probably Quality Time. And Maritza's is being bossy."

"Shut up," Maritza said, shoving him playfully. "I'm obviously Physical Touch."

Walgreens was bright and quiet. We followed JaKory to the greeting cards aisle, where I helped him pick through the Sympathy/Thinking of You section. Maritza got bored and wandered off to a different aisle.

"This one's got a strong spiritual theme, which Mom will appreciate," JaKory said, holding up a beige card, "but this one's *Dancing with the Stars*, and that's our favorite show to—"

"Heyooo!" Maritza yelled, popping around the corner with a plastic archery bow in her hand. "Look alive, bitches!"

She shot a plastic arrow at my hip, followed promptly by an arrow that hit a row of greeting cards. I chucked both arrows back at her while she loaded a third onto the plastic bow. JaKory turned on his heel and stomped away, grumbling about us making a scene.

"Stand still so I can practice!" Maritza yelled, her eyes tracking me in the aisle.

"Are you insane?!" I yelled back, grabbing a stray shopping cart and sending it careening toward her. She screeched and tripped into the endcap of stuffed animals, knocking several bears in Hawaiian T-shirts to the floor.

By the time we finished our arrow war and joined JaKory at the register, he'd already purchased both cards and a pack of Jujubes. It was only with the slightest trace of shame that Maritza pushed the archery set across the counter and retrieved her wallet to pay for it.

"You'll have to forgive my daughters," JaKory told the sour-faced cashier, who made a show of glaring at us. "They don't get out much."

We got back to the theater about fifteen minutes earlier than Grant had asked. Maritza turned off the ignition and we sat with the windows down, enjoying the warm summer air. People were spilling out of the movie theater, but there was no sign of my brother's shaggy brown hair or skinny stilt legs.

It was another few minutes before we spotted him. He was meshed in with a huge throng of kids who were trying to look older than they were. Grant was right in the middle of them, laughing and yelling, posing for pictures and fixing his hair between each take.

"Such a diva," JaKory snorted, shaking his head.

"How many fucking friends does he have?" Maritza said.

"My dad calls them his 'posse,'" I said sarcastically, and Maritza and JaKory laughed.

It was hard not to feel slighted when my parents fawned over

Grant's social life. My dad had been a total frat boy in college, the kind of guy who threw legendary parties and nicknamed all his friends. He still took a trip every winter to go skiing with "the boys." My mom wasn't extroverted like him—I guess I got that from her—but she was magnetic in her own way, always sure of how to speak to people, even if she was low-key about it. Case in point: She won homecoming queen in high school. Dad still teased her about it whenever they went on dates. Mom would come downstairs all dressed up, and Dad would spin her around and say, "Damn, honey, you could've been homecoming queen." Mom's eyes would sparkle, Grant would snort under his breath, and I'd stand in the corner and wonder how I wasn't adopted.

I looked hard at my brother, taking in his exuberant smile, trying to keep the negative swirling in my stomach at bay. Then I realized something seemed . . . *off*. Grant had wandered away from the group and over toward a pillar, and his mannerisms were stiff and jerky. He looked almost nervous.

A little current seared in my stomach.

"Who's he talking to?" I said, more to myself than my friends.

Maritza tapped an archery arrow on the steering wheel. "Probably Ryan, right? Or Brian? Whatever his doofy friend's name is."

"No," I said, trying to make her understand, "it's someone different. Look how he keeps touching his hair."

Maritza and JaKory went still, watching closely. All three of us were silent. Then Maritza said, "Do you think he's talking to a girl?"

I couldn't answer. My breathing was pinched; my nerves were on edge.

"He's moving again," JaKory said.

Grant stepped into the white lights streaming down from the

building. And then, as I'd known instinctively, a girl moved out from behind the pillar.

She was a skinny girl with braces and long, thick hair, and she was smiling at my little brother in a nervous, timid way. Grant was holding his arm to the side, nodding his head too much, and shifting his weight from one leg to the other.

"Holy shit," Maritza said slowly. "He's on a date."

My whole body felt cold and contracted. It was like the universe was playing a joke on me, and I had unwittingly participated in the setup. While my friends and I were lamenting our lack of romantic experience in the basement, my little brother had conned us into driving him to *a date*. I knew Grant was growing up, that he had started caring about girls, that pictures and popularity were part of his currency now . . . and yet I'd never stopped to consider that he was truly becoming a Teenager, and that he might be doing a better job of it than me.

The girl said something. She looked self-conscious. Grant inched a step closer, brushing his hair out of his eyes.

"He's gonna kiss her," JaKory said breathlessly.

I wanted to look away, to hide my face in my hands and pretend this wasn't happening, but I couldn't.

Grant hovered. The moment went on too long, and then it was lost. Finally, the girl leaned in and hugged him. She kissed him hastily on the cheek, then spun around and hurried off toward a group of giggling girls, a secret grin on her face.

Grant stood frozen. He dropped his head back and took a deep breath.

I took a deep breath, too, and looked around at Maritza and JaKory. They met my eyes immediately, and it was clear all three of us were feeling the same thing. I had an awful, twisted sense of relief, like I'd just gotten borrowed time on a deadline I hadn't realized was coming.

"Should we text him?" Maritza asked quietly.

Before I could answer, Grant looked our way. He watched us watching him, and his face froze.

"Shit," I said. My own voice sounded strange.

Grant looked away, glaring. Then he steeled himself and walked toward us, his head down, his posture rigid. His friends were calling after him, but he ignored them. He opened the car door and slid into the back seat without a word.

I wanted to say something, to channel my dad and make a joke that would burst the tension, but I'd never known how to do that. Maritza turned up her music to cover the awkward silence, and we drove out of the theater lot without speaking.

When we reached the first stoplight, Maritza broke the silence.

"So . . . how was the movie?"

Grant shifted in his seat. "Stupid."

I looked at my brother in the rearview mirror. He was slumped against the window, his cheek in his hand. The big sister in me wanted to comfort him, to offer my counsel like I had when we were younger, but I didn't have the experience needed for this kind of advice.

"Grant," Maritza said, in a would-be soothing voice, "we didn't mean to see that happen—"

"I don't wanna talk about it," Grant snapped.

My nerves were on edge again. I willed Maritza to drop it, to let us go home and pretend like nothing had happened, but Maritza wasn't the type to let things go.

"That girl obviously liked you," she said. "I could tell by the way she was looking at you."

Grant said nothing.

"I know it's scary to make a move," Maritza plowed on, "but you'll get another—"

"Maritza," I said loudly. "Do us all a favor and *shut up*."

Maritza looked scandalized. The light turned green, and she jerked the car forward.

"Just trying to be helpful," she spat, "considering his older sister isn't saying anything—"

"He doesn't need your help," I said, my face flushing.

"Yeah, well, he definitely doesn't need *yours*."

"What's that supposed to mean?"

"All right, hold on," JaKory said, spreading his arms between us. "Let's just take a second. We're all feeling a little vulnerable—"

"We're fine," Maritza barked.

"Maritza, stay in your lane—literally and figuratively. Codi, let it go. Grant's fine. He doesn't want anyone's help, and that's his prerogative."

"I wouldn't need *y'all's* help anyway," Grant huffed.

JaKory, offended now, threw up his hands and turned away toward the window.

Grant's words stung. It took me a beat to catch my breath, but then I twisted around to glare at him, my heart rearing. "You shouldn't need *anyone's* help," I said. "You're too young to be worrying about this anyway."

Grant glared back at me, not bothering to lift his head off the window. "I'm fourteen. Everyone my age is dating."

"Yeah, well, they shouldn't be."

"You're probably just saying that because *you've* never dated. I'll bet you've never even *kissed* anyone, none of you have—"

My whole body burned.

"Shut up, Grant! Of course I've kissed someone, and even if I hadn't, you can bet I'd never chicken out on it!"

"Fuck you, Codi!"

"HEY!" JaKory said, his voice booming. "Stop talking, all of you. Just *stop*."

A loaded, searing silence swept through the car. I faced the windshield without seeing it, my insides burning. I was angry, I was hurt, and I was embarrassed, but more than anything, I hated myself and the limited world I'd been living in.

"You should put your seat belt on, Grant," JaKory huffed.

Grant didn't move. I wanted nothing more to do with him, but the big sister in me couldn't let it go.

"Grant," I said, my voice hard. "Seat belt."

Still, Grant didn't move.

"What is wrong with you?" I said, whipping around to look at him again. "Put your seat belt on! Now!"

The way Grant looked at me then—murderous and resentful—confirmed we were strangers like never before. That my little brother had grown into a popular, self-possessed, too-cool-for-you Teenager who didn't need his dorky older sister for anything. He buckled his seat belt in one swift, angry motion, then dropped his forehead against the window and didn't speak again. When Maritza pulled into our driveway a few minutes later, he raced out of the car without bothering to shut the door.

My friends and I sat with the car still running, the music still playing. I didn't have anything to say, especially not to Maritza.

"I'll see you later," I said, getting out of the car. I didn't bother to invite them in.

My brother's room was the first off the upstairs landing. I stood in front of his door for a long minute, feeling the vibrations from his loud, blaring music. The hand-painted sign from my grandparents was still affixed to his door: a small wooden rectangle with footballs, trains, and *Grant's Room* written in swirly, child-friendly lettering.

I did something I'd never done before and held up my middle finger to his door.

Alone in my bedroom, I looked around and took stock of my world. Maritza's NASA sweatshirt that I'd stolen a month ago and kept forgetting to give back. A battered copy of a Doctor Who novel JaKory kept bugging me to read. Selfies of the three of us in my basement, in the school courtyard, in the Taco Bell drive-through.

No sign of a life any bigger than this. No wilted bouquets from the prom, no blurry photos from late nights I couldn't remember, no movie ticket stubs from a date with a pretty girl. The burning embarrassment I'd felt in the car was gone, but now there was a furtive pit of shame in my stomach, threatening every idea I had about myself.

My brother was becoming a real Teenager. He'd met up with a girl at the movies tonight, had probably paid for her ticket and bought her candy from the concession stand and held her hand in the dark space of the theater, and after the movie he'd spun her away from his sea of friends and come so, so close to kissing her, and I had watched from my spot in my best friend's car, fresh off an evening of playing with kids' toys at the pharmacy.

How had I gotten to be seventeen years old without anything *happening*? Surely my dad had enjoyed his share of wild adventures by the time he was my age. And surely Mom had kissed a few boys by the time she was crowned homecoming queen. They always talked about high school with that wistful tone in their voices, with that mischievous gleam in their eyes. What had their high school summers been like? What had they gotten up to on those late nights, in those fast cars? And what had their friends been like? Were they anything like mine?

Maritza and JaKory. They'd always been the center of my life, but suddenly my life felt so small. How much of that had to do with them, and how much of it had to do with me?

3

I WOKE EARLY THE NEXT MORNING. IT WAS RAINING again, and for a while I lay there listening to it, letting the feelings from last night wash over me. My parents had come home late from their gala, speaking in low rumbles, their dress shoes clacking on the kitchen floor. I'd pretended to be asleep when my mom had poked her head into my room.

When I finally came downstairs, the rain had let up and the sun was reaching through the windows, pearly white and timid as it stretched across our family room. Grant was in the kitchen, eating Froot Loops. He made a show of clanging his spoon around the bowl and keeping his eyes on the kitchen TV. I ignored him and poured my own bowl of cereal, but when I opened the fridge, something was missing.

"Are we out of milk?"

Grant said nothing, but when I looked at his bowl, I saw he'd

poured way more milk than he needed. His Froot Loops were practically drowning in it. The empty milk gallon was on the stool next
to him. I shoved the refrigerator door closed and grabbed a banana
instead.

JaKory called around noon, asking if I wanted to get coffee.

"Is this because you wanna talk about last night?" I asked.

JaKory sighed, long and pained. "Don't you?"

The small pit of shame still hummed in my stomach. "Maybe,"
I admitted.

"The sun's out," he said enticingly. "You could do some painting."

I laughed. He knew how to hook me. "I'll pick you up in fifteen
minutes."

The Chattahoochee River was the most underrated thing about
Atlanta. It wound through the northwest side of the city's perimeter,
long and sprawling and glistening. No one really talked about it, but
we drove past it all the time, even when crossing the interstate. It was
like an open secret, something we forgot was there.

Our favorite coffee shop was right on the banks of the Chattahoochee, in a quiet little haven nestled behind the highway.
The shop itself was in a huge, multistory cabin, and the grounds
stretched out along the river, carefully landscaped with close-
cropped grass that extended to the nettle-strewn tree line. You
could walk along the river rocks or sit in one of the Adirondack
chairs overlooking the water, listening to the steady rush of the
river sweeping past. Usually, when my friends and I came here,
we'd take our backpacks and stay for hours. Maritza would spread
a blanket and practice yoga, JaKory would sit at a picnic table and

lose himself in a book, and I'd sit across from him, painting the brightest colors I could find.

Our usual table was still damp from the rain. I brushed off my side without caring too much while JaKory methodically dabbed every part of his bench with a napkin. By the time he was finished, I had already dug my sketchbook and watercolors out of my bag. There was a patch of vibrant marigolds by the water that I was excited to paint.

We were quiet at first, but it wasn't strained—more like a gentle blanket. I could sense we were about to have a heart-to-heart. JaKory and I were good at those. We may have tried to save face with Maritza sometimes, but with each other, we always said exactly what we were feeling.

"Did you feel horrible yesterday, too?" JaKory asked.

I looked up from the colors I was mixing. "The worst I've felt in a long time."

JaKory was silent. Then he screwed up his mouth and said, "I went home and wrote a poem about it."

I smiled wryly. "'Course you did."

"There was one line I really liked. '*My youth is infinite but my fears are intimate.*'"

I mixed my orange and yellow paints. Such bursts of color, such vibrant promises, like the infinite youth JaKory spoke of. And yet those intimate fears loomed larger.

"I'm scared, too," I admitted. "Scared of . . . I don't even know what."

"I'm so pissed at myself," JaKory whispered. "I always knew I was different . . . black, nerdy, queer . . . but that's not why I'm missing out. It's because I'm standing in my own way. I know it."

I wilted. JaKory was speaking the same truth I felt in my bones. Did Maritza feel that way, too? Were all three of us stuck in a co-dependent friendship because it was easier than facing our individual inertia?

"What are we supposed to do?" I asked quietly.

JaKory held my eyes. "Maritza has a plan. She's on her way to meet us so we can talk about it."

I stared at him. "What do you mean, 'a plan'? I thought this was just you and me hanging out. You know I don't feel like talking to her after how she acted last night. Didn't you hear what she said to me? *He definitely doesn't need your help.*"

"She didn't mean it."

"You know she did."

"We're family, Codi. Families fight and make up."

"So you invited her without telling me?"

He looked past me. "Here she comes. Just listen and keep an open mind, okay?"

I spun around, caught off guard by this whole setup. Why was JaKory prepping me for a hangout with Maritza? Why did I feel like I was being ambushed?

Maritza approached cautiously, watching the ground like she might trip any second, even though she was the most graceful of the three of us. She sat next to JaKory and placed a large croissant on the table like a peace offering.

"How's it going?" she asked, looking directly at me.

"Fine," I said, not meeting her eyes. JaKory eyed the croissant, but I ignored it and went back to my painting.

"How was the dance camp meeting?" JaKory asked, clearly trying to break the tension.

Maritza was on our school's varsity dance team, and this summer she would be working as an assistant teacher at the middle school dance camp. It was a highly selective position that only a handful of dancers had been chosen for, and Maritza was elated, especially because it would help with her application to Georgia Tech in the fall. The only downside was that it was a full-summer commitment, which meant she'd be missing her family's annual Panama trip for the first time ever.

"Fine." Maritza shrugged. Her eyes darkened. "Except Vivien Chen was being a snotty bitch again."

Vivien Chen was Maritza's sworn enemy. She was in our class at Buchanan High School and was one of the smartest, most accomplished people around. Unfortunately, she had a knack for high performance in the same exact things as Maritza: science and dance. This past year, Maritza and Vivien had been in the same honors physics class *and* had competed for the position of dance team captain. And while Maritza had earned the better grades in physics, Vivien had ultimately won out as dance team captain. Maritza had taken it pretty hard; on the day their coach had announced it, back in April, she'd cried for two hours in my car.

"JaKory said you have a plan," I said pointedly, glaring at her. "I'd rather hear about that than Vivien Chen."

Maritza stared at me for a beat. Then her words tumbled out, loud and fast as ever. "Listen, I'm sorry about last night. I shouldn't have made that dig at you, Codi. I was just—I was caught off guard. I never imagined in a million years that your little brother would go on a date before I would. Before any of us would."

The only sound was the rushing of the river. I stared at my watercolors, trying to make sense of my emotions.

"Codi-kid," Maritza said, using the old nickname. She nudged the croissant toward me. "I'm sorry, okay? It was a dick thing to say. I was just feeling shitty about myself, and . . . well, I think we were all feeling shitty."

She tore the croissant and held out a piece to me. I was still annoyed, but my urge to hear her plan outweighed it. I met her eyes and took the piece she offered.

"Ha," she said, grinning. "Softening y'all with food always works."

"Shut up," I said, rolling my eyes and dipping my piece into her fresh coffee. "Are you gonna tell me what's going on, or what?"

She tapped her fingertips together, giddy. "Okay, so . . . you know that girl Rona, on my team?"

"The one who used to sit in Ben Reed's lap while Mr. Clanton 'rested his eyelids' during health class?" I asked. "Yeah."

"She was talking to me at the meeting just now, and she mentioned this party she's going to tonight. This guy Ricky Flint, he just graduated, is having it at his house. Rona said anyone could come. And guess where he lives?"

A sense of apprehension trickled over me. "Where?"

"In your neighborhood, Codi." She said it like a punch line, her eyes bright and fiery. Next to her, JaKory nodded triumphantly. It was obvious she'd already told him this part.

I knew where they were going with this, but it wasn't something I wanted to hear. We were falling into a conversation I wasn't ready for.

"And . . . you think we should avoid driving that way in case they accidentally set the house on fire?" I said.

"Ha, ha," Maritza said, rolling her eyes. "But for real, wanna go?"

They looked at me expectantly. JaKory nodded very slightly, like he was trying to encourage me.

"Not really," I said quietly.

"But think about it!" Maritza insisted. She moved to straddle the bench so she was facing me directly. "It's so close, we could *walk* there. That way we could drink!"

"Drink?" I repeated, feeling dazed. "Since when do we drink?"

"Since today, because I want to try something new. We'll drink, and we'll meet new people, and maybe—*maybe*—there will be a cute girl or guy that we can talk to, and flirt with, and *kiss*—I mean, isn't that what you want?"

I looked to JaKory for help, but he avoided my gaze.

"We can't just go to some random guy's party," I said.

"Why can't we?"

I struggled to articulate what I was feeling. "We—we don't—I mean, what are we gonna do, just waltz in there and act like we were invited? We won't know anyone. We've never even been to a party before."

Maritza leaned forward, an urgent energy about her. "Listen to me," she said. "Last night we picked up your little brother from a *date*, something none of us have ever experienced, and we watched him almost kiss a girl for the first time, something I've been wanting to do for *ages*. Didn't that feel as shitty for you as it did for me? I'm tired of feeling like I'm missing out. We keep hanging out just the three of us, doing the same shit we always do, watching bad movies we've already seen . . ." She clasped her hands in front of her and steeled herself. "We need to try something different, meet people who are different. It's like Einstein said: The definition of insanity is doing the same thing over and over again and hoping for a different result."

I looked between them. "This isn't an experiment, you guys," I said, trying to slow them down, to make them see reason. "We can't just throw stuff at the wall and hope it sticks. We need to think this through, figure out how to make ourselves ready—"

"Our entire adolescence is an experiment," Maritza cut in. "And it's time to try something new. Now. *Today.*"

I sat in silence, a wave of panic crashing over me.

"She's right, Codi," JaKory said quietly. "We're obviously not happy with how things are going, so we need to make a change."

I looked at Maritza. "Why did you tell JaKory the plan first? Why didn't you tell us together?"

They exchanged brief, meaningful looks that made my stomach turn.

"*What?*" I asked.

"Well—it's just—don't take this the wrong way, but I knew you'd be the harder one to convince. You're more . . . you know . . ."

"What?" I asked sharply.

"Complacent," JaKory said, wincing.

"I'm not complacent!" I yelled. "Not any more than *you*, anyway!"

JaKory's eyes sizzled. "Yeah, well, I'm done being complacent. I'm done being afraid."

Maritza's words had obviously gotten to him. She had drawn a line in the sand, marking herself as brave, daring, and adventurous on one side, and marking me as cowardly, weak, and stagnant on the other. JaKory was aligning himself with the side he wanted to be known for.

"I'm sorry," Maritza said, without sounding like it. "It just feels like I have to push you more. You're so content to flap around in your comfort zone."

"Don't talk to me like that," I said, my voice rising.

"Then stop acting like that," she countered, her voice matching mine.

"Like what?"

"Like you're *small*. Like you're afraid of everything."

"I'm not afraid—"

"I think you are. You've always been afraid to put yourself out there, even when you want something badly. Can't you see you deserve bigger things, Codi?"

My chest was heaving; my cheeks were burning. Never before had Maritza attacked me like this, going straight for my weak points like my brother did. I glowered at her, and she glowered back, and there was something more than anger in her eyes. It took me a beat to recognize it, but when I did, my stomach plummeted.

It was worse than anger, worse than pity: There was something in Maritza that was ashamed to be my friend.

All the breath seemed to go out of me. Just when I'd started to worry that I was outgrowing my best friends, *they* had rushed to the same conclusion about outgrowing me. They were ready to leave me in the dust and set off on their new adventure together. I stared at the two of them like I'd never seen them before. In a way, I felt like I'd never truly seen myself before.

"Well?" Maritza said after a heavy pause. "Are we gonna go tonight?"

There was silence for a long, hanging moment. I watched the rushing river. The moment stretched on.

"No," I said. "If this is really how you guys think of me, then I don't want any part of your stupid plan. Y'all have fun."

As I stood up, I caught them looking away from each other. An impenetrable wall seemed to solidify in my chest, and suddenly I was desperate to get away from them.

I stayed in my room that night, playing music and sketching for hours. It was comforting and familiar, but several times I found myself staring at my sketchbook without seeing it, lost in visions of Maritza and JaKory at that party. They were somewhere here, in my neighborhood, but not to hang out with me. That had never happened before.

Were they relieved I wasn't with them? Were they meeting new friends who were cool and outgoing? Were they sneaking off into dark corners for those make-out sessions they were so desperate for?

Around midnight I decided to go to bed, but just as I got up to brush my teeth, my phone chimed with a text.

> **Maritza Vargas:** *Are you up? I know I'm not your favorite right now but I drank too much and can't drive home, can you come meet us and drive my car back to your house??*

I stared at the message for a while. Competing emotions jostled for attention inside me: hurt, resentment, even a bitter desire to say no. But then I imagined Maritza trying to drive them home after she'd been drinking, and I thought of what could happen to them, and that thought was unbearable to me.

I pulled on my shoes and answered before I lost my nerve.

> *Send me the address.*

4

IT WAS A HUMID NIGHT. THE STREETLAMPS WERE ON,
casting light onto the pavement below. I hurried along the sidewalk,
checking the directions on my phone. The address Maritza had sent
was just past the clubhouse, so I knew where to go until I reached that
point. It was the same familiar path the three of us had walked a
hundred times.

I wasn't nervous until I came upon the street where this guy lived.
I didn't know him, but the idea of anyone who was bold enough
to throw a party in his parents' house was intimidating to me. It
was strange to realize that this guy made the same drive home from
school that I made every day, that he grew up swimming in the same
neighborhood pool as me, and yet his whole approach to life seemed
to be vastly different from my own.

My phone led me to the end of the street, where the cul-de-sac
was. I walked slowly, making my way toward a long line of cars, cars

that I knew must belong to people at the party. How did it feel to be one of those people? What was it like to lie to your parents about where you were going, and to pick up your friends along the way, and to hope—maybe even know—you'd hook up with someone cute once you got there?

Just before I reached the first car, I passed a cluster of towering magnolia trees, their leaves whispering in the night. I hastened to move past them, gripping my phone tightly, still lost in my daydream about the party.

Then I heard something. It was a boy's voice, low and agitated.

"We've been out here ten minutes already—"

Another boy's voice, even lower than the first one, broke in. "It's fine, they won't notice we're gone—"

"Dude, you always say that, but we've had more than one close call already—"

The voices were coming from the trees. I stood frozen on the sidewalk, my heart hammering in my chest, listening without meaning to.

"I'm going back," the first voice said. "I'll catch you later."

And then, before I could move, his dark shape emerged from the trees.

I was about to say something, to make my presence known so I wouldn't alarm him, when—

"Wait," said the other boy, darting out to catch up with the first. I saw the outline of his arm reaching for the first boy's, trying to hold on to him, and a moment later their bodies were fused together, mere feet from me, and I heard sounds I'd only heard in movies.

The only thought in my head was *kissing*. These two guys were *kissing*. And I was standing there, paralyzed in the dark, witnessing it.

"Okay, okay," the first boy said, his voice softer now. He took a breath and pulled away. "Enough for now."

And then he turned, and he took a rough step forward, and he saw me.

My mouth was open, ready to explain, but—

"Who is that?!" he yelled, jumping back.

The second boy, the one who had darted after the first, hurried forward. For an infinite second, he was silent and still, hovering over me. Then he shone his phone flashlight right into my face.

I threw my arms up, trying to block out the glaring white light, but it was everywhere.

"Who are you?" the second boy asked, his voice harsh on my ears.

I felt a strangling panic in my chest. My mind wasn't working properly. Neither was my voice.

"I said, *Who are you?*" the second boy repeated. "What are you doing here?"

"Sorry," I managed, my heart thudding painfully, my hands over my face. "I was just—I was—I was walking."

"You were *walking*?"

"Yeah," I breathed. "To the end of the street."

"Why?"

"My friends are at a party down there. They're drunk and need me to drive them home. I walked here from my house."

"Your house?"

"I live in the back of this neighborhood."

There was silence, but then: "Whose party are they at?"

"I don't know, some guy from Buchanan, I can't remember his name."

The boy went quiet. A beat passed. My heart was still drilling against my ribs.

"Could you—" I began, trying to sound confident. "Could you turn off that light?"

There was silence for a long beat, and then the light went off. I lowered my hands and blinked into the darkness, but all I could see were white spots.

"Goddamnit," whispered the first boy. He was breathing shallowly. "I told you something like this would happen."

"Don't worry," said the second boy. "She's not gonna say anything to anybody, are you? You probably can't even see us, right?"

"No, I can't," I said quickly.

"I'm going back," the first boy said. "Don't let her follow me."

"Wait," said the second boy. "Wait, dude, come on!"

My eyes readjusted to the darkness. I could see the first boy running off, fading into the night, and the second boy watching him go. Then the second boy turned back to me. We stared at each other through the darkness. The silence between us was pressing.

"I'm sorry," I said finally. "I didn't mean to walk up on you."

He ignored me and walked back to the trees. I could just see his outline, tall and broad in the dark. He stood absolutely still, and then, without warning, he rammed his hand against a tree.

My pulse quickened in alarm. This guy was a stranger, and he was clearly unstable. I took a hasty step back, but then—

He was whimpering. I could hear it from where I stood on the sidewalk. He slumped against the tree, cradling his injured hand.

I froze for the second time, torn between two instincts.

The night was loud in my ears. The streetlamp ahead was bright and beckoning. Behind me, the guy was drawing pained, ragged breaths.

I walked back to him.

He was shaking his hand in the air, cursing under his breath. I hovered next to him, poised to run in case he got violent again.

"I'm fine," he grumbled, without looking at me. "Go find your friends."

He sounded lonely, dejected, almost like he'd expected to end up in this very spot. He was still breathing hard, flexing his hand gingerly. I stepped closer and grabbed his wrist.

"Stop moving," I said.

He stilled. I held his hand and shone my own phone light now. His palm was torn open and covered in blood, but the back of his hand and his knuckles were fine.

"You didn't punch it?" I asked. "You just hit it?"

"I knew not to punch it," he snarked. "Not a fan of broken knuckles."

"But you're a fan of broken skin?" I asked, unable to help myself.

He yanked his hand away. I lowered my phone, and we stood facing each other beneath the tree.

"Who are you?" he said.

It was the third time he'd asked, but his tone was softer now.

I blinked at him. I was still nervous, but I knew it was only fair to tell him, especially now that I'd witnessed such a vulnerable moment.

"I'm Codi. Teller."

"Codi Teller," he repeated, like he was testing it out. "And you go to Buchanan?"

"Yeah, I'm a junior—I mean, rising senior. Who are you?"

It took him a few seconds to answer. "Ricky Flint," he said at last. "I'm the guy whose party you're trying to get to."

For a second I couldn't think at all. This whole incident already felt surreal, and now it was almost comically absurd. I couldn't believe the boy whose party I'd been thinking about all day, the boy I'd imagined to be the very essence of a Teenager, popular and cool and inherently *straight*, was out here hiding in the trees after kissing another boy.

"Are you gonna tell anyone?" he asked.

I could tell he was trying to keep his voice steady, but there was the faintest crack in it.

"It doesn't matter to me," he went on, "but it—it matters to him."

It was unexpected, the way he said it. It wasn't in a guilt-tripping kind of way; it was more like he was acknowledging me as an equal, like he knew I had witnessed this private, delicate thing that I could use against him and the other boy if I wanted to, and he was laying it out there, giving me the choice.

"No," I said, looking over at him. "I'm not gonna tell anyone."

He stared at me for a long moment.

"Really, I promise." I hesitated, feeling my way into the words that followed. "I mean, I get it. If I was the one having a party—which, just, wouldn't happen, but if it did—I'd be out here, too, trying to kiss a girl."

He didn't react at first. Then he asked, in an uncertain voice, "A girl?"

"I like girls," I said, with a confidence I didn't feel.

Until that moment, I didn't appreciate how big of a deal it would be to tell someone other than Maritza and JaKory. I felt vulnerable and powerful in the same breath.

"Oh," he said finally. "Yeah. Cool."

I'd hoped for a grander reaction, but maybe he didn't realize what it meant for me to share something like that with a stranger.

"Um . . . that other guy . . ." I said. "Is he . . . your boyfriend?"

"No," he said, very definitively. "No, we're just . . ."

He lapsed into silence, shaking his head. I was burning with follow-up questions about the two of them, but I kept them to myself.

"What are you gonna do about your hand?" I asked.

"Oh," he said, as if suddenly remembering it. "It's not a big deal. I've been hurt worse in football."

Football. This was the kind of guy who was engaged in extracurricular life, who was known for doing big things, who probably had a ton of friends even if I couldn't imagine it right now.

"I'm gonna get something to clean this up," he said, turning away from the trees. "Um. Are you still coming to my party?"

"Oh, right, yeah," I said, following after him.

It was an abrupt change from the moment we had just shared by the trees. All of a sudden we were walking down the sidewalk together as if it was something we did every day, like two friends walking to our next class. I felt that jarring sense of intimacy that comes with walking in step with someone you don't know; I was almost bizarrely aware of how my body moved, and how his moved next to mine.

We passed several houses before we reached the heart of the cul-de-sac. The streetlamps were more concentrated here and I could better see what he looked like. He was a tall, muscular black boy with heavy-lidded eyes, and when he looked sideways at me, I could see he was handsome.

"Why didn't you come to the party earlier?" he asked. "With your friends?"

"Oh. Um." I wasn't sure how to answer without revealing how uncool I was. "Parties aren't really my thing."

He nodded. "I get that. Parties can be hit-or-miss."

I looked at him. "Have you had parties before?"

"Once or twice. My older sister got away with it tons of times, so I figured I'd carry on the legacy. I don't like hosting all that much, but nothing else was going on, and my parents are out of town for the long weekend, so I thought it would be good to . . . you know . . ." He gestured awkwardly. "Have a chance to see people."

The way he said it, I wondered if "people" meant the boy he was with in the trees. We reached his driveway and stood together beside the mailbox looking up the small incline toward his house. The lights were on and the distant pulse of music drifted down to us. There was a sign in the front yard like the ones that every graduating senior in our neighborhood had on display—CONGRATULATIONS, RICKY! BUCHANAN HIGH SCHOOL GRADUATE—and next to that, a University of Georgia garden flag planted in the grass.

"You're going to UGA?" I asked, impressed. The University of Georgia was almost impossibly hard to get into; only the best students from our school were admitted. I was already dreading the application I'd have to complete in the fall.

"Yeah," Ricky said, as if it was no big deal, "been dying to go there since I was little."

"Wow."

He didn't elaborate. He was looking down at his hand, still covered in blood.

"Hey, Codi?" He hesitated, looking carefully at me. "Before you leave with your friends . . . could you do me a favor? Could you sneak in there and grab some antibiotic and bandages?"

I stared at him. He couldn't possibly have understood the enormity of what he was asking me—of how terrified I'd be to venture into a party by myself—but I didn't know how to explain it to him.

"I'd do it myself," he said apologetically, "but I don't want to deal with all the questions."

"I—I would," I said, "but—but I don't know anyone in there."

He looked at me for a long beat. I felt small and insignificant, doomed to be the same limited person I'd always been, the same person Maritza and JaKory seemed to believe I was.

Ricky nodded like he realized he'd made a mistake. "Right, no worries, I get it. Um . . . it was nice to meet you."

He offered me his good hand. I stood still, not wanting to say goodbye to him, not wanting to say goodbye to the version of me he'd met by the trees.

My youth is infinite but my fears are intimate.

The definition of insanity is doing the same thing over and over again and hoping for a different result.

This was my chance to make a different choice, even if—especially if—it scared me.

"Actually . . ." I said, looking up at him. "Where do you keep your first aid kit?"

The music was loud; that was the first thing I noticed. The second was the sheer number of people filling the house. Most of them were concentrated back in the kitchen, at least as far as I could tell, but there were still kids clustered in the hallway and the foyer. Some of them were groups of people talking; others were guys and girls brazenly making out in front of everyone. I felt like I was watching the kids in the pool again—except this time I was in the water with them, and I didn't know how to swim.

My heart was hammering and my hands were sweaty. The staircase was on the opposite wall, and I moved in that direction, focusing on nothing but the picture frames hanging above it. I had to excuse myself past a crowd of girls who were huddled together, laughing and yelling in high-pitched voices, but none of them seemed to notice me. I was just about to reach the bottom step when someone grabbed me from behind.

"Heyyyyy! You made it!"

Maritza was squeezing me too hard, talking too loudly in my ear. Then JaKory was hanging all over me, yelling, "This party's amazing, Codi! I feel gregarious! I feel *fun!*"

I'd never seen my friends drunk before. Maritza's eyes were heavy and unfocused; JaKory's grin was wide and worry-free. They seemed slightly drunker than everyone around them, but no one seemed to notice.

"I can't believe you came inside!" Maritza beamed. "Let's get you a drink!"

"No, that's okay—" I tried to say, but they dragged me through the foyer and into the kitchen, where the music was loudest and where the air was hot and swampy from all the people gathered together. Before I could refuse, Maritza pushed a beer into my hand.

"There are so many attractive people here," she whispered. Her breath smelled like straight alcohol. "Hot guys *and* hot girls, but I don't know how to talk to any of them!"

"She got shot down," JaKory said, hanging off my shoulder. "It was so heartbreaking, Codi, I could feel it in my chest."

"JaKory thinks that short white guy is hot, but he won't go anywhere near him!"

"I can't be a failure," JaKory whispered, wobbling where he stood. "Am I a coward, Codi? Tell me I'm not a coward."

"Are you driving us home, Codi? I'm sorry we got drunk, I didn't mean to, but I was nervous, and I'm sorry I was an asshole, but you can't forget that we're best friends and I love you to the moon, okay?"

I looked into their hazy eyes. The hurt I felt from earlier was still fresh in my chest, but I didn't have time to deal with it right now. I needed to get back to Ricky. "Look, guys, I have to use the bathroom, okay? Wait here and I'll be right back."

I handed them my untouched beer and pushed my way through all the hot, sweaty bodies until I was back at the staircase again. I hurried up it, praying no one would be at the top.

"Hey!" someone yelled from below. "Upstairs is off-limits! Ricky's rules!"

I could feel my neck burning, my heart pounding harder, but all I did was glance back for the quickest second, mouth *Bathroom*, and hope the guy wouldn't yell at me again.

I found the bathroom easily. It took all of two seconds to locate the antibiotic ointment and bandages inside the medicine cabinet and another few seconds to wet a hand towel from the closet, and then I was faced with going back downstairs. I took a deep, calming breath and pushed myself to leave before I could think twice about it.

No one said anything as I came rushing down the stairs, but right before I reached the front door I had to stop. A girl I vaguely recognized was trying to take a picture of some other girls, and I had almost walked right into it.

"Oh, sorry—" I said.

"Sorry, go ahead—" she said.

"No, you go ahead—"

"Thanks—"

"Do you want me to take it? So you can be in it, too?"

I said it automatically, impulsively, forgetting that I didn't want to be there, forgetting that my hands were full of first aid supplies and a wet towel. It was almost like this casual, cool part of my brain spoke before the real me could take over, and for a moment I was stunned by my own voice.

And then the others reacted. I could tell instantly that I had said the wrong thing: The girls who were lined up for the photo shifted uncomfortably, and the girl taking their picture smiled like she was trying to recover from being stung.

"No, that's okay," she said in an overly bright way, "but thank you."

She turned back to take the picture. I waited for them to finish, knowing my face and neck were red and blotchy. *This* was why I didn't go to parties or talk to anyone other than Maritza and JaKory: because I didn't know what to say, or do, or even how to *be* around other people my age.

"Have at it," the girl said, handing her phone off to the other girls, and then she turned and looked at me.

"Thanks for waiting," she said. "They've been asking me to take that picture for like ten minutes."

It was hard to look straight at her. She had beautiful sea-green eyes and a warm smile I didn't feel I had earned.

"I'm sorry if I said something awkward," I blurted out.

She shook her head. "You didn't. It's just . . ." She checked behind her and lowered her voice. "They're all going to UGA next year, so they wanted a pic together, and I . . . um . . . didn't get in."

I blinked at her, unsure of what to say. She smiled a small, close-lipped smile that told me she was devastated but trying to keep perspective on the whole thing, and I couldn't believe she was trusting me, a person she didn't know, with this thing that was obviously paining her.

"That was shitty of them to make you take it, then," I said.

She broke into a looser, more genuine smile. "Yeah, it was, right? I'm not even that close of friends with them." She looked intently at me, and her eyes took in my face in a way I wasn't expecting. "I know you from school, right?"

A warm wave spread across my chest. Ricky hadn't known me, and no one at this party had looked twice at me, but here was a girl with a pretty smile who recognized me and knew I belonged.

"Yeah," I said, "I'm a junior—"

Before I could go on, two people swooped in behind the girl and started tugging her away, laughing and shouting. One of them was a short, happy girl with red hair, and the other was a big, beefy guy with a buzz cut and twinkling eyes. They were clearly two of her good friends.

"Come on!" the redhead shouted. "Leo and Samuel are shotgunning!"

The girl I'd been talking to was laughing, even as she tried to resist their pulling. "Hold on, guys, I'm trying to talk to—"

"We'll bring her right back!" the guy with the buzz cut told me, spinning her away. "Hey, has anyone seen Ricky?!"

There was a commotion in the foyer as everyone started heading for the kitchen, and suddenly I was the only person left standing there. For a moment, I forgot where I was—forgot, until I looked down to the antibiotics in my hand, that I had ventured into this crazy party to grab first aid for Ricky. I turned away from the raucous sea of people swelling toward the kitchen, and a moment later I was back outside, breathing clear air, letting my nerves settle in the silence.

Ricky was still at the base of the driveway, waiting for me. "Everything all right?" he asked. "It sounded really loud in there just now."

"People are shotgunning?" I said. "Whatever that means."

"Are you serious? Damn it, I told them shotgunning was off-limits."

"They were looking for you, I heard some guy asking if anyone had seen you. Here,"—I handed over his supplies—"let me give you some light."

I shone my phone flashlight as he cleaned his hand, and while I watched him, the heady adrenaline rush I'd felt inside the house seemed to cool and wash away. I felt odd, but it was a good kind of odd—like I'd surprised myself in the best way.

"Thanks," Ricky said, crumpling up the bandage wrapper. "I owe you one. Do you wanna come back in for a while?"

I was caught off guard by him asking. It felt so possible, so clearly within my reach . . . I mean, hadn't I just been in there? Hadn't I talked to someone I didn't know? Couldn't I walk back in there, side by side with the guy who was hosting this party, and feel like I belonged in that space?

I wanted it—and for the first time, I could *admit* that I wanted it—but I didn't want to overdo it. Not tonight.

"I should probably go," I said. "Maybe next time."

Ricky looked like he was trying to figure me out. "All right," he said finally. "It was really cool to meet you, Codi. Maybe we can hang out sometime."

"I'd really like that," I told him.

"And thanks for—um—not telling anyone what you saw."

He looked at me one more time, his eyes serious and careful. Then he turned and disappeared into the house, and I was left on the driveway with a subtly different version of myself.

"This girl was so *hot*, Codi, you have no *idea*—"

"—Where are we? Can we get a cheeseburger?"

"—She had this gorgeous mouth, and eyes that cut straight to my soul, I don't know why she had to walk away like that—"

"—Or nachos! We should get nachos!"

"Will you two SHUT UP!" I yelled, swatting JaKory into the back seat.

We were one turn away from my house, and Maritza and JaKory were even drunker than when I'd first run into them at the party. I'd been trying to drive carefully, not wanting to mess up Maritza's car, but the two of them had been yelling in my ear from the moment they'd met me in the driveway.

"We're home," I announced, turning off Maritza's headlights as I rolled up to my house. "Now listen." I turned to stare them down. "The two of you are *very* drunk, and you're being *very* loud, and my parents are going to be *very* upset if they catch us sneaking in right now. So you're going to follow me down through the basement without talking, got it?"

JaKory giggled in the back seat. Maritza sighed dramatically and said, "You just don't understand how hot this girl was, though."

"Yeah, Maritza, I get it, and I'm sorry you didn't make out with her, but it's time for us to go to bed."

"Will you make us nachos?" JaKory asked.

I sighed. A few days ago, I would have found drunk Maritza and JaKory to be hilarious. But now, after the conversation we'd had by the river, and after the big night I'd had without them, all I wanted was to be alone with my thoughts.

I managed to get them down the driveway pretty easily; JaKory only tripped twice. I got them inside, got all three of us waters and a bag of pretzels, and pulled extra blankets and pillows from the basement closet.

JaKory burrowed into a sleeping bag on the floor while Maritza and I curled up on the couches. For a few minutes we didn't talk, just ate our pretzels and gulped down water. Then Maritza rubbed her hand down her face and said, "It was really fun, Codi. You should've come earlier."

I didn't answer. This was the point where I normally would have told them about Ricky, this raw, three-dimensional boy I'd crossed paths with tonight, and about the moment I decided to walk into the party despite my gnawing fear. But lying there in the darkness, any desire I had to share my experience evaporated into the air. Tonight I'd proved that I could be bigger than they believed. That I could be brave, and daring, and maybe even a hint of a real Teenager. And for now, the only person who needed to know that was me.

"I don't want you to miss out on things," Maritza went on, peering at me through her drunken haze. "You gotta have experiences, you know?"

"Experiences," JaKory echoed from the floor. His eyes were closed and he was breathing through his mouth.

I got up, turned off the light, and curled deeper into my fleece blanket. Within three minutes both of my friends were snoring. I was used to their nighttime breathing, but tonight I couldn't sleep, couldn't turn off my mind.

For the first time I could remember, I left my friends in the basement and went to sleep in my own bed.

5

I HAD TO WORK AT NINE O'CLOCK THE NEXT MORNING, which meant I had to wake Maritza and JaKory up well before they'd finished sleeping off their hangovers. They were groggy and slow-moving, and JaKory wouldn't stop talking about how much he was craving hash browns. I snuck them out through the basement so my family wouldn't notice their obvious hangovers.

"Feels like there's an elephant on my head," Maritza said, hanging over her car door.

"Two elephants," JaKory groaned, rubbing his eyes.

"Yeah, and nothing even came of it," Maritza grumbled. She peered at me from beneath her messy hair. "We missed you, though, Codi-kid."

She said it sincerely, almost like she'd forgotten our heated conversation from the day before. Maritza had always been good at glossing over our sore spots. Usually I appreciated that, but something in me had switched this time.

"Yeah, y'all mentioned that last night," I said brusquely.

Maritza looked hard at me. It was clear she realized I wasn't over our argument yet. "Well, it's true, we really did miss you."

There was a hanging silence. I didn't care to say anything back.

JaKory's eyes went soft. He came over and wrapped me in a hug. "Forgive us, okay? We needed to try something new. Obviously nothing worked out, but at least we gave it a shot."

I returned his hug half-heartedly and backed away from the car. "Y'all get going. I'm gonna be late for work."

Maritza looked like she wanted to press the matter, but for once, she let it go. "And I'm gonna be late for my coffee-within-fifteen-minutes-of-waking-up window," she said. "Come on, JaKory."

"Ugh," JaKory said, tucking himself into the passenger seat, "I can't fathom drinking a scalding-hot coffee right now."

"So let's get iced ones, genius," Maritza said, snapping the door shut.

I watched them pull away from the curb, still squabbling, and as I walked down the driveway to my own car, I couldn't help but feel relieved that they were gone.

I worked at a retail store called Totes-n-Goats. It was a small boutique in a shopping plaza where the main clientele consisted of suburban families and where the developers decorated the lampposts with signs like STEP INTO SUMMER! At Totes-n-Goats, we sold purses, patterned handbags, and pretty much anything that featured a decorative animal on it. I'm not sure who had the genius idea to combine these two things, but many women in the area seemed to love it. They'd come in to buy hand towels with alligators on them, salt and pepper shakers shaped like bunny rabbits, even lip balm with owls on the label. One lady came in every week to ask whether we'd "gotten our paws" on any gazelle items yet.

My proper title was "Sales Associate," but I'm not sure it was all that fitting, considering I never spoke to customers if I could help it. "Creeper Who Lingers in the Back of the Store and Gets Flustered When Customers Ask for Help" might have been a better title. I think the only reason they kept me around was because I knew how to work the register and I never complained when they asked me to pick up another shift.

That Saturday was the start of Memorial Day weekend, so we were expecting heavy sales. My manager, Tammy, made me follow her around the store after we opened. She wanted to coach me, once again, on how to approach customers with a "bubbly" attitude.

"Smile bigger, Codi, bigger," she said, pointing her fingers at the corners of her mouth. "You can't look like you're on your way to the dentist."

Tammy could be patronizing sometimes, but I knew she was grateful that I'd agreed to pick up extra shifts that weekend. Two of the other sales associates, who were in college, were going to the lake to celebrate the long weekend with friends, and they'd called out last minute.

"Thank Jesus we can count on you," Tammy said, smoothing a zebra sticker onto my name tag. "You're not another one of these young people who put partying and friends over showing up and being responsible."

I didn't reply. A group of kids my age was hovering in front of the store window, passing a cigarette between them. They were laughing and smacking each other's shoulders, obviously enjoying an inside joke.

Tammy followed my line of sight, and her face darkened immediately. "Oooh, these yahoos," she muttered, marching toward the door. "Come on, Codi."

"Oh, no, I'll just—"

"You need to learn how to handle these situations," she said, tugging me by the arm.

We spilled outside the door. The group of kids looked up, not bothering to hide their cigarette.

"Y'all are loitering," Tammy said, hands on her hips, "and I'll need you to leave before I call plaza security."

One of them laughed in her face. I recognized him as an underclassman from my school. "We're just having breakfast," he said, rumpling his hair.

"Oooh, and nicotine counts as a breakfast food now, huh?" Tammy asked shrilly.

"All part of a balanced diet, ma'am," one of the girls said with a smirk.

"There are benches down that way," Tammy said, pointing with a stubby finger. "Why don't you take a little walk and have a nice *sit-down* breakfast."

It was clear she thought that was a real mic-drop kind of line. The kids snorted at her, kicking their feet off the wall. Their eyes skirted over me as they slouched away, and I averted my gaze, trying to be invisible.

"Damn yahoos," Tammy repeated once we were back inside the

store. "I tell you what, I don't miss that stage of life at all. Not for a second. I used to wake up hungover as all hell, sprawled on the floor of my friend's room, thinking I was such a badass. You see this little beast?"

She rolled up her sleeve and showed me a discolored tattoo on her forearm.

"It's a Mexican tequila worm," she said. "That's what happens when you mess around at that age."

"I kinda like it," I told her, my cheeks still flushed.

"Ah, well," she said, with a faraway look in her eyes. "We're all young once, I guess."

I couldn't believe it. Even *Tammy*, with her animal stickers and goat sweaters, had once been more fun and outgoing than me.

I felt on edge for the rest of my shift. When I finished at one o'clock, I drove back to my neighborhood and made a full stop at the clubhouse stop sign. I sat there for a minute, my car idling, until another car pulled up behind me and honked.

My house was toward the right. On impulse, I turned left instead.

Ricky's house was different in the daylight. No line of cars, no pulsing music. It even looked smaller, maybe because there weren't dozens of teenagers inside.

I wasn't sure what I was doing there. Ricky probably wasn't even home; he was probably out with his friends, or maybe with that guy. And if he was home, he had probably only said we should hang out to be polite.

Still, there was something inside me that wanted to be there. I remembered that brave, wild buzz of dashing into his house last night, and I wanted that feeling back.

I stepped hesitantly up to the front door. Last night I'd pushed it open in a rush, anxious to break through the throng of people. Today I'd have to ring the doorbell and wait for Ricky to find me standing there with my armpits sweating and my khaki work shorts sticking to my thighs.

I pressed the doorbell. A muffled musical note sounded inside the house, and a few seconds later, Ricky opened the door.

"Codi," he said, his tone surprised. He looked tired and hazy, like he hadn't gotten much sleep.

"Hey," I said casually. "How's your hand?"

He seemed caught off guard by the question, or maybe by my being there altogether. "Oh. It's all right," he said, showing me the fresh bandages. "Probably good that I put antibiotic on it right away. Thanks for that."

"No problem."

He nodded, and I nodded, and I had no idea what to say next. "So, uh . . ."

"Did you and your friends get home okay?" he asked.

"Oh, yeah. They were pretty drunk, but it was a quick drive, just two minutes to the back of the neighborhood."

He was watching me curiously, just as he had last night, like he still wasn't sure what to make of me.

"So . . . did you come over to hang out?" he asked.

"Oh, yeah, um . . . I just thought maybe you'd want some help cleaning up. There were a lot of people here, and it's probably annoying to have to clean up by yourself . . ."

He watched me again. There was something guarded in his expression. But after a beat, he swung the door back and said, "You know how to clean a place without making it look suspiciously perfect, right?"

He stood aside and let me into the house.

Cleaning up that party was like showing up to an archaeological dig. Every spill, stain, and half-drunk beer told a story of the people who'd been there last night. Ricky had an answer for everything I found. The half-eaten pizza with Sour Patch Kids on top was the work of Julie Nguyen, whose culinary concoctions got more and more bizarre at every party; the cheap black cape belonged to a guy I knew from lit class, Daniel Parrilla, who had earned the nickname "Magic Dan" because he liked to perform magic tricks whenever he got drunk ("Kid's a crock," Ricky said); the bright green thong I found in a potted plant was probably Aliza Saylor's, who apparently couldn't stand to wear underwear once she got three Lime-A-Ritas deep.

"So she just starts stripping?" I asked, using a paper towel to drop the thong into a trash bag.

Ricky laughed, his eyes on me. "You sound terrified."

"I mean, it's . . ."

"Weird," he said, nodding. "Yeah, her friends always joke they're on 'Panty Patrol.'"

I glanced at the thong again, heat creeping up the back of my neck. "I assumed someone lost it from, like, hooking up in here."

"In the corner of the family room?" He looked amused, like he thought I was trying to be funny. "Nah. I'm pretty sure the hookups were happening in the laundry room, 'cause my friend Leo was staked out there all night. He always shows up early for a party, finds the spot where people are most likely to hook up, stands there like a bouncer, and charges everyone ten dollars to use it."

"You're kidding."

"It's how he pays for his weed. Leo's a businessman."

I felt pretty out of my element, hearing all this stuff, but Ricky didn't seem to be judging me. He played James Brown's greatest hits while we scrubbed the kitchen floor, and he sang along enthusiastically, dancing on his hands and knees. He caught my eye, daring me to dance with him, but I could only laugh and scrub harder at the floor.

"You need to loosen up," he said, sitting back on his feet. "Can't even dance to James Brown? Do I need to switch to Enya or something?"

"Very funny."

"Come on, show me some moves."

I blushed and shook my head, going back to my scrubbing. Ricky seemed perplexed, but he didn't say anything more. He turned up the music and moved to clean a spill off the kitchen stools.

We worked without talking until I found a collection of aluminum beer tabs on one of the counters.

"Do we need to throw these away?" I asked.

Ricky went still. "Oh . . . yeah," he said, staring hard at the tabs. "That was probably Tucker—um, the guy that—that you saw me with. He always does that."

He scooped them into the trash bag he was holding. I got the impression he would have saved them if I hadn't been there.

"I'm hungry," he said, not quite looking at me. "Do you want some lunch?"

He made us grilled ham and cheese sandwiches. I sat plopped on a stool at the now-clean counter, leaning on my elbows while he hovered next to the stove. He flipped the sandwiches more than he needed to, and when he wasn't flipping them, he tapped the handle of the spatula against the counter like someone doing Morse code. I could tell he was agitated, but I didn't know why.

"I never add ham," I said, trying to get the flow of conversation back. "I just make straight-up grilled cheese."

"You've been missing out."

"My best friend won't eat grilled cheese at all. He says it's disgusting."

"Huh," Ricky said, like he wasn't truly listening. "Remind me not to hang out with him."

"Yeah." I paused. "He's gay, too, though."

Ricky made a stilted movement. I waited for him to say something, but he didn't.

"He's the one I came to pick up last night," I went on. "Him and my other best friend, who's bi. You didn't meet them, did you? Maritza Vargas and JaKory Green?"

Ricky separated our sandwiches onto patterned ceramic plates. He wasn't meeting my eyes. "No, I don't think I did."

"Oh. Well, they said they had a great time." I paused. "Do you, um—do you always get to see that guy—Tucker—at parties?"

Ricky paused in the middle of passing my plate over. He looked up at me, his eyes careful and hard.

"Codi," he said, "do you think I need you or something?"

I looked back at him, completely thrown by his serious tone. "What?"

"You think I'm, like, the closeted kid that needs someone to talk to? Is that why you came over?"

"No—?"

"Because it's fine that you know about me and Tucker, but I don't *need* anyone to know. It's not a big deal. We're not a serious thing. I'm not worried about it. I'm fine."

I felt the heat rise in my face. Just like last night, with the girl who was trying to take the picture, I had somehow said the wrong thing.

"I'm not . . ." I said, struggling to explain. "I mean, I didn't come over for that."

He stared at me. "What did you come over for?"

It was rough, the way he asked it, and it left me feeling so stupid and small that all I wanted was to curl up from the shame of it. How foolish had I been to show up here? How presumptuous, how silly, to believe this boy would want to invite me into his world? Ricky's dancing, his teasing, all of that felt a million miles away. I wanted nothing more than to bolt out of his house and never come back.

But then I remembered, with a clawing at my stomach, the accusation Maritza had leveled at me by the river:

You've always been afraid to put yourself out there, even when you want something badly.

I steadied myself. Whatever happened, I wasn't going to lose this chance at friendship because I was too chickenshit to put myself out there.

"I'm not trying to help you, or whatever," I said slowly. "I mean,

I've never even—I've never even kissed anyone, or dated, so how would I be helpful to talk to? My friends wanted to come to your party so they could meet new people, and I—I didn't want to come, but then . . . Look, I don't really know how to do this, okay? I don't hang out with anyone other than Maritza and JaKory, but last night I met you and . . . and you seemed like someone I wanted to know. And I haven't wanted that in a long time. Okay? That's it. That's why I'm here."

Silence. Neither one of us had touched our sandwich. I wanted to look away from him, to be anywhere but in this vulnerable moment, but I forced myself to hold his gaze.

"Should I go?" I asked.

Ricky looked hard at me. The music blared in the silence between us.

On impulse, I reached for his phone and turned up the music. James Brown's "I Got You" roared through the kitchen, and I began to dance without thinking. I threw in as many moves as I could remember from my friends' Celine Dion choreography days, but mostly I was just making shit up, letting myself be a complete fool. I even grabbed Magic Dan's cape off the table and whirled it around like a dance partner.

At first Ricky looked embarrassed for me, and I almost stopped. But then he started to laugh.

"All right," he said, nodding along. "All right."

Before I knew it, he was dancing with me. His moves were smooth at first, but then he devolved into goofiness, matching my energy. We danced until the end of the song, and when James Brown screamed the last "Hey!" I did a kind of crazy pirouette and landed in a heap on the floor, the song's final note ringing in my ears.

Ricky pressed pausc as the next song started up. He was all smiles when he looked over at me.

"Okay," he said, like he'd finally made up his mind about me. "That was definitely unexpected."

I grinned.

He stood watching me for another moment, and then a smirk took over his face. "Let's go out to the deck. I'm gonna show you something."

The deck was bright and burning compared to the coolness of the house. I hovered by the screen door while Ricky stepped his way over to a mess of scattered beer cans. I couldn't help but answer his mischievous look with a smile.

"Last night you said you didn't know what shotgunning was," Ricky said, looking pointedly at me. He walked over to an open box of beer cans and fished two of them out. "I'm gonna fix that."

He was grinning again, like he liked being a bad influence and knew it was exactly what I needed.

A wave of nervousness swept over me. "Right now?"

"You got anything better to do?"

I rubbed my neck. "I mean, I *was* looking forward to that sandwich . . ."

He rolled his eyes. "Come over here."

I went and stood next to him. He held out a beer, and I hesitated.

"Is it gonna make me drunk?"

"A little tipsy, maybe, but not drunk. You'd have to have a few of these for that to happen."

I couldn't figure out what I wanted. I'd never drunk a beer before, but I'd also never *wanted* a beer before, and this seemed like a safe place to try it.

"I won't let anything happen to you," Ricky said. "And obviously you shouldn't do this unless you want to, but for what it's worth, I think you might have fun."

I nodded and accepted the beer he handed me.

"These are gonna be warm," Ricky said, "so it's gonna taste nasty, but that doesn't matter when you're chugging."

"We're chugging?"

"Yeah, we're chugging."

He pulled his car keys out of his pocket and explained what we were going to do. I listened carefully, trying to make sure I understood.

"Dude," he said, clapping a hand to my shoulder. "Breathe. It's not rocket science."

"Right," I said, trying to steady myself.

"You ready?"

I nodded and turned my can horizontally. Ricky stabbed a hole in the bottom of my can, then his can, and we held them to our mouths like we were about to eat corn on the cob.

"Ready . . . and . . . pop the tab!" Ricky yelled.

I popped it open and chugged from the hole in the bottom, throwing my head back wildly. The beer was warm and tasted vaguely of aluminum, but I chugged it down as fast as I could, ignoring the dribble that spilled onto my neck and T-shirt.

"YES!" Ricky shouted, his own face and T-shirt spotless. "You got it! Keep going!"

I drank the last of it and let the can clatter to the deck. I bent forward, hands on my knees, wiping my mouth like a boy would do. Ricky roared with delight and pulled me into a hug.

"That," he said, with his arms around me, "was fucking awesome."

It turned out drinking beer left my stomach feeling swollen and carbonated like I'd been drinking soda, but with one special side effect.

"So this is what being drunk feels like," I laughed, spraying the hose over the beer stains on the deck.

"You're not drunk," Ricky said, chowing down on his sandwich. "You're *maybe* tipsy."

"Either way, it feels good. I'm starting to understand why that girl wants to take her underwear off all the time."

"Please don't do that."

I snorted. "I'll spare you."

Ricky had been right that the beer was gross-tasting, but I was enjoying the effect nonetheless. I felt like I could laugh more easily, like I wasn't so trapped in my head.

"You missed a spot," Ricky said, pointing toward the corner of the deck.

I turned the hose on him, spraying his legs and bare feet, laughing when he dropped his sandwich in shock.

"I'm eating this anyway," he said, picking up the soggy sandwich and stuffing it in his mouth. "Now, c'mere, we'd better spray those beer stains off your shirt."

He wrangled the hose from me and sprayed straight at my torso, drenching my work shirt. I screamed and stole the hose back from him, drenching his T-shirt and athletic shorts.

We dashed around the deck, chasing each other, until we were both soaked through to our skin.

"Shit," I said, pulling off my Vans and stretching my bare feet into the sun. "What now? Do we have more to clean?"

"Fuck cleaning," Ricky said. "It's time for a drive."

Ricky lent me a size XXL T-shirt to wear over my damp shorts. We spread pool towels over the seats of his truck and climbed inside in our bare feet. The interior smelled like *boy*, like sweaty football pads mixed with cologne, and there were hints of Ricky throughout: a brush in the cup holder, a strip of photo-booth pictures sticking out from the side compartment, a graduation tassel hanging from the rearview mirror.

We drove to Sonic, where Ricky ordered us popcorn chicken, Tater Tots, and Snickers Blasts. We sat with the windows down, gorging ourselves on the hot food and fending off brain freezes from the ice cream. Ricky played Nina Simone's "Feeling Good," singing unabashedly along, bragging about how he'd gotten the other football guys interested in her music. Then he kept driving, going nowhere in particular, making turns whenever he seemed to feel like it.

After a while, we ended up along the river. Ricky parked with his truck facing the water, and we kicked our feet up on the dash, slurping the last of the ice cream from the bottoms of our cups.

"So what do you and Maritza and JaKory do when you hang out?" Ricky asked. "Is it anything like this?"

I told him. I talked about our movies, and swimming, and our annual Halloween sleepovers, and how Maritza couldn't make it through a Harry Potter movie without losing her shit laughing at the centaurs, and how JaKory once wrote a poem for every person in my family. I kept checking his expression the whole time, worrying that

I was boring him, but he had this open look on his face that made me feel like he cared what I had to say.

When I'd said enough, I asked him, "What about your friends? What's your favorite thing about them?"

He looked out over the river. A whole minute must have passed, but he didn't seem pressed to come up with the answer right away. Finally, he started nodding to himself and said, "That I feel like I could have met them in kindergarten."

"What do you mean?"

"I didn't meet most of my friends until high school, but every single one of them is someone I could have met on the kindergarten playground—it's natural and easy, nothing held against each other. Remember how easy it was to make friends at that age?"

I let that settle into me; it felt like something I'd forgotten a long time ago, but I knew what he meant. I wondered if Maritza and JaKory felt that way about me, and, more important, if I felt that way about them.

We got back to his house around dinnertime. I changed into my own T-shirt, now dry after lying in the sun. Ricky walked me out to my car and hugged me close like we'd been friends for ages.

"Text me about hanging out again," he said.

"I will," I said, and I meant it.

6

SUMMER KICKED INTO FULL SWING AFTER MEMORIAL
Day. The days became sunny and scorching; my thighs burned when
I plopped into the seat of my car. My dad wore cotton polo shirts to
the office and my mom walked barefoot to the mailbox when she got
home from work. The neighborhood pool was busy with swim meets
and birthday parties, and Totes-n-Goats was flooded with moms
pulling elementary-school-age kids behind them. I worked nearly
every day, rubbing my arms to keep warm in the store's freezing air-
conditioning, then immediately sweating when I stepped into the
parking lot at the end of a shift.

Maritza, JaKory, and I usually spent our summer days together,
but this year, with my job at Totes-n-Goats and Maritza's job at
dance camp, we saw each other much less. Part of me was sad about
it—nostalgic, almost—but another part of me didn't mind having
some space, especially after that day by the river. JaKory, however,

was at a loss for what to do with himself. Unlike Maritza and me, he wasn't working a summer job—he'd never gotten his license, and we didn't have the best public transportation in the suburbs. He was so bored without our usual swimming dates that he took to texting us a running monologue of his thoughts throughout the day.

> **JaKory Green:** *I've decided I'm going to curate my own summer reading list featuring both classic novels and the latest movers and shakers, and maybe once the school realizes how much better it is than their deplorable compilation, they'll ask me to sell it to the district. That'll give me something to do while you two are "working," a.k.a. betraying our childhood.*
> **Maritza Vargas:** *If you were any more dramatic, you'd have your own Bravo show.*

My brother spent those first few days of June at a basketball camp for rising high schoolers. My parents dropped him off before work in the morning, but it was my job to pick him up in the afternoon. Every day I'd wait outside the gym, and Grant would come trudging into the car stinking of sweat, and we'd make the ten-minute drive home speaking only about what our family was eating for dinner. Sometimes there would be a pocket of silence when I would want to say something interesting or funny, anything to make him look at me the way he did when he was younger, but I could never bring myself to do it.

The most exciting thing in my life quickly became Ricky's friendship. We went for more drives, sometimes to pick up milkshakes, other times just to talk. He told me more about his family, his football stats, even the bad dreams he had sometimes; I told him about my art, my brother, and the fear I felt when speaking to people I didn't know. When he scored free Braves tickets from his part-time job at his dad's software sales company, he asked me to go with him to the game, and we ate hot dogs and nachos with our feet kicked up on the empty seats in front of us.

Part of me longed to tell Maritza and JaKory about Ricky, but a bigger part knew to hold it inside for myself. For one thing, Ricky had asked me not to tell anyone about him and Tucker, and I didn't know how I could explain meeting him without bringing that up. But there was a deeper reason that I wasn't really letting myself think about. There was something about hanging out with Ricky that made me feel like a newer, better version of myself, and I wasn't ready to share that version with anyone else, not even—maybe especially not—my two best friends.

On the first Thursday of June, after Maritza and I got off work, we picked up JaKory and went to a park on the Chattahoochee, several miles down from the coffee shop. It was brilliantly sunny, the sky pure blue and cloudless.

We meandered around the people on the park trail, Maritza plucking JaKory away from the speedy runners trying to slip past him. After we'd walked a good distance and the trail had become denser with trees, Maritza found a narrow dirt path that opened onto the river. There was a craggy boulder jutting into the water where we could all sit comfortably, so we plopped down and hung our legs off the sides and watched the kayakers going past.

"We should learn how to kayak," Maritza said, squinting ahead. "It looks like one of those things you do to 'feel alive.'"

"Absolutely not," JaKory said, stretching his gangly legs in front of him. "It creeps me out, how you have to hide half your body in that little boat."

"You're a weirdo."

"I have anxiety."

"About weird things."

It was a gentle day with a breeze coming off the water. I leaned back onto my hands and felt the warm stone beneath my skin. JaKory looked just as content as me, his chin tilted toward the sky, the sunlight gleaming off his new fade. Maritza, however, seemed restless and agitated. She kept tapping a stick against her knee.

"I'm thinking about girls," she announced.

"Gross," JaKory said, with his eyes still closed.

"Are you *not* thinking about guys?"

"No, I was thinking about kayaking accidents."

"You're fucked up," Maritza said breezily. She pivoted to face us better, shielding her eyes with her hand. "So what's gonna be our next move to meet people? I say we go scouting around this park."

I snorted without meaning to.

"What?" she asked.

"You want to meet someone *here*? It's two o'clock on a Thursday. Everyone here is either retired or parents with preschoolers."

"No, I've seen a bunch of hot girls."

"Okay, well, they're probably all in college."

"So? I could date someone college-age."

"No, no, hell no," JaKory said, shaking his head. "I can't date up that far. Too nerve-racking."

"JaKory, of *course* you could," Maritza said. "You're handsome and smart and—well, *sometimes* you're funny—"

"Shut up."

"We can't force something that's supposed to be organic," I said. "It's creepy to just go up to someone in the park."

"We wouldn't be *creepy* about it," Maritza said, though she looked doubtful. "We'd just try to make friends first. How are we supposed to meet someone if we're not trying?"

JaKory and I huffed and whined, but, as usual, Maritza had her way. We walked the park for half an hour, shooting awkward glances at every person we came across. I'd been mostly right: Nearly everyone we passed looked like they were either in retirement or their early child-rearing years. There was one guy who looked like he could be near our age, but JaKory refused to go up to him, much to Maritza's annoyance.

"Sweet salvation," JaKory said as we came upon a taco truck. He turned to Maritza. "Let's accept that this particular experiment failed and it's time to eat our feelings."

"Fine," Maritza sighed. "I should have known this was a stupid idea. There must be something I'm doing wrong . . ."

She trailed off, lost in her thoughts, and I patted her back and steered her toward the taco truck. We got in line behind a gaggle of people who were craning their necks to read the menu board. JaKory grabbed my shoulders and started chanting *Sriracha* under his breath. Maritza, however, was suddenly distracted by something else.

"Dude, look, she's hot," she whispered, nudging me to check out the girl inside the taco truck.

She was a cute girl, it was true: somewhere around our age, with long dark hair beneath a hunter-green baseball cap. Maritza grinned at her like an idiot.

"Let's talk to her," she whispered again.

My stomach jumped with a tiny thrill, but the rational part of me knew how this would turn out. "You go ahead," I told her. "I'll just watch, try to pick up some pointers."

I grinned, trying to show her I was teasing, but Maritza frowned. "You're gonna make me do this alone?"

She sounded serious, like I was truly abandoning her.

"Come on, Maritza, I can't just flirt with someone I don't know."

"But that's the whole point of this exercise. How else would we get to know her?"

"But she's probably not even—I mean, look at her, she looks straight."

"You're stereotyping," Maritza said, crossing her arms, but there was the slightest trace of doubt in her voice.

We reached the truck window. The girl was even prettier up close, and I struggled to hold eye contact as I placed my order, feeling Maritza's and JaKory's eyes on me. JaKory ordered next, smug and cocky, impervious to a gorgeous girl's charm. Then it was Maritza's turn.

"Do you like the chorizo?" she asked the girl in a strange voice.

"Yeah, it's pretty good," the girl said nonchalantly.

"Cool." Maritza hesitated. "Um . . . do you like the carne asada?"

"Yep, that one's good, too."

"Sweet," Maritza said, attempting a brave smile. The girl smiled blandly back. "Um—what about the veggie?"

"Yeah, it's . . . full of great veggies," the girl said. She tapped her fingers, waiting expectantly. Maritza's cheeks turned the faintest shade of pink.

"I'll just have a shredded chicken," she said quickly, ducking her head to busy herself with her wallet.

JaKory and I said nothing as the three of us traipsed to a picnic table. Maritza seemed embarrassed, and we ate our tacos with subdued energy. JaKory overcompensated by exclaiming over every part of his meal.

"Wow, this lettuce is *fresh*," he said. "So green, so *verdant*—"

Maritza swallowed and looked back to the food truck. The line had dwindled and the cute girl was still in the window.

"I'm gonna try again," she said with a steely look in her eye. She turned to me. "Will you come?"

I grimaced. JaKory shot me a look that said *You're fucked.*

"Sorry, Maritza, but I don't think we stand a chance," I said quietly.

Maritza crossed her arms and looked at the girl, then at us, then back at the girl again. For a moment I thought she was going to give in, but then she got up and stalked off toward the food truck, her posture upright and cool.

"What is she *doing*," JaKory moaned.

We watched anxiously as Maritza approached the girl at the window. The girl looked up with a politely puzzled expression when Maritza started talking.

The whole thing took less than thirty seconds. Maritza was wearing her forced-confidence smile, and the girl was forced-laughing, and my chest was locked with stress, and then Maritza was heading back toward us.

JaKory and I looked at each other, waiting for her to sit down, but she marched right past us. We got up and chased after her, flanking her on either side as the grass turned into asphalt.

"What happened?" JaKory asked.

"Are you okay?" I asked.

Maritza stormed all the way to her car, turning to us only once she'd grabbed the door handle. "She wasn't interested."

JaKory and I fell back, looking at each other.

"Why not?" I tried.

Maritza exhaled, long and pained. "She has a boyfriend."

I offered her a sympathetic look. "Was she mean about it?"

"No," she said, avoiding eye contact. She crossed her arms over her chest. "She was really nice."

We stood in a circle, an awkward silence hovering between us. Everything felt stilted and weird.

JaKory wrapped one of his long, lanky arms around Maritza's shoulders. "You tried," he said. "Now you won't spend the rest of the day wondering *what if,* and that's more than Codi and I can say."

Maritza didn't let herself sink into JaKory's hug. She squeezed her arms together and said, "Sorry I tried to force that on you guys. I'm just—I'm *so* tired of feeling like this."

"Like what?" JaKory asked gently.

"Like . . . like I don't know how to do the whole girls thing."

I swallowed. I'd never heard Maritza describe it that way. "I'm sorry," I told her in a small voice.

"For what?" she asked, rolling her eyes at herself. "For not making a fool out of yourself? Forget it, Codi-kid."

I couldn't come up with any words of comfort for her. We climbed into her car and left the park in silence.

"What do you want out of this summer?" Ricky asked the following afternoon. We were sitting at Starbucks, drinking iced coffees with extra sweetener. Ricky had been up at six A.M. the last few days in a row; he'd had some early trainings for his software sales internship, and it was a long haul down to the city, especially with rush-hour traffic. He seemed tired, but the coffee was bringing him around.

"What do you mean?" I said.

"Well, I mean, you've already tried shotgunning . . ." He grinned. "What else are you gonna try? Bungee jumping? Cow tipping?"

"Jewelry heists, maybe."

"Good one."

"I don't know, who says I need to try more stuff?"

He narrowed his eyes at me. "I'm starting to figure you out, Codi Teller, and I know you want more out of this summer than just working at Purses-n-Pigs."

"Totes-n-Goats," I laughed.

He raised his eyebrows, waiting for my answer. "I'm asking because you seem kind of down today. Restless, almost. What's going on?"

I sighed and scooted my chair closer to his, making sure we wouldn't be overheard. "Maritza tried to hit on this girl in the park yesterday, but she got shot down," I told him in a low voice. "And Maritza's *pretty*. Like, a lot prettier than me."

Ricky looked confused, so I elaborated.

"I don't know if I'll ever meet a girl," I told him. "The odds are impossible."

"Says who?"

I stared him down. "Come on, don't patronize me."

"I'm not. Why can't you meet a girl?"

I scoffed. "First of all, how many girls like other girls? Not many, at least compared to the number of girls who like boys. And then how am I supposed to find those girls? I mean, sometimes it's obvious, but sometimes it's not! Like that girl in the park yesterday—I told Maritza she seemed straight, and it turned out she was, but that can't always be the case, right? Like, if I didn't know Maritza, I would have no idea she was into girls. She's been my best friend since sixth grade, but I didn't pick up on it until she flat-out told me. It was obvious with JaKory, but I literally had no idea with her. And *then*, even if I find a girl who likes girls, what are the odds she's gonna like me? What if I'm not her type? What if I'm too boring, or quiet, or—"

"Or kind? Or interesting? Or earnest? Come on, Codi, you're being too hard on yourself. And why are you worried about being *her* type? What if she's not *your* type?"

I met his eyes. "How did you meet Tucker?"

He glanced away, shaking his head. "That's different. It's not a real thing."

"But you've still kissed him."

He looked wildly around, making sure no one had overheard us. "I'm telling you, it's not a thing," he said in a low, hard voice. "I only know him through my friend Samuel because they were on the baseball team together. He and Samuel got to be really tight this year, so we'd hang out with him at parties. That's it."

"Wait. So you've only hung out with him at parties?"

Ricky wasn't looking at me. "Pretty much."

"How did you end up kissing him?"

"What's with the inquisition, Codi?"

He asked it with an edge to his voice, and I shrunk back in my seat.

"Sorry," I said quietly. "I was just wondering."

That defensive look stayed in his eyes for a minute, but then it faded and he shook his head rapidly. "No, that's okay. I'm just not used to . . ."

He trailed off, and there was a swell of pressure between us.

"I'm sorry," he said. "I just don't think you should base anything off my random hookups with Tucker. We barely know each other. The most he ever talked to me was this one day at Sonic, when Samuel went off to call his girlfriend. We sat there by ourselves for a few minutes, and he told me he felt like he didn't fit in on the baseball team, and I was blown away by that. Tucker's the best baseball player our school has, you know? It took me forever to realize what he was talking about. But I didn't even have his phone number until the other day, and it's only because he texted me to make sure you hadn't told anyone what you saw."

It was jarring for me to hear that; I hadn't even considered that Tucker would worry about it afterward. "Is that all he said?"

"Yep," Ricky said bitterly. He fidgeted, tapping the lid on his coffee.

"Well . . ." I said, trying to fill the silence between us. "You're right about me wanting something out of this summer."

He chanced a look at me. "Yeah?"

"Yeah, I mean . . ." I trailed off, shaking my head. It was embarrassing to admit this to him, but I pushed myself to do it anyway. "I want to grow," I said slowly. "I want to become a braver, more outgoing person. I want to *scare* myself, you know? I'm tired of being the quiet artist type."

Ricky blinked, considering me. "What's wrong with being an artist?"

I shrugged. "Don't get me wrong, I love painting. I love my creative side; I'm grateful for it. But I also don't want that to be the only way that I . . . you know . . . engage with the world."

Ricky frowned. "What do Maritza and JaKory think about this?"

I jammed my straw up and down in the coffee. "I haven't talked to them about it."

"Why not?"

"Because they . . . they could never believe that I would be anything more than who I am right now."

Ricky fell quiet, watching me. "Shouldn't your friends see your potential more than anyone?"

I hesitated, trying to decide whether I wanted to have this conversation. I'd never spoken of Maritza and JaKory's shortcomings to anyone, especially not another person our age, but I'd also never had anyone else I could confide in.

I took a deep breath and made up my mind.

"Look, do you know what my favorite thing to paint is?"

"What?" Ricky asked.

"Portraits. I love painting people, trying to capture those little details that make them who they are. Chicken pox scars, or a certain way they move their eyebrows, whatever. I used to paint Maritza's and JaKory's portraits every year when we were in middle school."

"That's really sweet—"

"But a few months ago, we found the very first portraits I painted of them, and they were totally wrong. Maritza and JaKory thought it was hilarious, but I was embarrassed."

Ricky frowned. "But how old were you when you painted those?"

"Twelve, but that's not the point. It wasn't the technical skill that was embarrassing, it was my perception. I painted them like they were *perfect*. I didn't capture any of their flaws. But you know what I found later that night? I found a self-portrait I'd done around the same time, and I had painted myself with *so* many flaws. The longer I looked at it, the better I remembered how I felt that day, when I was looking in the mirror and painting what I saw. I felt like *shit*."

I paused, taking another breath. Ricky watched me heavily.

"I never even told Maritza and JaKory about it. And now I just keep thinking, like, what kind of twelve-year-old knows herself so poorly, or has such low self-esteem, that she glorifies her friends in her artwork but can't even really see herself? And I think maybe that—that I'm still doing that." I took a deep breath. "I've been holding on to Maritza and JaKory *so* tightly, like they're all I could ever have, when deep down I really want the space to try something new, to make new friends, to meet a girl who sees a side of me they'll never see."

Ricky looked steadfastly at me. "Damn," he said quietly. "That's a lot to keep bottled up."

I looked away from him, self-conscious. "It's all hitting me recently. I feel so torn about it. I love Maritza and JaKory, but I also feel this . . . this . . ."

"Resentment?"

"*Yeah*," I said, like it was the most shameful thing I could imagine.

Ricky reached across the table and squeezed my wrist. "I think that's okay, Codi. Sounds normal to me."

I snorted humorlessly. "You said it feels like you've known your friends since kindergarten."

His expression changed; he looked solemn and thoughtful. "I

do feel like that," he said, "but there are still things I need to work through with them. Fears and insecurities I have around them."

I waited for him to continue, but he said nothing else. I let the silence grow around us.

"Ricky?"

"Yeah?"

I breathed in, knowing my question was risky. "Do your friends . . . do they know about Tucker?"

He looked at the ground. I didn't know him well enough to say for sure, but he almost looked embarrassed.

"No," he said.

I nodded. I knew not to press the issue.

"Do Maritza and JaKory know about me?" he asked. He didn't bother hiding the apprehension in his voice.

"No. They don't even know we hang out."

"At all?"

"At all."

He searched my expression. "Trying to keep something for yourself?"

"Yeah," I said apologetically.

He nodded. "I get that. I mean, I keep certain things for myself, too."

I knew he was talking about Tucker, and I took that as his way of telling me not to press him about it any more.

We slipped into silence, taking long drags from our coffee. Then Ricky looked over at me.

"For what it's worth, I think you're a pretty cool person, and I think you can grow into whomever you want to be. Maybe you'll do it with Maritza and JaKory on the sidelines, or maybe they'll be right there on the field with you, but either way, you'll figure it out. I know they have to be good people, because they're friends with you."

I breathed deep into my stomach. "Thanks, Ricky."

He smiled a soft, knowing smile. "Now, about the girl thing . . ."

I laughed. "Yeah?"

"Isn't there anyone you can think of that you might have a chance with?"

"No."

"Even with all the pretty girls at school? You've really never met anyone who caught your attention?"

Something stirred in my mind. I thought of the girl I'd spoken to at Ricky's party, the girl who had recognized me from school, but I didn't know who she was or whether she even liked girls.

"What?" Ricky said.

"Nothing."

"What?" he pressed.

"Well . . . there was a girl at your party. A cute girl. But I don't know her name."

"Did you talk to her?"

"For a second."

"And?"

I told him all about my picture faux pas, and how the girl had been so nice about it. "And she recognized me," I said, trying not to sound too pleased about it. "She knew I went to Buchanan."

"But you didn't get her name?"

"We got interrupted by her friends. They came over and started tugging her away to watch those guys shotgun."

"What'd they look like?"

I described the girl and her friends. Ricky's eyes grew bright.

"Do you know her?" I asked, half hopeful, half terrified.

He grinned, a mischievous glint in his eyes. "I might."

"Ricky—please don't tell her—"

"Relax, Codi," he laughed, holding up his hand. His usual warm energy was back, like he'd drunk some sunshine along with his coffee. "I'll take care of you."

I pestered Ricky with questions on the drive back to our neighborhood, but he refused to tell me anything else. "You'll see," he said, over and over. "I'm gonna make it worth your while."

It wasn't until we turned onto my street that he switched the conversation to something else.

"You know how you said it was obvious with JaKory?" he asked, suddenly low-key again.

"What?"

"When you were talking about Maritza liking girls, you said it shocked you."

"Yeah . . ."

"But JaKory wasn't shocking to you."

I knew where he was going with this, and I tried to sound nonchalant with my answer. "No, Maritza and I thought he was gay for a while."

Ricky glanced at me. "Why?"

I didn't know how to phrase it without making him read into it. "Well . . . the way you can just tell with some guys."

Ricky was silent for a long moment. Then he asked, "I'm not one of those guys, right?"

I wasn't sure how to answer. The truth was he *wasn't* one of those guys, at least not as far as I could tell, but I didn't want him dwelling on that as if it mattered.

"No . . ." I said uncertainly. "I don't think so. But it's not a bad thing or a good thing, it's just . . . you know . . ."

His expression was inscrutable. He didn't take his eyes off my driveway, but he nodded very slightly. "Cool," he said, though he sounded anything but. "Catch you later, Codi."

He gave me a stiff smile, and I clambered out of his truck.

7

JaKory Green: *What's the plan tonight, comrades? I'm thinking Indian take-out and another ~special~ movie*
Maritza Vargas: *You make it sound like we're watching porn. But I'm down. There's that one I wanna watch with the two girls and the spotted unicorn*
JaKory Green: *Sounds kinky but okay*

It was Saturday night, and I was working the closing shift at Totes-n-Goats with nothing to occupy me but my phone.

Until Ricky showed up out of nowhere.

"What are you doing here?" I asked, looking up at the sound of the bell tinkling.

He wandered curiously into the store. "I wanted to buy a goat."

"Funny."

He was dressed like he was on his way out somewhere. He stepped up to the register, his eyes roaming over the line of handbags behind me, and I recognized the crisp cologne he'd worn the night of his party. Was he on his way to another party? And if so, would he invite me to tag along?

"Got a big night planned?" I asked, trying not to sound too eager.

Before he could answer, Tammy swept in from the stockroom, breathless. It had been a slow night, and her eyes popped at the sight of a potential customer. "Hi, can we help you find something? How'd you like to see our panda oven mitts?"

Ricky gave her a polite smile, but the corners of his mouth were twitching. "Uh, no, thank you. I just came by to talk to Codi real quick."

Tammy's expression sank. She threw me a look like I'd offered her a piece of pie and then yanked it away. "Of course," she said, giving him an awkward little bow before she dipped off to the kitchen section.

Ricky turned to me, eyebrows raised in a way that said *That bitch is crazy*. "Is it okay that I came in?"

"It's fine," I said, shaking my head. "She's just not used to me having visitors."

"What time do you get off?"

"Nine."

He smirked like that was exactly what he wanted to hear, and I could tell he was going to spring something on me.

"Wanna come out with me and my friends?"

I processed his invitation slowly. Ricky and I had been hanging out a lot, but it was always the two of us by ourselves. I'd never met any of his friends before. I was flattered—and terrified—that he would even suggest it.

"Do you have something else going on?" he pressed.

I thought of the texts Maritza, JaKory, and I had been sending about our plans to hang out later.

"Maritza and JaKory wanted to watch a movie," I said, biting my lip.

"One of the same old movies you always watch?"

He had me there. I gaped at him, stalling with my answer.

That knowing smirk was still on his face. "Well, if you change your mind, it's shaping up to be a good night. We're grabbing food at Taco Mac, and then who knows what'll happen." He paused, his eyes twinkling. "I'm gonna wait in my car. You can ride with me if you decide to come."

I hesitated. I'd already said yes to Maritza and JaKory, but I knew exactly how a night with them would go. Ricky's offer promised something new.

I exhaled and rolled my eyes at him. "You know I'm gonna say yes."

"I know it," he singsonged. He held up a pack of cocktail napkins featuring a pig in a pearl necklace. "You'll get these for my college going-away party, right?"

Before I could do more than laugh, he turned around and ambled out the door, setting the bell tinkling again.

Tammy reappeared and looked at me nosily. "Is that your boyfriend?" she asked, like she couldn't quite believe it.

"No," I snorted, cleaning a stain off the checkout counter, "not even close."

Ricky played an Aretha Franklin album on the way to Taco Mac. There were a few artists I'd come to realize he played when he was feeling good, and Aretha Franklin was one of them. Even after we'd pulled into the parking lot at the back of the restaurant, he didn't turn off the ignition until the song ended.

"Ready?" he asked.

My stomach was in knots. I had no idea what Ricky's friends were like—what if they were snotty, or mean, or way too cool for me? What if they didn't like me? What if they made him realize he didn't actually like me, either?

"Codi," he said firmly, as if reading my mind. "Relax. My friends are nice. You'll like them." He jumped out of the truck. "Take off your name tag, though."

"Ricky," I said, following him toward the restaurant, "how many people are gonna be here?"

"Just a few," he said, shrugging. "Come on, I've been craving this queso all day."

He steered me into the restaurant. I tried to walk all cool and casual like him, but my heart was hammering and I wasn't sure what to do with my arms.

There was a small group of people stretched across a table in the center of the restaurant, and as Ricky and I approached, they turned toward us with raised arms and goofy grins. I took them in without really seeing them; I was too focused on sitting down so they'd stop looking at me.

"Where've you been?" a loud guy asked. I recognized him as the guy with the buzz cut from Ricky's party.

"I was meeting up with Codi," Ricky said, gesturing toward me. "Everyone knows Codi, right?"

My face burned as everyone looked at me, but Ricky didn't give me time to feel embarrassed: He pulled out my chair, turned to the buzz cut guy, and said, "Cliff, introduce yourself."

Ricky's friends didn't miss a beat. They all smiled and told me their names, and none of them questioned why Ricky had brought me along. Cliff, Samuel, and Leo had been on the football team with Ricky; they looked like they worked out as much as he did, except maybe Leo, who was short and skinny. Terrica bounced in her seat when she said hello; she had delicate shoulders and perfect teeth and looked like she could have been a model. Then there was Natalie, the pretty redhead I remembered from the party, who offered me some of her salsa. And finally, tucked on Natalie's other side—

It was her. The girl I'd talked to at the party. The girl I'd told Ricky about.

"Lydia," she said, giving me a little wave. "Nice to officially meet you, Codi."

I blushed all over.

Under cover of the others talking, I shot Ricky a questioning look, wondering if he realized that Lydia was the same girl I'd been talking about at Starbucks. The smirk he returned told me he knew exactly who she was.

"I hate you," I muttered under my breath.

"You're welcome," he muttered back.

The table was loud and crazy. I was almost overwhelmed, watching them all shout back and forth and steal each other's fries. Terrica was trying to corral everyone into a game, but she was so soft-spoken she had to bang on the table to get their attention.

"*Thank you*," she said, raising her eyebrows. "Can we keep going? It was Leo's turn."

"Noooo," Leo said, shaking his head fast, "it was Natalie's turn." He exaggerated his features to show he was lying.

"You're a fucking liar," Terrica said, "but fine, Nat can go."

"What are we playing?" Ricky asked.

"Don't Judge Me, But."

Samuel leaned forward, addressing me. "You gotta excuse Terrica. She's obsessed with games. Never lets us rest."

"Excuse *me*," Terrica said, smacking his arm. "You can shut up, asshole, 'cause this is an amazing game. Codi, have you ever played?"

I blushed again, surprised at the attention. "Um, no, I haven't."

"Awesome, awesome," Terrica said, clapping her hands while everyone else let out dramatic groans.

"Terrica *loves* explaining things," Ricky said.

"Ignore them, Codi," Terrica said, holding her hands up like she was blocking her friends out. "Okay, so it's pretty simple. Whoever's turn it is says, 'Don't judge me, but . . .' and they follow it with something that's embarrassing or gross or weird about themselves. If that sentence applies to you, too, then you have to drink. The goal is to get as many people to drink with you as you can. Obviously we're playing with sweet tea instead of alcohol—"

"—Which means it's taking longer to get to the sexual stuff," Cliff said, to laughter from the others.

I laughed uncomfortably. "Um . . . cool. Sounds good."

"Right?" Terrica said happily. "Okay, Nat, you're up."

Natalie shook her long red hair. She had a relaxed, self-possessed air about her, as if she didn't take shit from anyone. "Okay . . ." she said, like it was the easiest thing in the world. "Don't judge me, but . . . last year I had a sex dream about the Keebler Elf."

The table erupted in shouts of laughter. I sat still, watching them all, trying to smile so I didn't look out of place. I'd never confessed a sex dream to *anyone*; come to think of it, I wasn't sure I'd even had one yet. Maybe this had been a bad idea, and I should have stuck to my original plan to hang out with Maritza and JaKory. I could just imagine them in this same situation: JaKory would sit silently, arms around his torso, completely out of his element; Maritza would overcompensate by naming the craziest sex dream imaginable, even though it'd be obvious she made it up. They would both be just as awkward as me.

I was deep in my head, still wishing Maritza and JaKory were there, when a sudden pain brought me back to the moment. Ricky had pinched my arm. I looked up at him, startled.

"You good?" he whispered, tipping his head toward his friends, reminding me to be present with them.

I breathed.

Next to him, Cliff was looking fake-horrified, his eyes wide and his mouth hanging open. "This changes everything," he was saying to Natalie, scooting his chair away from her. "We have to break up."

Natalie shrugged and popped a chip in her mouth, completely unfazed. Next to her, Lydia was losing her shit laughing. She had a big, bursting laugh that made her whole face turn pink. Without meaning to, I found myself smiling.

"Should I shrink myself?" Cliff went on, curling up in his chair. "Would that turn you on?!"

Natalie laughed in spite of herself. She grabbed for Cliff's hand, and he pretended to recoil from her, turning to Ricky instead.

"Rick, Rick, can you find me a red hat?"

"Get him a green jacket!" Samuel shouted.

I was laughing now, picturing Cliff, with his meaty arms and square chin, as the tiny little Keebler Elf. Before I could stop it, my voice was out of my mouth, joining in on the joke:

"You'll need pointy ears, too."

It was like time froze: For a second I was free-falling, bracing for the worst. Then everyone laughed. Ricky beamed at me, and my heart soared.

"All right, all right, Cliff's turn!" Terrica said.

Cliff cleared his throat. He was smirking, his eyes dancing. "Don't judge me, but . . . I've hooked up in Samuel's house."

"What the fuck, man?" Samuel said.

"Was it with Samuel?" Leo asked, deadpan, and Terrica swatted him.

"That's at least four of you who have to drink," Lydia said. She looked at Natalie. "I mean, I'm assuming."

"Um, *yeah*," Natalie said, rounding on Cliff. "You'd better mean with me."

Cliff laughed and wrapped his arm around her. "Of course I mean with you."

I looked at the rest of the table, trying to figure out who the two other people were.

"Well, come on, lovebirds," Cliff said. "Or are you trying to tell me you've never hooked up there before?"

He was talking to Samuel and Terrica. They looked at each other, rolled their eyes, and drank.

"Thanks, dickhead," Samuel said.

"You're welcome. Anyone else?"

There was a pause. Then Ricky sighed and took a sip of his Dr Pepper.

"Whoa!" the guys shouted. "Hold up, hold up, hold up!"

"Who'd you get with?" Leo asked.

Ricky shook his head. "I'm not saying."

He was playing it cool—acting like he was the kind of guy who didn't kiss and tell—but I had an instinct about his answer. He'd told me before that he met Tucker through Samuel, and my guess was Ricky had hooked up with Tucker at Samuel's house.

"Typical Ricky," Cliff said, shaking his head. "Won't trust us with his hookups."

"My business is my business," Ricky said.

"Not anymore it's not," Terrica said, "'cause it's your turn."

The table fell quiet. I watched Ricky, waiting to see what he would say, wondering how deep he would go with his friends. Had he *ever* offered a hint of his sexuality?

"All right," he said, clearing his throat. He looked thoughtful for a moment, then gave a slow, careful answer.

"Don't judge me, but . . . sometimes, when I'm alone . . ." He took a breath. "I listen to Nickelback."

The table exploded with shrieks of laughter.

"Come on, man!" Leo shouted. "There are some things you just don't say!"

"I know, I know," Ricky said, burying his face in his hands. "I've never been so ashamed."

It was the first time I'd truly laughed during the game. Nickelback sucking was one of those culture-wide jokes I actually understood, and I knew Ricky well enough by now to appreciate how funny it was that he secretly liked their music.

"And to think," I said, surprising myself again, "you were totally feeling yourself with Aretha Franklin earlier."

His friends roared with laughter again, clapping their hands together like my teasing was the best thing they'd ever heard. I could feel my neck flushing, but in the best way.

"So who's drinking to that?" Terrica said, eyebrows raised.

There was a pause, and then every single one of us took a drink.

"That's what I fucking thought," Ricky said, pretending to glower.

It was my turn now. I took a deep breath, my heart rate picking up. I'd been trying to figure out what to say since Terrica had first explained the game. Natalie and Cliff had made me nervous with their confessions of sex dreams and hookups, but Ricky had given me an opening by talking about music.

"Okay," I said, trying to keep my voice strong, "don't judge me, but . . . I used to think that TLC song was about a boy named Jason Waterfalls."

"Wait, what?" Natalie asked, but I barely heard her over another voice: Lydia had shouted, "What, me too!" at the exact same moment. We locked eyes, and she beamed at me.

"What are y'all talking about?" Cliff asked.

Lydia turned to him, still beaming. "You know that song about chasing waterfalls?"

"I thought they were singing to a guy named Jason Waterfalls," I said, laughing. "Like, 'Don't go, Jason Waterfalls!'"

"Exactly!" Lydia said. "I thought Jason Waterfalls was some really cool, really cute boy, and they were begging him not to leave them."

"Yeah! I didn't even realize it was 'chasing' until, like, seventh grade," I said.

"You are the *only* other person I've met who thought that!"

Natalie cut in, spreading her arms between us. "All right, weirdos, take a drink," she said easily. "The rest of us have ears that actually work."

Lydia caught my eye as we each took a sip of our sweet tea. I had a feeling then, the same kind of feeling I'd had when she recognized me at Ricky's party: a warm, hopeful anchoring, like maybe I did belong.

The game went on, and now, for the first time, I felt I was truly a part of it. I laughed easily, held eye contact when they addressed me, and even accepted the buffalo wing Cliff offered me. I was in the flow of the experience, taking it all in, dazzled to find myself holding my own. If I could have painted that moment to keep it forever, I would have made every texture and color pop with life. Scrunched eyebrows, draped arms, crumpled napkins shot across the table. Yellow lemons, green peppers, brown hands, soft pink lips. Every one of them a small, infinite miracle I never thought I'd know.

By ten thirty, the Taco Mac parking lot was nearly deserted. We clustered around the few remaining cars while everyone debated what to do next. In the end, Leo's insistence to "hit the roof" won out.

"What's the roof?" I asked once Ricky and I were back in his car.

"Leo's mom works for this graphic design firm that's, like, all hipster and 'open office' or whatever. They have access to the roof of the building, so sometimes we go there and hang out."

"And we're allowed to?"

Ricky glanced at me, hedging his answer. "We're not *not* allowed to."

We followed Leo's car, with Samuel and Terrica behind us and Cliff, Natalie, and Lydia behind them. It was only a ten-minute drive, but that was long enough for me to lose some of the confidence I'd built up at Taco Mac. I was nervous about sneaking onto an office roof late on a Saturday night.

We parked our cars side by side in the back corner of the parking lot. Leo swung a backpack over his shoulder, casual and breezy while he took a hit from his vape, and we followed him into the building like it was nothing. I could tell from everyone's chatter that they'd done this a million times before.

"Everyone in?" Leo asked as we crammed into the elevator.

Cliff was holding tight to Natalie; Samuel was doing the same to Terrica. I hung in the corner with Ricky, trying to keep myself relaxed. Lydia slipped into the spot in front of me, and when she turned to face the doors, I caught a whiff of her shampoo.

"Selfie!" Terrica sang, holding her phone aloft.

We squeezed ourselves into the camera frame as the elevator pulled us upward. Natalie pinched Cliff's ass just as Terrica took the photo, and he squirmed and squealed in a goofy, high-pitched voice. The doors opened onto the fourth floor, and before I knew it, we were on the roof.

"Wow," I said, taking it all in.

The others streamed past, giddy with energy, but Leo came up to me and swept his arm over the view.

"What do you think?" he asked.

"It's beautiful," I said, forgetting my nervousness.

Across the treetops and stretches of interstate, the city skyline was glittering. It was miles away, far enough to seem mythical and imposing.

"That's Buckhead," Leo said, pointing off to the left, "and Midtown's over there, and downtown's, you know, down there."

I turned to him. "Thanks for bringing me."

"'Course," he said, laughing. "It's obvious you can hang."

I wasn't sure how to answer that, but Samuel saved me. "Hey, Le," he called, gesturing Leo over, "let's get this going."

We hung in a pack around the railing, talking and laughing while Leo pulled beers from his backpack. He handed them out in a routine way, and I accepted one like it was no big deal, but I looked to Ricky for affirmation. He winked at me and popped the tab of his open, and I followed his lead. The beer tasted just like the one I'd shotgunned on his deck.

Leo produced a joint next. He lit it up and passed it around, but I turned it down, blushing. For a split second I worried that someone might call me on it, but nobody even noticed. They all seemed to be doing their own thing, letting the night carry them wherever they wanted to go.

"Ricky, Codi, wanna join us?" Lydia called. She was lying flat on her back on the concrete, with Natalie stretched out next to her. The others were still by the railing, taking turns smoking.

Ricky raised his eyebrows at me. He was letting me decide.

"Yeah," I said boldly, leading the way to them.

I lay down next to Lydia, my chest buzzing. The concrete was hard on my skull and back, but I eased into it, trying to be graceful. Ricky spread out next to me, keeping his knees up, folding his hands over his stomach.

The sky was velvet blue, streaked with milky patches, sprinkled with stars. I breathed in and felt contentment flooding into my arms and legs, loosening everything.

"Nat and I do this thing," Lydia said, her voice clear in the stillness. She turned toward me, and I could smell her shampoo again. "We give the stars as many names as we can."

"You mean, like . . . you name the constellations?" I asked.

"No, it's way better than that." She shifted and pointed up to the right. "Like, that little guy is Mr. Potato Head."

"He's right next to Shrek," Natalie said. "And there's Donkey."

"And that's Harry Styles."

"What was the one you came up with that one night?" Natalie asked her. "The little pig?"

"Peppa Pig," Lydia said. "She's a nasty woman."

I laughed out loud. Lydia turned to grin at me, her eyes bright, her eyelashes long.

"That's Ariana Grande," Ricky said, pointing.

"No," Natalie said, "Ariana Pequeña. She's a *little* star."

"Twinkle, twinkle," Lydia giggled.

I raised my arm, spreading my fingers over the night sky. "Look, Ricky, there's Nickelback."

Lydia and Natalie burst out laughing. Ricky swatted me sideways, dragging his hand across my face as I sputtered with laughter.

We went on like that for a few minutes, throwing up the most outlandish names we could think of, Lydia making me choke with laughter when she proclaimed one of them to be Edward Cullen, "because he sparkles." We finished our beers and drank another round, and everything became funnier and funnier, and I found myself talking more and more freely.

We finally sat up when the others came over to join us. They plopped down with their feet spread out in front of them, their eyes red from smoking, Terrica giggling like crazy. Natalie filled them in on our star names and Samuel laughed so hard he cried. We were in a loose circle, the breeze swirling around us, the summer crickets buzzing and whirring far below. I caught a glimpse of Ricky's glowing smile, his relaxed laugh, and I finally understood what he meant about feeling like he'd known his friends since kindergarten.

"So, Codi," Cliff said, "what's your story? What are you into?"

I laughed, tipsy and relaxed. "I'm still figuring that out."

"Codi's a painter," Ricky announced, and the group gasped like they'd never heard anything so impressive.

"A painter?" Leo repeated, his eyes glazed over. "Like *Monet*? Duuuude."

"Nowhere near that good," I said quickly. "It's just a hobby."

"She's awesome at it," Ricky said, even though he'd never seen my paintings. "She does people's portraits."

"*Whoa*," everyone said again.

"Um . . . yeah . . . I haven't done that in a while, though . . ."

"Can you paint *our* portraits?" Terrica asked, like it would be the most meaningful thing in the world.

"Yeah, that would be insane!" Natalie said. "I've always wanted to have my portrait done!"

Cliff snorted. "Narcissistic much?"

"Shut up, dickhead," she said, smacking him. "Seriously, though, I've wanted one since I was little. My aunt and uncle had this ginormous portrait of my cousin hanging in their house, but when I asked my parents if I could do something like that, my brother said you had to be pretty to have your portrait done."

"I'll fucking kill him," Cliff said, kissing her goofily.

"It's fine," Natalie said nonchalantly. "He turned out to be the ugly one."

Everyone roared with laughter; Lydia swatted at Natalie's forearm like she was too much for her to handle.

"So?" Natalie asked brightly, looking at me. "What do you think, Codi?"

"She charges for her portraits," Ricky said protectively.

"Then it's a good thing I've got that serving job," Natalie said, undeterred.

I hesitated. I could feel Ricky's eyes on me and half hoped he would step in again.

Then Lydia spoke, looking directly at me. "Could I come watch?"

My heart drummed. I could still feel Ricky looking at me, but I didn't need to catch his eye this time. The way forward was clear.

"Yeah, okay," I said casually, trying to contain my grin. "Let's do it."

It was after midnight by the time we left the rooftop. Ricky's friends hugged me goodbye and made me promise I'd hang out with them again. It was the easiest promise I'd ever made.

"We'll text you about the portrait," Natalie said, punching her number into my phone. "Lyd, here, put yours in."

Lydia typed her number in, her fingers moving fast, her pretty lip between her teeth. When she finished, she held my phone out with a mischievous smile.

"What?" I asked, smiling without even trying.

She nodded at the phone, and I saw how she'd entered her contact info: *Lydia Kaufman aka Jason Waterfalls.*

"Amazing," I said, grinning at her.

"Right?" she said, grinning back.

"So," Ricky said as he drove me back to my car at Totes-n-Goats. "My friends are pretty great, huh?"

I smiled at him. "They're incredible."

"And?"

"And what?"

He looked sideways at me. "Don't be a punk. How'd it go with Lydia?"

I couldn't help but laugh. "You knew it was her I was describing, didn't you?"

He grinned. "I narrowed it down, yeah, and then after you told me about the redhead and the buzz cut guy, I knew I had it on lock."

"You didn't tell any of them, did you?"

"Of course not." He hesitated and sighed. "Actually, the guys were trying to ask if you and I were a thing, but I shut that down fast."

"Ew. I didn't even think of that. Did you tell them I'm gay?"

"No, just said we're friends."

I fell silent, wondering how Ricky's friends would react if I told them. They seemed like they wouldn't care at all, and I wondered, yet again, why he couldn't tell them the truth about himself.

"Lydia told me about meeting you at my party," Ricky said.

I whipped around. "She remembered me?"

"Yeah. She said you were really awesome and she was glad she got to meet you for real this time."

I felt like I'd been swept up on a wave.

"Are you gonna say anything?" Ricky laughed.

I laughed, too. "What's there to say? I mean, she's super cute, but I just met her. Do you even know if she likes girls?"

Ricky shrugged, his eyes thoughtful in the glow of the street-lights. "I guess you'll find out, won't you?"

8

MARITZA AND JAKORY WEREN'T HAPPY WITH ME FOR blowing them off on Saturday night.

"I *told* you," I said as we hovered around my kitchen counter on Sunday afternoon, "I wasn't feeling well. I just wanted to sleep after work."

"But you're feeling better now?" JaKory asked, genuinely concerned.

"Yeah," I said, not looking at either one of them. "I probably just ate something weird."

My brother was standing in front of the pantry, most likely scoping out the canned ravioli he was so obsessed with, and as I spoke, he turned around to stare at me. The look on his face was accusatory. He must have been awake when I'd gotten home last night and knew I hadn't been sick at all.

"Anyway," I said hastily, trying to keep Grant out of the conversation, "are we going to the pool, or what?"

We spent the afternoon swimming, playing games, and sunbathing in our favorite section of the lounge chairs. It was comforting, it was familiar, and it was quintessential summer, but it also felt dissonant to be there with Maritza and JaKory, doing the same things we always did, when I'd been with Ricky and his friends just last night, doing something new. It seemed like a glaringly big omission not to tell my two best friends about it.

Much later, when my friends had gone home and I was watching TV on the couch, my brother walked past me and said, "Since when do you lie to Maritza and JaKory?"

I wasn't quick enough to come up with a retort. Instead I let my mouth hang open, another lie halfway out of my throat, but my brother shook his head and continued on past me.

Two nights later, when I was getting ready for bed, Natalie texted me.

> **Natalie Novak:** *Hey Codi, so when are you gonna paint me like one of your French girls??*

I noticed she'd sent it to a group chat—and the other person included was Lydia.

"Shit," I said under my breath, pacing in loops around my bed. My heart was beating way too fast, thrilled by the prospect of texting Lydia, even if it was technically in a group chat. I couldn't shake the feeling that it was the start of something.

Before I could reply, Lydia's response showed up. She sent a GIF from *Titanic* of Old Rose saying, "It's been eighty-four years."

I stared at my phone, trying to think of a funny or clever response. In the end I settled for something safe:

Hahaha, whenever you want! I'm working morning shifts for the next three days but other than that I'm free.

I read over my message, trying to see it through their eyes. Did saying "whenever you want" sound too eager, too desperate? Should I have played more hard to get?

Natalie Novak: *Yaaaassssss! How about tomorrow after Lyd and I finish at the restaurant? We're on the breakfast shift til 2.*

I hadn't known Lydia and Natalie worked at the restaurant together, but the idea settled perfectly in my head: Lydia wearing a server's apron, popping up to a table with that bright, beaming smile, asking old folks whether they wanted bacon with their eggs. I pictured myself seated at one of her tables, trying not to blush when her hand grazed mine as she collected my menu.

I agreed to meet them at the restaurant, Natalie gave me the name and address, and I figured that was the end of it. I tucked myself into bed, already imagining how it would go the next day, and was just about to fall asleep when my phone glowed blue in the darkness. Lydia had sent one more text.

Lydia Kaufman aka Jason Waterfalls: *Can't wait. Thanks Codi!*

Below that, she sent a GIF from TLC's "Waterfalls" video.

I closed my eyes, smiling to myself. Despite having to work a nine A.M. shift the next day, I couldn't wait to wake up.

Work dragged and dragged and dragged. The store was dead, so Tammy asked me to refold a wall of T-shirts. It was miserable, and I was exhausted, but every few minutes I'd remember that I was going to see Lydia afterward and suddenly I'd feel buoyant.

When my shift ended, I went straight to my car, took off my goofy name tag, and tried to make my hair look cuter. This annoying little voice in my head kept saying, *None of this matters, she's probably straight*, but another voice, one that reminded me of Ricky, said, *Stop worrying and enjoy this feeling.*

The Court Café's parking lot was emptying out by the time I got there. I waited in my car, savoring the air-conditioning, but as soon as the clock hit two I got out and leaned against the car door, trying to look casual while the staff slipped out the back exit.

Lydia and Natalie were the last to leave, laughing together as they spilled out of the restaurant. The moment they stepped off the sidewalk, Lydia noticed me and broke into that big smile.

"Hey," she called, walking toward me. She was wearing a sky-blue polo shirt with the restaurant logo on it, and her hair was up in a messy ponytail with these little flyaway hairs dancing around her face. I had a tender, visceral urge to tuck them behind her ear.

"Wanna come inside?" Natalie asked, pulling up behind Lydia. "We're closed until dinner at five, so it's super chill in there. I was thinking we could do the portrait on the back porch."

"Yeah, okay," I said, grabbing my stuff out of the car. "That sounds perfect."

Lydia offered me a hand with my supplies. I gave her the sketchpad to carry, and our fingertips touched for the briefest second. A tingling sensation ran up my neck, and I blushed, but thankfully she didn't seem to notice.

"Sorry we took so long," Lydia said as they led me inside. "We were swamped today. There's some national Little League tournament going on, so all these families came in at the same time. One of my tables was from Vermont, and I don't think they'd ever been to the South before, because they got all excited about ordering grits."

I found myself smiling at her. "Did they like them?"

"No, they thought they were gross. But I affected a cute little accent so they could still have an *authentic* southern experience. I've said 'y'all' about a hundred times in the last two hours."

Natalie snorted. "You're such an exaggerator. You're not even southern!" She turned to look at me. "Her family's from Michigan."

"Yeah, and yours is from New Jersey," Lydia said, poking her in the back, "but you still drink *swayt tay* like it's your job."

We filed onto the restaurant's enclosed porch, looking out over a forest of trees. The tables were clean and set for the dinner shift, but Lydia and Natalie had created an opening where we could work on the portrait.

"How's this?" Natalie said, plopping down in a chair by the porch screen.

Lydia hovered by the table next to her, and for the first time, I realized I hadn't thought this through. I usually worked alone, removed from everyone else. Now I'd be trying to create something with two people watching me, one of whom was the cutest girl I'd ever met.

As if she could read my mind, Lydia asked, "Are you comfortable, Codi?"

"Oh, um, yeah," I said, trying to play it cool. "Just trying to get in the zone."

"I can leave if it's distracting."

"No, no, not at all," I assured her. It was a blatant lie, but they didn't know me well enough to sense it. If Maritza and JaKory were here, they'd be smirking behind their hands, able to feel every wave of nervousness radiating off me. Maritza would crack some dry joke like, *Distracting? Why would you worry that you're distracting her, Lydia?*

Natalie was now rummaging in a tote bag, pulling out clothes and a makeup kit. Without warning, she stripped out of her restaurant polo and stood there in a neon-pink push-up bra, showing Lydia the shirt options she'd brought. I averted my eyes, busying myself with setting up my materials.

Natalie seated herself back on the chair, now dressed in a navy silk top, her hair freshly sprayed and angled perfectly over her face. At first she looked poised, but then I noticed she kept fidgeting with her hair. Her eyes were flitting around like she wasn't sure where to rest them.

Lydia had noticed, too. "Nat," she said firmly. "Look alive."

Natalie rolled her eyes and crossed one leg over the other, her posture tight. She was trying to play it cool, but I could tell she was uncomfortable. It gave me an idea.

"Hey, actually . . ." I said to Lydia, "could you sit next to Natalie and talk?"

"Talk?"

"Yeah, just have a natural conversation. Bring out the authentic Natalie."

Lydia raised her eyebrows, her expression mischievous as she turned to Natalie. "Codi thinks I bring out your authentic side."

It made my stomach swoop, hearing her say my name. I'd never liked it as much as I did in that moment.

Natalie rolled her eyes again. "Shut up, Lyd, just come talk to me."

They sat next to each other, two best friends making each other laugh, and I began to paint.

"Codi, this is insane," Natalie said, eyes wide as she took in her portrait. "I'm, like, creeped out by how good it is."

The time had passed in a flowing, meditative way. Lydia and Natalie had talked and laughed about everything imaginable, from how they'd run late to their own graduation to how much they loved Lydia's grandma Mimi to the day last October when they'd gotten caught leaving campus in the middle of third period ("We got three days of detention for that one," Natalie snickered). I'd painted Natalie with all the vibrancy I could see in her. The bright red hair was the easy part; it was her confident, sunny face I had truly wanted to capture, and Lydia had coaxed it out.

"Codi, this is just . . . *wow*," Lydia said. "I love that you painted her midlaugh."

I smiled self-consciously. "It felt right."

She looked intently at me. "You have really good instincts."

I could actually feel my face turning red, and I hastened to look away from her. "Thanks."

We traipsed out to the parking lot, Natalie carrying her portrait in front of her like a treasure. "I can't wait to show Cliff," she said in an awed voice. "He'll love it. He'll want you to paint me naked."

I snorted, hoping to god she was kidding.

We waved Natalie off, and then it was only Lydia and me, standing together in the bright, scorching parking lot, completely alone for the first time.

"You really are talented," she said, her warm arm brushing against mine as we plopped against her car. "Oh, sorry," she said, scooting away. "I probably smell like grease."

"No, you don't," I said hastily. My skin buzzed from where she'd touched it. "I like grease, anyway."

It was the stupidest thing I'd ever said, and I fought hard to keep my face neutral.

"I mean, you know, like hash browns and french fries," I muttered.

Lydia laughed. "Yeah, and bacon."

"Yeah, bacon, exactly." I paused, trying to think of a subject change. "I'm surprised Natalie wanted to do the portrait here."

Lydia frowned, and I could tell she was going to reveal something about her best friend. "Yeah . . ." she said hesitantly. "She doesn't really like being at home. Her family situation is kind of shitty."

I wasn't sure what to say to that. Natalie was such a cool, outgoing person; it was hard to believe she struggled with anything.

"But I also think she low-key loves the café," Lydia went on, her voice brighter. "It's our third summer working here, and everyone kinda feels like family at this point, even when they're driving you crazy." She smirked and met my eyes. "So whose portrait are you doing next?"

"Oh," I said, caught off guard by the question. "Um . . . I don't know. I guess I'll see if there's any demand."

She nodded, her expression thoughtful. "Cliff will probably ask next. Natalie will make him because she'll want to see what you do." She paused. "Maybe you could paint mine sometime, too."

I'd been hoping she would offer that, but I was also overwhelmed by the idea. I couldn't imagine being alone with her for such a long stretch of time. All I managed to say was "Yeah, definitely."

There was a pause, and I wondered if she had wanted me to give a more specific answer. I tried to think of a follow-up, something that would give me a guaranteed reason to see her, but it was like trying to summon an answer for a pop quiz.

"I should get going," Lydia said finally, peeling herself off the car. "I have class in an hour."

"Class?" I asked, my heart sinking.

"Yeah, I'm taking some credits at the community college. I'm going to GCSU next year, and they have a bunch of math requirements for freshmen, so I'm trying to get a few out of the way this summer."

I could tell from the way she said it that it was the last thing she wanted to do. I thought back to the night we'd met at Ricky's party, when she'd confided in me about not getting into UGA. It seemed like school was a point of sensitivity for her.

"I hate math," I told her. "My best friend is a genius at it—she, like, wants to be an astrophysicist—but I despise it."

Lydia's eyes settled, and I could tell I had said the right thing. "Really?" she asked. "Me too. My mom is an accountant, and she can't figure out how the math gene skipped over me. Everyone says I have her work ethic and smile, but somehow I didn't get her brains."

"You have an amazing smile," I blurted out.

She gave me a funny look, almost like she knew I'd said that by accident, and my face and neck burned all over. "I mean . . . I'm sure you have a great work ethic, too," I said stupidly.

She laughed lightly, not quite looking at me. "Thanks. Um, so . . . I'll see you soon? Are you coming to Samuel's party on Friday?"

I blinked. This was the first I'd heard of Samuel's party, and I didn't know how invites to these things were supposed to work.

My confusion must have shown on my face, because Lydia smiled and said, "He just texted about it this morning. I'm sure Ricky will give you the details."

"Oh," I said, blushing. "Yeah, I'll ask him about it."

"Cool. Well hey, thanks for letting me watch today."

"Oh, yeah, no problem," I said, nodding too much. "It was really helpful, having you there to talk to Natalie—I mean, just having you there in general, 'cause I think it helped us be more loose and relaxed . . ."

She grinned at my rambling. "Yeah, it was awesome."

"Yeah." I paused. "Um, well . . . see you Friday."

"Friday," she agreed, ducking into her car. "Catch you later, Codi."

"Bye, Lydia," I said, slinking off before she could see me blush.

The whole way home, I imagined myself painting Lydia's portrait. We were on the Court Café's porch again, with her in that sky-blue polo, and I was making her laugh while I painted her long, honey-colored hair. The moment I finished, she stepped up next to me, dropped her head on my shoulder, and whispered how perfect it was.

My stomach was whirling all over the place by the time I walked into the house. Mom and Dad were still at work, and I didn't know where Grant was, so I sat down at the kitchen table, pulled out my sketchbook, and began a preliminary sketch of how Lydia's portrait might look. Even though she'd raved about Natalie's, I had to make sure the one I painted of her—if it ever happened—was exceptional.

My phone was buzzing with a slew of texts from Maritza and JaKory, but I switched it to Do Not Disturb mode and popped my headphones in, playing the same song on repeat while I practiced. Sunshine streamed through the windows and spilled across the table, inching its way toward my drawing, and I took off my watch and forgot about everything other than the paper girl in front of me.

Then, all of a sudden, someone was peering over my shoulder. Grant.

"What the hell!" I yelled, ripping my headphones out.

Grant was unfazed. "Who's that?"

I flipped the drawing over, my heart hammering. "No one."

"Is that someone you know?"

"It's *no one*, Grant. Go away."

"You're being weird."

"You smell like BO. Go take a shower."

"I was *outside*," he snipped. "That's the place where *normal* people go."

He said it with a mean edge to his voice. My heart was still pounding from his sneaking up on something so private, so revealing, but before I could say anything to shoo him away, he shocked me with another question.

"Do you have a boyfriend?"

His tone had changed to nosy curiosity, almost like we hadn't been picking at each other only seconds before. I froze, a feeling of dread creeping over my stomach.

"I've seen you go out with that guy," he went on. "The one with the truck."

My heart pounded faster. Grant knew about Ricky, which meant he might tell my parents I had a boyfriend, and that would lead to a labyrinth of conversations I wasn't ready to navigate; or, worse, he might let something slip to Maritza and JaKory, and I wasn't ready to explain why I'd been hanging out with a new friend without them.

"Have you been spying on me?" I growled.

"It's not spying if your room looks out over the driveway. What kind of truck does he have?"

"I don't know, Grant. Stop asking about—"

"You don't know what your boyfriend drives?"

"He's not my boyfriend, dumbass," I said harshly. "He's just a— he's a coworker from Totes-n-Goats who picks me up for work sometimes."

It was a good lie that would hopefully prevent him from mentioning Ricky to my parents *and* friends, but he raised his eyebrows like he didn't believe me. "Do Mom and Dad know him?"

"Of course they do," I snapped. "Now will you get out of my face? Seriously, you smell. I hope you don't hang around your girlfriend like this."

In a flash, his expression soured. He stepped away from the table, smacking his hands against the chairbacks. "You used to be nice, Codi," he said, his tone acidic again. "Now you're an asshole."

He loped out of the kitchen, shaking his hair out of his eyes. I tried to refocus on my sketch, but his words kept replaying in my head. I checked the texts Maritza and JaKory had been sending instead.

> **JaKory Green:** *What am I supposed to pack for this Florida trip? The father figure will want to bro out with sports-ball activities but I don't own a single pair of those godforsaken athletic shorts*

I had forgotten about JaKory's upcoming visit with his dad. He was going to Florida for four days, like he did every summer, and he wasn't exactly thrilled about it.

> **Maritza Vargas:** *Pack allllll the gay outfits. Troll that man haaaard*
> **Maritza Vargas:** *Codi what should we do while he's gone? Wanna stay over Friday night?*

I stared at my phone, my stomach pinching uncomfortably. Friday night was Samuel's party, and even though I hadn't confirmed with Ricky yet, I was pretty sure I was going. More to the point, I *wanted* to go. But what was I supposed to tell Maritza?

> *Can't dude, sorry, Mom wants to have a family movie night.*

It was a weak lie, and I prayed she wouldn't overthink it.

> **Maritza Vargas:** *You guys and your damn family values*

I set my phone down, a mixture of guilt and relief settling over me.

On Thursday afternoon, Ricky and I met at our neighborhood pool, both of us fresh off work. There were tons of little kids there, shrieking and jumping and running around, so we grabbed chairs in the far corner of the lounge area and threw our clothes on the free chairs so no one would bother us.

"Of course you're invited," Ricky said, after I mentioned Lydia's invitation to Samuel's party. "I texted you that last night."

"Yeah, I know, but I wanted to make sure it's not, like . . . a pity invite."

"Were you not listening when my friends made you promise to hang out with them again?"

"No, I was—"

"So stop second-guessing yourself. Tell me more about the portrait party."

I filled him in on how Natalie's portrait had turned out, including how Lydia had suggested I could paint hers sometime.

"And you said yes, right?" Ricky said, staring me down.

I winced, already knowing how he'd react. "I sort of left it open-ended."

He sighed and dropped his head back like I was impossible. "*Why?* She offered you a ready-made chance to hang out with her!"

"Yeah, but I don't know her well enough yet! It felt too—you know—*soon*. I want to know her better before I commit to something like that."

"Girls," Ricky huffed, shaking his head. "Can't take an opportunity when it's right in front of you—always need that *emotional connection* first—"

"What, you think I won't get another opportunity?" I asked testily. "I'm not trying to rush into something here. I like this girl, and I like all your friends, but I want to feel my way into it at my own pace. I can't act like someone I'm not."

Ricky snorted. "You're not capable of acting like someone you're not."

"Is that an insult?"

Ricky lowered his sunglasses. "Why are you being so defensive? I'm saying you're a very genuine person."

I looked away from him and watched the kids splashing in the water. Maritza, JaKory, and I were usually in there with them, Maritza picking fights with the brashest eleven-year-olds and JaKory begging everyone to play Categories. I had never come to the pool with anyone but them before. The thought of it made my throat ache.

"I don't know, Ricky," I sighed. "I don't feel very genuine lately, not with the way I'm keeping things from Maritza and JaKory. I lied to Maritza about why I can't hang out with her tomorrow night." I paused. "And I lied to my brother yesterday, too."

Ricky was quiet, his hand splayed over the pages of his UGA course catalog. "Listen. You have to understand why you're doing it. Sometimes we lie because we have to take care of ourselves first."

I knew he wasn't only talking about me anymore. His hand had stilled on the page.

"Are you ever gonna tell your friends about . . . you?" I asked gently. "'Cause now that I've met them, I don't think they're the type of people who would have a problem with it."

He was silent again, thinking. "Maybe you're right," he said carefully. "But there's no point telling them about something that only happened a few times."

"So you don't think it'll happen again?"

"No."

He said it in a way that shut down the conversation. I exhaled and stared out at the water, thinking of my two best friends. Ja-Kory was in Tallahassee by now, trying to keep up with his dad and half brother; Maritza was still at dance camp, probably straining to outshine Vivien Chen. I hadn't seen either one of them since Sunday, which was the longest we'd ever gone during a standard summer week, and I felt weird about it: On the one hand, I was discombobulated because it was so different from our normal routine, but on the other, I found myself missing them much less than I'd thought I would.

"Hey," Ricky said, interrupting my thoughts. "We're gonna have fun tomorrow night, all right? My sister got me a fifth of vodka for helping her move out of her dorm, and I know you're dying to try vodka."

I narrowed my eyes at him, trying to figure out his game, but all he did was waggle his eyebrows and lean back into the sun.

9

THE WORLD FELT VERY IMPORTANT ON FRIDAY NIGHT.

I told Ricky I would drive, mostly because I didn't want to feel like his accessory this time. I picked him up after dinner, and he came hustling out of the garage with his mom on his heels, fussing at him to fix his shirt collar. She stood in the driveway and watched him squeeze into my car.

Talking to parents made me more nervous than anything, but I didn't want to be rude or awkward. I rolled down my window and smiled as I said hello.

Mrs. Flint had Ricky's warm eyes, but they turned serious after she finished greeting me.

"Y'all be good," she said, looking meaningfully at us.

"We will be," Ricky said, grinning like a Cheshire cat.

It was smushed with the two of us in my little sedan, but Ricky seemed perfectly at ease, even with his long legs bumping up against the dashboard. He tapped his fingers on his knees and hummed along to the Ben Howard playlist I had going through the aux cable, and his contentedness made me feel more at ease, too.

Samuel's party looked and sounded a lot like Ricky's had, but I was more confident walking in this time. Cliff, Natalie, Samuel, and Terrica rushed to hug me, and before I knew it, they were pressing a drink into my hand. "Vodka LaCroix," Terrica informed me, cheersing our cups together. "We're bougie bitches like that."

I took a sip, and it burned like nothing I'd ever tasted before. I stuck my tongue out without meaning to.

"People *like* this stuff?" I said, and Ricky laughed and wrapped an arm around my shoulders.

"Just sip it. It'll get better."

Samuel took me on a tour of the house, which was smaller than Ricky's and mine but full of knickknacks and kitschy art that his parents were into. Terrica came with us, shooing people out of the way and twirling like Vanna White every time Samuel pointed out something new. When we got to the upstairs, Samuel pulled up short at the sight of Leo standing assertively near the banister.

"Dude. You blocked off the entire floor?"

Leo crossed his arms. "Yeah? I'm only letting them use the bathroom. Your parents' and sister's rooms are off-limits."

I remembered what Ricky had told me after that first party: that Leo always found the spot where people were most likely to hook up and charged them ten dollars to use it.

"Are you fucking kidding me, man?" Samuel said. "How much have you made so far?"

"Thirty bucks."

Samuel hesitated. "Fine. But I get half of what you make. And obviously we"—he gestured between Terrica and himself—"don't have to pay."

"I'll give you twenty percent."

"Seriously, dickhead?"

Leo shrugged. "Dude, you know I'm gonna use the money to share more weed with y'all anyway."

"All right, all right," Samuel said. "Carry on."

We trailed back downstairs, where Ricky, Natalie, and Cliff were hanging out in the kitchen. Samuel filled them in on Leo's latest business venture, but I hardly listened: I was looking for Lydia, but she was nowhere to be found.

"Hey, Natalie," I said as quietly as I could, "where's Lydia tonight?"

"Oh," Natalie said breezily, pouring more LaCroix into her cup, "she's at the movies with her family."

"Her family?"

"They go one Friday night a month, isn't that cute? Usually it's just her and her parents, but both her brothers are home this weekend, so it's like a big deal. I always give her shit about it, but that's because my parents are divorced and I'm jealous. Anyway, she'll probably roll in around eleven with a big thing of popcorn under her arm."

I raised an eyebrow. "What?"

"She loves movie theater popcorn, so she gets it to go," Natalie said, rolling her eyes. "And then she'll try to grab my phone with that greasy butter all over her fingers, just watch."

The party picked up its pace, with Samuel blasting Latin hip-hop that made my ears pound. More and more people arrived, and the shrieks of laughter grew louder, and the smell of sweat and heavy cologne was everywhere. I sipped my way through a second vodka and LaCroix, feeling more relaxed by the minute, even talking to someone I didn't know in the bathroom line. Then Magic Dan pulled me over to show me card tricks in the family room, and Natalie had to come to my rescue by pretending she needed something from my car.

An hour later, Tucker showed up. I didn't realize it was him at first because I hadn't been able to see him that night in the dark, but I got a good look at him when he came into the warm light of the kitchen. He was a lanky, awkward-looking guy—there was almost something birdlike about him—but he had a kind of easy confidence about him, too. He went right up to a group of guys I didn't know, who bro-hugged him and handed him a beer, and within seconds it was clear he was commanding the conversation. I kept waiting for him to come talk to Ricky, but he stayed planted where he was, as if Ricky were invisible to him.

Then I saw him looking furtively in our direction a few minutes later.

"Tucker's here," I murmured to Ricky.

Ricky didn't take his eyes off Samuel, who was in the middle of telling a story. "I know," he said through clenched teeth.

I didn't say another word about it.

A while later I ended up in the family room, sprawled on the floor with Ricky, Samuel, Natalie, and Cliff. Samuel was telling us about his family cat, Burgermeister, who was tucked away in his room upstairs, and who was so fat they were having to track him on a diet plan. Ricky laughed hysterically into his hands as Samuel acted out Burgermeister's attempts to climb the stairs.

"I've got hiccups," Ricky said, giggling and wiping tears from his eyes. He paused and took a breath. "Man, I think I need some water."

He ambled into the kitchen and didn't come back. I was pretty sure he must have been looking for Tucker, but none of his friends seemed to notice.

"Ha!" Natalie said, pointing across the room. "As promised, Codi."

I turned to look and saw Lydia heading our way, a giant tub of popcorn under her arm. She looked radiant. I wish I could explain the way she lit up the room, how she had this natural energy about her, how she stopped to chat with almost everyone she passed. When she plopped down on the family room carpet with us, she was almost breathless.

"Here," she said, passing off the popcorn bucket, which Cliff grabbed immediately. "What are we drinking?"

"*Vodka*," Natalie said in a Russian accent.

"I'll make you one," I said, and hopped to my feet before she could tell me no.

I mixed the drink the way I'd seen Natalie do, crossing my fingers that I got it right. When I got back to the family room, Samuel, Cliff, and Natalie were absorbed in conversation again, but Lydia looked directly at me with a grin that made my heart leap. I caught a whiff of her perfume, sweet and floral and distinctly her.

At some point our group ended up on the deck, where we found Ricky chatting with Tucker by himself. Their energy changed the moment we walked out. Tucker looked at me with mild horror in his eyes, then looked to Ricky with an almost imperceptible question. Ricky shook his head and muttered something in hushed tones, and Tucker's shoulders relaxed.

Cliff and Samuel converged on Ricky and Tucker, and I knew to anyone else it must have just looked like a bunch of guys hanging out, but I could see the subtle resistance in Ricky's and Tucker's body language: how Ricky took a second too long to angle his hips away from Tucker, how Tucker crossed his arms over his chest, how their grins looked a little too forced.

"Are you people-watching?" someone asked.

I turned to find Lydia standing there with a cold beer in her hand. She held it out to me, and I took it and popped it open like a pro.

"Nah, just waiting for you," I said, feeling bold. "I wanted to play the star game again. What do you think of the name 'Kris Jenner'?"

Lydia choked with laughter, dribbling beer onto the deck. Everyone looked up as we hopped backward from the splash, Lydia still choking, me laughing and thumping her on the back. Her bare shoulders were like sparks beneath my fingertips.

"Damn, that was embarrassing," Lydia said, coughing between laughs, but she seemed perfectly at ease.

"Good thing I'm not wearing sandals," I said, shaking the beer-covered toe of my Vans.

She rolled her eyes, but she was grinning. "It could be worse, trust me. The other day a customer sneezed scrambled eggs onto my thigh, and my manager scolded me for not telling him 'Bless you.'"

"My brother threw up ice-cream cake on my arm once. At my own birthday party."

"Seriously? You win."

"Anytime my family tells the story, my dad is always like, 'Yeah, Grant, you really take the cake for that one.'"

"Dad jokes are simultaneously the best and worst thing in life."

"They really are."

We turned to lean against the deck railing, facing outward toward the trees. It felt like the world had shrunk to just the two of us. Her elbow bumped against mine, and my body hummed at the touch.

"Are you having a good time?" Lydia asked.

It was easy to be honest with her. "Actually, yeah, I am. Would you believe this is my first real party?"

"You're kidding," Lydia said, but there was no judgment in her eyes, only spark.

"Big groups of people aren't really my thing. But I really like your friends, so it's easy to be here with you all."

Lydia smiled. "They're really awesome people. I didn't even hang out with them until this past year."

"Really?" I asked, surprised.

"Well, excluding Natalie. She and I have been friends for years. We used to hang out with a different group of girls, but then something happened and we kind of . . . went our separate ways. Last summer she started dating Cliff and hanging around his friends—you know, the boys—so I started hanging around with them, too, and then Samuel and Terrica started dating, and we all just kind of fit together."

I paused, letting the narrative sink into me. "Can I ask what happened with the other girls?"

Lydia crossed her arms. "It was a big, stupid thing, but the gist of it was they thought they were better than Natalie and me. I'd been trying to make it work with them since freshman year, ever since it was decided that we were, like, a 'group,' but the truth is they acted like my frenemies more than my friends. Finally my brothers pulled me aside and were like, 'Why are you letting your "friends" treat you like this?' And I thought, you know, *they're right.*"

I was quiet, thinking of Maritza and JaKory. They were nothing like Lydia's frenemies had been, but there was still a part of me that wanted to pull away from them.

"I'm going through a lesser version of that with my two best friends," I told her. "I love them more than anything in the world, but sometimes when I'm around them I feel like—like I'm less than the person I want to be. Then I met Ricky and the rest of you, and it was like this whole new side of me got to breathe."

Lydia's eyes were on me, studying me. I felt it like a heat lamp.

"Can I tell you about my friends?" I asked her, and in that moment I felt more vulnerable than ever.

"Yeah," she said, her eyes intent on mine. "Of course you can."

I took a long, deep breath, and then everything came spilling out, everything I loved about Maritza and JaKory even with the complicated feelings I had right now. I told her about how quirky and genuine they were, and how Maritza dressed up as Janice from *Friends* for Halloween one year, and how JaKory used to have a pet rabbit named Robert Frost, and how they sang me a song when I couldn't stop crying after I sprained my wrist in PE class, and how we called ourselves JaCoMa for all of seventh grade . . .

"They sound amazing, Codi," Lydia said. "I don't think they're going anywhere. Maybe you need to breathe right now, but that doesn't mean you don't love them."

I swallowed. The vodka and beer were making me emotional, and I didn't want to be emotional tonight.

"Well, anyway . . ." I said, feeling self-conscious. "I'm just glad I met you and your friends."

Lydia looked hard at me. "You're really cool, Codi."

I met her gaze. "I'm not sure that's true."

"Sure it is. Everybody's cool in their own way, once you give them the chance to show you."

I smiled back at her. "You think so?"

"Yeah, don't you think that's how high school works? You go through it with your head up your ass, making judgments about people you don't even know, but if you can get out of your own way and make room for the people you weren't expecting, then everything finally clicks." She shook her head, and the smile slipped from her face. "It takes forever to find your people, and then as soon as you do, you graduate and head to different colleges. You lose each other right when you're getting to the good stuff."

I watched her for a moment, how her body went still and her eyelashes caught the glow of the porch lights.

"I'm sorry," I said quietly.

She looked at me. "Don't be. It's just life. And hopefully"—she took a deep breath—"there will be some cool new people waiting for me at GCSU."

"There will be," I told her. "You're going to make a million new friends in college. They'll flock to you." I took a breath, feeling my way into something that would make her smile. "Especially if you keep bringing giant popcorn buckets to parties."

Her mouth twitched. It looked like she was thinking for a second, and then she turned to me and said, "I hope there's a *kernel* of truth to that."

I shook my head, laughing. "Terrible dad joke."

"Completely terrible," she agreed, her eyes bright, "but you're laughing, aren't you?"

The night went on. Samuel and Terrica talked me into a game of beer pong, which I played with Leo, who had finally retired from guarding the upstairs, and then Natalie invited me to play King's Cup with her, Lydia, and a group of people on the family room floor. I'd never played that game before, but it was really funny, especially when people made up rules like "Everyone has to speak in a British accent" and "No pointing at anyone," which, it turned out, was way harder than you'd think. Then I downed another beer and made some friends in the bathroom line, including the infamous Aliza Saylor, who tried to pull her thong off while we stood there talking.

I barely saw Ricky during any of this, but when I was out in the garage, getting more beer, Tucker stepped out behind me. He stood in the doorway with his hands in his pockets, scuffing his shoe into the floor. I waited, the cold beer cans pressing against my shirt.

"Codi," he said, clearing his throat.

I nodded at him. "Hi, Tucker."

He kept standing there, scuffing his shoe harder, and I could physically feel how uncomfortable he was.

"I like your Hawaiian shirt," I said, my voice carrying across the garage.

He looked up at me. It was almost like he was checking to see if I was serious.

"Really." I shrugged, unable to believe this popular athlete thought I was making fun of him. "It's a good shirt. It's fun."

He cleared his throat again. "Thanks. I found it in my dad's Goodwill pile. Thought it would get some laughs."

There was a beat of awkward silence where he just stood there looking at me.

"Look, Tucker—" I began.

"No, hold on," he said, going still. "Please, let me try this."

"Okay."

"I didn't mean to follow you, but, uh . . . I just wanted to apologize for freaking out on you a few weeks ago. I was worried you would tell someone what you saw, but he—um, Ricky—says you haven't done that."

"No, I haven't," I said, watching his anxious face. "And I won't."

"Thanks. It's not that I'm embarrassed or whatever, but—it's just that it's no one else's business, right? I'm still trying to figure things out, and I don't want other people making judgments."

The beer cans were too cold; I set them on the floor and rubbed my hands into my shirt, trying to warm them. "Ricky told me you're the best baseball player our school has."

"He said that?"

"Yeah."

Tucker bit his lip. "Ricky exaggerates, I think."

I met his eyes. "No, I don't think so."

He gave me a pained half smile. Then he took a few steps forward and plucked the beer cans off the floor. "Who are these for? I'll carry them."

"You don't have to."

"Nah, I'm happy to. I need to look like I came out here for a reason, anyway." He took a step toward the door and then turned back to face me. "Listen, Codi . . . if things don't pan out with Ricky and me, please don't hold it against me, okay?"

And on that cryptic note, he opened the door and led me back into the house.

The party started winding down, and it was a damn good thing, because I was *drunk*. From what I could tell, everyone else was, too. We were sprawled out on the family room floor again, this time playing a girls-only round of King's Cup while Cliff, Leo, and Samuel snored on the couches behind us.

Lydia was stretched out next to me, her thigh occasionally brushing against mine, my skin buzzing wherever she touched it. Her hair kept falling over her face, and every time she pushed it back, I wondered what it would be like to kiss her.

"New rule," Lydia said, flinging down a king of spades. "Everyone has to be addressed as 'bro' instead of their name."

"Why, bro?" Natalie slurred.

"Because, bro, I declared it." She pointed at Terrica. "You're up, bro."

"Bro, *thank you*," Terrica said, slumping toward the card pile.

Our voices got deeper and deeper the more we said "bro," and it was stupid, but we were giddy and drunk and having a good time. Lydia was laughing harder than anyone. "Your turn, Codi," she said, bumping my elbow.

"Whoa, whoa, whoa," Terrica said, pointing at her. "Take a drink, bro. You said her name."

"What? Shit. Sorry, bro." She looped an arm around my shoulders, and my whole belly swooped. She was mere inches from my face, and I could see her lips so clearly.

"No sweat, bro," I said, leaning into her arm.

A few minutes later, I glanced into the kitchen and saw a girl standing very close to Tucker. I hadn't seen her until now, but she was hard to miss: She kept grabbing Tucker's arm and sweeping her hair back as she laughed.

"Who's that?" I asked.

The other three looked up lazily. "Oh, that's Bianca," Natalie said. She burped without seeming to notice, then lowered her voice conspiratorially. "She and Tucker kinda have a thing."

They resumed the card game, but I was only half paying attention. I had just noticed Ricky standing in the corner of the kitchen, not far from Tucker and Bianca. His whole body seemed to be contracting in on itself, his arms wrapped around his torso like he was trying to hug warmth into his body.

I caught his eye, and he pushed his way across the kitchen, staring determinedly away from Tucker.

"Let's go, Codi, I'll drive your car," he said stormily. Then he swept out of the house without looking back.

"Is he okay?" Terrica asked.

"He's fine," I said with a wave of my hand. "You know how dramatic boys can be."

It wasn't until I hugged the girls goodbye that I realized the true extent of our drunkenness. Terrica held on to me and started crying like she would never see me again. Natalie rubbed my head like I was a cat, muttering about how soft my hair was.

And then it was just Lydia.

She hugged me tightly, her hair pressing against my face. She smelled like shampoo and perfume and every pretty thing. "Drink lots of water when you get home," she whispered into my neck. "And eat carbs. Lots of carbs."

"You got it, bro," I said, tugging on a strand of her hair.

She grinned and hugged me one more time, and I turned and made my way out the door.

The night was loud. Crickets were trilling and whirring, cars were whooshing by on distant streets, even the heat itself seemed layered with heavy sound. Ricky said nothing as we drove down dark, winding streets. He lowered my car windows but didn't turn the music on, which even my drunk ass knew was out of character for him. It wasn't until he parked in my driveway that he made any sound at all.

"All right," he said, handing me the keys. "Have a good night."

He moved to get out of the car, but I held him back. "How're you getting home?"

"I'll walk. No big deal."

"Are you sure you're okay?"

His voice was gruff, strained. "I'm fine."

I held on to his forearm, trying to seem more in command of myself than I was. "I saw Tucker with that girl," I said quietly. "Bianca."

A muscle twitched in Ricky's jaw. "That's nothing."

"Okay."

We sat there in the driveway, the night enveloping us.

"He's just a fucking coward," Ricky said suddenly, his voice searing through the quiet. "Makes no difference to me how he wants to live his life, but it's aggravating to see him with someone he doesn't give two shits about."

"*Ricky.*"

"What?" he snapped, his voice shaking.

"He means something to you," I said softly. "It's okay. I think you mean something to him, too."

Ricky was staring through my windshield. I could hardly see his face in the darkness.

"Sorry for yelling," he said abruptly. "Get some sleep."

He got out of my car before I could say another word.

I snuck into my house as quietly as I could, half-afraid that my parents would be waiting up for me, even though I'd lied to them that I was watching a movie with Maritza tonight. I was relieved to see the lights turned off in the kitchen, no sound except for the air-conditioning humming steadily in the background. I tiptoed to the sink, poured myself a glass of water, and grabbed a box of cheese crackers from the pantry. Then I crept up the stairs and headed toward my room, eager to lie in bed and replay the night in my head.

But as I crossed the hallway, my brother's light switched on.

I froze where I was, standing halfway between his room and mine, looking at him where he stood in the doorway. He was squinting as his eyes adjusted to the light, wearing a T-shirt he'd clearly outgrown months ago.

"What are you doing?" he grumbled.

"Shhh. I told Mom and Dad I'd be home late. Go back to sleep."

"I wasn't sleeping, I was watching Netflix. Why do you look all guilty?"

"What?"

"Were you drinking?"

I cursed inwardly. Could he tell by my voice? By my body language?

"I wouldn't tell on you," he said defiantly.

The crazy thing was, I believed him. But it didn't matter: My defenses were too high to let him in.

"Don't be an idiot, Grant," I growled. "I was just watching a movie with Maritza. Stop being so nosy."

He stared me down for a few seconds, and I stared back, and then he shook his head and snapped his door shut like I wasn't worth another breath.

10

LET'S JUST SAY MY FIRST HANGOVER WAS A SHOCK.

I woke up with a pounding head, dry mouth, and queasy stomach. For a moment I hoped I was the only person home, but then I remembered it was Saturday, and I could hear my parents bustling around downstairs, their favorite nineties rock playing in the background. I chugged the water on my nightstand and went back to sleep.

A while later, someone was rubbing my back. I rolled over, hazy-eyed, to find my mom peering down at me.

"Do you feel okay, honey? It's almost noon."

"Yeah," I croaked. I wasn't sure whether I sounded hungover or just tired, but I didn't have the energy to care.

"You came home late last night," Mom said. She left it hanging, and I tensed up, expecting her to put the pieces together, to deduce that I'd been out drinking like a typical teenager. In that moment, I wasn't sure whether I wanted her to know or not.

But then: "You and Maritza must have watched more than one movie, huh?"

I swallowed. I didn't know if she was handing me the lie for my sake or her sake, or if she realized it was a lie at all. Maybe it was just outside her realm of possibility to consider that I'd been drunk—that her shy little artist had started rebelling after all. I remembered my brother standing in the hall last night, accusing me of drinking. At least he thought it could actually happen.

"Yeah," I said finally. "A few movies. You know how Maritza gets."

"Mm-hm," Mom cooed. "Well, why don't you take a shower to help yourself wake up, and then come down and help us clean out the garage."

I finally saw Maritza and JaKory on Monday night, after JaKory got back from Florida. We went to Chick-fil-A and sat on the patio and talked as loud as we wanted to. I hadn't seen them in days, but neither one of them asked much about what I'd been up to. I was somewhat relieved, since I wouldn't have to lie through my teeth again—but their assumption that I'd merely been working and painting also reinforced how boring and predictable they thought I was, and I resented it.

"Y'all should drop by the dance studio one of these days," Maritza said, stirring her strawberry milkshake. "There's always something dramatic going on. Did I tell you about the seventh-grader who got her period for the first time the other day? She ran out of the bathroom screaming that she was dying. Didn't even know what was happening. *Absurd.* Coach Leslie had to take her into the bathroom and tell her what to do through the stall door, and the other girls were trying to act all compassionate, but mostly they were acting superior, and—"

"Did anyone have something to give her?" I asked.

"I had some tampons with me, but she was too freaked out to try that, so Coach Leslie said we should get her a pad instead—"

"Ugh," JaKory interrupted. "Can we talk about something else?"

"Stop being such a boy," Maritza said, kicking his ankle. "How many times do we have to tell you that we'll be talking about period stuff in front of you until your dying day? So anyway, Coach Leslie's like, 'We need to get her a pad,' but none of the girls had one, so *of course* fucking Vivien Chen went to CVS to buy her some—"

"That was nice of her, though," I said.

"She didn't do it to be nice," Maritza said exasperatedly, "she did it to suck up to Coach Leslie and prove that she's all captain-y or whatever."

"Isn't she just *the worst*?" I said, catching JaKory's eye.

"An absolute she-devil."

"Y'all don't know her like I do," Maritza said darkly.

"You're so dramatic," I told her, trading out our milkshakes. "Tell us something good about the dance job."

Maritza shrugged. "It's pretty great, overall. I mostly hang out with Rona. She's perfected her impression of Vivien, even down to the bizarre way she holds her water bottle—"

"I've started talking to this guy," JaKory interrupted. He said it in a rush, and I got the impression he'd wanted to tell us since the moment we'd sat down.

"What?" I asked breathlessly.

"Who?" Maritza squealed, swatting his knee.

"His name's Daveon." JaKory's eyes were shining, but he looked away from us. There was a pause. "We met on Tumblr."

His words hung in the air. Maritza and I traded looks, and I hurried to speak before she could.

"Wow," I said in the most neutral tone I could muster. "What's the story?"

JaKory started talking so fast he could barely breathe. "He writes the funniest, most sarcastic posts about, like, everything. He's in the Doctor Who fandom, too, so he's always reblogging GIF sets and fan art and really incisive commentary. But he's into serious stuff, too, like LGBT issues and Black Lives Matter and international politics. A couple of days ago he wrote this post about how annoying it is to be gay in Alabama, and I didn't even know he was from Alabama, but I reblogged his post and was like, 'This. this. this. except Georgia,' so then he messaged me like, 'You're from Georgia?' and we got to talking, and he's so brilliant and *interesting*, and he makes these clever jokes all the time, and . . ." He let out a deep sigh. "I just can't stop talking to him."

Maritza and I stayed silent. We'd seen this feverish side of JaKory many times before—usually about the latest book or TV show he was obsessed with—and there was always an infinite, voracious nature to his yearning, like nothing could ever truly satisfy him. We usually had to ride out each obsession until he moved on to the next one.

"But . . . he lives in Alabama," Maritza said reasonably.

JaKory gave her a challenging look. "Yeah, I realize that. But it's only one state over."

"But you don't have a car."

I cut in before JaKory could snap at her. "How old is he?"

"Our age," JaKory said pointedly, as if that outweighed the car problem.

"Well . . . how do you even know he's attractive?" Maritza said. "He could be ugly."

"Ugh, he's *not*," JaKory said, rubbing his hands down his face. "He's posted pictures of himself before. On a scale of one to ten, he's a number we've never even heard of."

He pulled out his phone and handed it to Maritza.

"You saved his pictures?" she asked.

"Only two of them!"

"He is handsome," she said fairly. "Look at that jawline."

"I know. You could cut diamonds with his jawline."

I reached for the phone. "He's cute," I said, scrolling between the two pictures. "I mean, for a boy."

"Oh, you sweet ingénue," JaKory said, taking the phone back. "You could never appreciate an Adonis like him."

"Let's just hope that's actually him," Maritza said, "and he's not some weirdo trying to catfish you."

"It *is* him," JaKory insisted. "I have good instincts about these things."

Maritza shot me a look. I glanced away from her before JaKory could notice.

We finished our milkshakes and wandered over to Target. It was Maritza's mom's birthday that week, so we helped her search through the jewelry section. "Something Christian," Maritza instructed us, "but anything flashy works, too."

I stood side by side with her, picking through the necklaces to find something Mrs. Vargas would love, until I realized JaKory was missing.

"Hey," I said, knocking her elbow. "Where'd lover boy go?"

We found him in the men's section, trying on a fedora that made his skinny head look even smaller.

"Please don't buy that," Maritza said. "You look like a Bruno Mars wannabe."

"Daveon will love it," JaKory said, modeling for himself in the mirror.

Maritza looked meaningfully at me, urging me to step in, but I shook my head and kept quiet.

"JaKory . . ." Maritza implored, "do you really need to spend money to impress a guy on *Tumblr*?"

"I can't hear you," JaKory said, tilting the brim of the fedora over his eyes. "Love makes me immune to negative energy."

After we'd dropped JaKory off at his house, fedora and all, Maritza exploded.

"He's living in la-la land," she said without preamble. "He's such an idealist, never thinks about the practical side of things. It's not gonna work with this Daveon guy—if he's even *real*—and then JaKory's going to be heartbroken, and we'll be left to pick up the pieces."

I bit my lip. "What if there's a chance it could work?"

Maritza looked at me like I was crazy. "*How?*"

"Maybe Daveon has a car—or maybe their emotional connection is enough for now—I don't know, shouldn't we just be happy that he's found someone he likes? Isn't that what you've been talking about this whole time?"

"I've been talking about something that could actually *work*. For every action, there is an equal but opposite reaction, right? You put forth effort into the universe, and the universe gives you something back. But how does fantasizing about someone on the internet lead to practical application?" She sighed, long and pained. "It's just wish fulfillment. He's letting himself get excited about this because there's no actual *risk* involved."

I fell silent, absorbing her words. I often forgot how wise Maritza could be, and then in moments like this, it walloped me in the face.

"You're really smart," I said, shaking my head. "Sometimes I kind of hate it."

She laughed a pure, bright laugh, and for one shining second our friendship was golden again.

"So what about you and me?" she asked. "We're deep into summer and neither one of us has any prospects."

I fidgeted in my seat. Could I tell her about Lydia? Maritza would understand better than anybody. She'd ask a million questions, demand to see her picture, make me offer up every detail so we could analyze it together. She might be the only person who could help me figure out if Lydia liked me back.

But I couldn't explain Lydia without explaining Ricky and Cliff and Natalie and everyone and everything else I now had in my life, including the fact that I'd been lying to Maritza and JaKory for weeks now.

"I don't know, dude, I've just been working a lot," I lied, even though I knew she would judge me as soon as I said it.

"Yeah, well, you're not gonna meet anyone there, unless you count those weirdos who come in looking for kitty cat overalls."

"You had kitty cat pajamas until eighth grade," I pointed out.

"They were cashmere," she said, her mouth twitching.

"They were the most ridiculous thing you've ever owned, and you know it."

Her smile lingered for a beat, but then her expression turned heavy again. "I don't know, Codi-kid," she sighed. "We need to find some other way to meet people. We could try to hit the bars down in the city, but neither one of us has a fake."

"I'm not interested in that."

"What *are* you interested in?"

I shook off the question. "You haven't met anyone around here that you like?"

She snorted humorlessly. "Yeah, I've got a major crush on the new barista at Starbucks, but he's twenty-five and has a girlfriend."

"At least he's someone cute to talk to."

"Aren't you listening to what I've been saying? I don't want to just *talk* to someone cute, I want to *date* someone cute. Someone I can get excited about, who makes this long-ass summer feel special and meaningful and new . . ."

We fell quiet, nothing but plain suburban roads in front of us. I didn't know what—or who—Maritza was thinking about, but I knew what was on my mind.

Just as Lydia had predicted, Cliff asked me to paint his portrait next. He'd already gushed about Natalie's portrait when we were hanging out at Samuel's, but he texted another slew of compliments that had me blushing with pride.

Cliff Broward: *My favorite thing about that girl is her spunk and somehow you made that come thru in a painting. I'm ready to pay that bigggg cashhhh moneyyyy for mine!!!*

I agreed that we could meet up on Wednesday afternoon, after my morning shift, and that Natalie should come to help him relax just as Lydia had done for her.

The sky was overcast as I drove out to Cliff's house. He'd texted me to come around the back, where the basement door was, so I parked in the driveway and traipsed down the back path, hearing blaring music from the inside. I stepped in through the open door and felt more like I was in a gym than a basement: There were weight machines, treadmills, and exercise mats everywhere.

"Ayyyy!" Cliff roared, springing off the rowing machine. He hustled toward me and high-fived me with a slap that turned my hand red. "Whoops, sorry. How's it going?"

Natalie eased herself off the bench press, where she'd been lounging with her phone. "What's up?" she asked, pulling me in for a hug. "Welcome to Cliff's sandbox."

Cliff laughed and paused the music. He was drenched in sweat and stinking like hell, and as I watched, he squirted water sloppily into his mouth, wiping his chin on his sweaty bicep.

"So I figured you could paint me like this, huh?" He grinned. "Fresh off the circuit."

"*How* do you have so much exercise equipment?" I asked.

"My parents own a gym. That's, like, what they do. My whole family's really into fitness."

"They're masochists," Natalie said, deadpan. "It's revolting."

"Do you actually want me to paint you like this?" I asked, gesturing to his sweaty man-tank.

"No," Cliff and Natalie said at the same time.

"If you can give me five minutes," Cliff panted, "I'll take a super-fast shower and put some real clothes on. Babe—you saw the chicken salad in the fridge, right?"

Natalie made us sandwiches while Cliff got ready. We laughed about how silly we'd gotten at Samuel's party, then hovered around the exercise equipment, setting up an area in the corner where I'd be able to paint Cliff's portrait.

"Sorry about this shit everywhere," Natalie said, flinging a pair of weight-lifting gloves out of the way, "but he'll be most himself if you paint him here."

I grinned. "You know all my tricks now."

"Hire me as your assistant," she said, flicking her hair back theatrically. "I'd have to fight Terrica for it, though; she's dying to get in on this. Don't be shocked when she asks for her portrait next."

Cliff bounded down the stairs in a black button-up shirt, beads of water still clinging around his scalp. "I told you it'd only be five minutes," he panted, fastening his top button.

"Cliff," Natalie said, staring at the garish red Nike shorts he was wearing. "What's with the shorts?"

"What? It's not like Codi's gonna paint my legs," he said, charming her with a big smile. "And if I'm gonna be sitting for hours and hours, I gotta keep the boys comfortable."

"Oh god, shut up and get your butt on the chair," Natalie said as I tried to block out any image of Cliff's *boys*.

We played music this time, keeping it low in the background while Natalie sat a few feet from Cliff and talked to him about the drama from her shift that morning. Cliff grinned through all of it, but he kept glancing at me self-consciously, his shoulders pulled tight.

"Sorry, Codi," he said. "Just feels a little weird to be paying someone to draw my face."

"It's gonna be awesome," Natalie said, rubbing his knee. "And if you don't want it, *I'll* buy it. Just stay loose and show Codi that adorable smile of yours."

Cliff's smile became softer, in what I assumed was his version of a blush. His shoulders relaxed, and for several minutes I was able to see the real him.

"So, Codi," he said after a quarter of an hour, "I heard Ricky freaked out on Friday night."

I paused with my brush in midair. Cliff's voice was light, casual, but he and Natalie were both watching me intently.

"Um. What do you mean?" I asked.

Cliff shrugged. "Nat said he was acting all moody when y'all left Sam's house."

We looked at each other. He was still smiling, but there was strain behind it: He was fishing for information. I remembered what he had said that first night at Taco Mac: *Typical Ricky. Won't trust us with his hookups.*

"Oh," I said, wondering how to play it off. "Yeah, I think he was just tired."

"Hm," Cliff said, wrinkling his nose. "Yeah, sometimes he gets like that." He made eye contact with Natalie, and I could tell this was a conversation they'd had many times before.

Natalie turned to me. "Cliff worries about him."

"Babe—" Cliff began.

"No, Cliff, it's okay," Natalie insisted. "You should be allowed to say how you feel. He's your best friend."

Cliff sighed. His shoulders were tight again, and he glanced at me almost like he was embarrassed. "I just didn't know if you had any insight," he mumbled.

I lowered my eyes, trying to keep my expression neutral. I wished there was something I could offer Cliff—some hint of what was going on with Ricky, of what Ricky might need from him—but I knew it wasn't my place.

"I don't," I said, wincing apologetically. "Sorry."

Cliff shook his head too fast. "Nah, don't worry about it."

Natalie gave me a sad, knowing smile, and I returned it—two girls wishing these boys could say how they felt.

"What the fuck," Cliff said in an awestruck voice, gazing at his portrait.

Natalie was beaming, her arm around Cliff's back. She kept shaking her head like she couldn't believe how well the painting had turned out.

"Damn, Codi," Cliff muttered. "You really are something else."

I laughed lightly. "Do you want anything changed?"

"Hellllll no. You made me look awesome."

"Look at this," Natalie told him, pointing at the cheeks of portrait-Cliff. "She got your dimples and everything." She turned to me, still shaking her head. "Two for two, Codi. You're incredible."

"Damn," Cliff said again, still staring at his likeness. He took it in for another thirty seconds, then looked around at us. "Well, shit, I'm starving. Who wants tacos?"

We went for Mexican at Los Bravos, just the three of us, and I was surprised to find how comfortable it was even with me playing third wheel. Cliff made us laugh with old stories from the football team—"I've heard this one before," Natalie muttered to me, "so be prepared to hear about Samuel's naked ass"—and eventually, to my delight, the conversation turned to Lydia.

"That asshole could've been here right now," Natalie said, shaking her hair back. "I texted her to come, but she's stressing about her math class. She's got a midterm tomorrow."

"Oh, damn," I said, trying not to sound too disappointed. "Is she okay? She told me how she hates math."

"She puts too much pressure on herself," Natalie said sympathetically. "She's *so* smart, but she gets in her head about it. She's always been able to see the good in other people, but she doesn't see it in herself."

My heart felt tender, like I was holding Lydia inside it and trying to wrap her up with all the softness I could muster.

"She thinks you're awesome, by the way," Natalie told me, munching through another chip. "She won't stop talking about what a genius you are with painting, and how we all should've hung out with you sooner."

I felt sunbeams shoot through me from my scalp to my heels. It was all I could do not to flush red on the spot.

"So anyway," Natalie said, like she hadn't just given me the world, "what are you up to this weekend?"

I stammered out something about working and taking it easy, and after that Cliff changed the subject to the renovations at his parents' gym. We hung out until the restaurant swelled with the dinner shift, and then I hugged them and took in more of their profuse compliments before we parted to our separate cars.

Ricky and I met up at the neighborhood clubhouse on Thursday night. We sat in his car with the windows rolled down, right next to a gardenia bush whose sweet scent wafted toward us on the breeze. It was the first time I'd seen him since Samuel's party, and he seemed like himself again, or at least he was doing a really good job of acting like it. I told him about my experience painting Cliff's portrait, and how Natalie had offhandedly mentioned that Lydia thought I was awesome.

"You are awesome," Ricky said, smiling at my delight.

I rolled my head back. "Ugh, I've got such a bad crush on her."

He laughed through his nose. "I already know that."

"Yeah, but . . . it's *bad*. I'm worried I'm reading too far into things with her, that I'm getting excited for nothing. How can I tell if she's interested in me?"

"Do you get any vibes?"

"Vibes?"

"Yeah, *vibes*."

"I mean, she acts like she enjoys being around me, but she's like that with all your friends. I mean, what if—what if she's not—"

"What if she's not like you?" Ricky suggested.

I stared at him. "I was going to say 'like us.'"

He shifted in his seat but didn't acknowledge what I'd said. "You'll never know unless you try. And after you've tried for a little while, you'll feel it in your gut if she likes you. Have you followed up on her suggestion to paint her portrait?"

"No . . ." I began, and he frowned at me. "Well, what if I don't get it right?"

"You got Natalie's and Cliff's right."

"Yeah, but I can *see* them, you know? Natalie and Cliff put their whole selves out there. I feel like I have a read on them, like I can stand back enough to see who they really are. It's harder to do that with someone who means something to you—or could mean something to you."

Ricky's eyes flitted between mine. "Like . . . it would be harder for you to paint my portrait than theirs?"

"Yeah," I said emphatically. "I mean, if you wanted me to I could, obviously, but it would take me—"

"No," he said abruptly. He paused. "I mean, no thank you. Maybe later."

I stared at him, trying to figure out what that meant. Was Ricky worried about how I perceived him?

He seemed to read the question on my face. "Ignore that," he said, sweeping his hand over the steering wheel.

I chewed my lip, thinking. I knew he could tell I had follow-up questions, but he didn't help me get there.

"I wasn't gonna mention this," I said, watching him carefully, "but Cliff asked me if everything was okay with you at Samuel's."

The whites of his eyes shone in the dim light. "What did you tell him?"

"That I thought you were tired."

He searched my eyes. "That's it?"

"That's it. I promise."

He nodded, his eyes flitting away from me. "Thanks."

"Of course." I hesitated. "But are you sure you don't want to talk about Tucker and that girl?"

He huffed in frustration, dropping his head back against the headrest. "Yes, I'm sure. I don't want to be your project, or Cliff's, or anyone else's. You said you wanted to be my friend just to be my friend, remember?"

Now I shifted in my seat, angling away from him. "Sorry," I said, without meaning it. "I just want to be there for you with the Tucker thing the same way you're there for me with the Lydia thing."

"I don't need you to be. They're not the same situation."

"Yeah, okay, got it."

I wasn't sure why I was getting so worked up about it, but it rankled me every time Ricky shut down this conversation. I wanted him to trust me—just like Cliff did—and selfishly I wanted to know how it felt to have someone like Tucker, even if Ricky claimed it wasn't real.

We were sitting in a loaded silence when his phone rang. He cleared his throat and answered it, affecting a more upbeat voice. From what I could tell, it was one of his friends, calling to make plans with him. All I heard was a series of Ricky saying "Uh-huh" and "Yeah." The only real question he asked was, "Who else is invited?"

"What's up?" I asked after he hung up. I thought I might be pushing my luck, but he'd taken the call in front of me, after all.

Ricky seemed torn about something. He had his thinking face on.

"What?" I pressed.

"That was Cliff. He wanted to see if I was free for a party at Lydia's Saturday night."

"Lydia's?" I repeated.

"Yeah, did she mention it to you?"

My heart sank. "No."

"It might not mean anything," Ricky said quickly. "Cliff said Natalie and Lydia were organizing it, trying to find out if people were free. Maybe they just haven't asked you yet."

"You asked Cliff who else was invited, though. Did he say?"

"He said he didn't know," Ricky said evenly.

The hopeful feeling I'd had since talking with Natalie evaporated. I tried to keep my expression passive, but I knew Ricky could read the disappointment in my face.

"Don't react yet," Ricky said bracingly. "Wait and see if she texts you."

Ricky dropped me off around ten thirty P.M., staring down my dark driveway with a faraway look in his eyes. I moved to get out of the car, but he called me back.

"Yeah?"

He looked at me for a second. "Did Cliff seem, like . . ." He bit his lip, struggling with the question. "Did he seem suspicious? About me?"

I clutched the car door handle. Ricky's expression was very serious, and I remembered the first night I met him, when he'd asked if I was going to tell anyone about him and Tucker kissing in the trees.

"No," I said, speaking as clearly and meaningfully as I could. "He seemed like he cares about his best friend."

Ricky blinked a few times. "All right," he said, swallowing. "I'll think it over."

I figured that was the best I was going to get. We waved good night, and I'd turned to go when he called me back a second time.

"Yeah?" I asked, perplexed by the smile inching up his face.

He looked up from his phone. "Just got more details about Saturday night. You should check your phone."

It turned out I'd been worrying for nothing. There was a missed call from Lydia on my phone, and when I called her back, she answered breathlessly.

"Codi," she said, her voice ringing brightly through the line. "What are you doing Saturday night?"

THE LAST STREAKS OF DAYLIGHT WERE COLORING THE
sky as Ricky and I drove to Lydia's house. She lived about fifteen minutes from us, off a winding road close to the Chattahoochee, in the
depths of a wooded area with trees that had stood there for centuries.
Only a few cars breezed past as we followed the curving, quiet road.

"What are you doing?" I asked as Ricky pulled off into a secluded
parking lot.

"We're meeting here," he said, grabbing a bag from the back seat.
"It's right next to the park."

"We're not going to her house?"

"Her house is around the corner, but it's easier to start things here."

I wasn't sure what he was talking about, but I figured it had something to do with the casual clothes we'd been told to wear. Cliff's and
Samuel's cars were parked next to us, but there was no sign of them
or anyone else. I followed Ricky out of the truck and up an earthy

hill, my sneakers scraping against the dirt. Voices floated down to us from the other side of the hill.

"Here we go," Ricky said as we came upon an open field.

Lydia, Natalie, Cliff, Samuel, Terrica, and Leo were already there, lounging in the grass. They jumped up as we approached, shouting our names across the field. Terrica did a cartwheel just for the hell of it.

"Papa was starting to worry," Leo said in a fake-nervous tone, grabbing Ricky and me for hugs.

"Don't start with the 'Papa' stuff," Samuel said, shaking his head.

The girls hugged me in quick succession: first Terrica, then Natalie—who, for some reason, looked more closely at me than usual—and then, before my heart could beat hard enough, Lydia.

"Hey," Lydia said, leaving one arm hanging off my shoulders. "Ready for some Manhunt?"

"Of course," I said, grinning even though I had no idea what she was talking about. She looked so cute that I thought I might combust at the sight of her; she wore an old, faded pair of jean shorts and a vintage Atlanta Braves jersey with the top button undone. I tore my eyes away from the glinting skin at her collarbone.

"Are we really starting with Manhunt?" Ricky asked, digging in his bag.

"Damn right!" Terrica trilled, at the same time that Samuel muttered, "Terrica's request."

"Did you bring a flashlight?" Cliff asked.

"Two of 'em," Ricky said, handing one to me.

I looked around at everyone's loose, laid-back clothes. The boys wore dark, grubby man-tanks, their bare chests showing through the giant armholes; Samuel was sporting a maroon bandana over his curls. Terrica had braved a long-sleeve T-shirt, despite the humidity, and

Natalie was rocking an Adidas workout tank. I was glad I'd dressed in a T-shirt and sneakers.

"How do we play?" I asked.

As if they'd expected me to ask, the boys parted around Terrica, Leo going so far as to bow to her.

"I could get used to this," Terrica said, observing them with her hands on her hips. She raised her eyebrows and locked eyes with me. "Okay, Codi, here are the rules."

We split off into teams: Cliff captained one, and Terrica, of course, captained the other. Everyone argued about how to split up evenly, with multiple people pointing out that Leo was a detriment because he was sure to get bored and wander off on his own.

"Y'all can take me or leave me," Leo droned, holding up his palms. "This stallion was born to run his own path."

"At least we can put the 'stallion' on firepit duty," Samuel said, pointing at the portable firepit that Cliff had carried from his truck. "If you're gonna clock out, at least help out, huh?"

"Yeah, yeah, I'll set it up when I get tired of playing," Leo said.

"So in ten minutes," Natalie clarified.

In the end, we decided to play boys against girls. Cliff insisted it would be unfair to the girls, but Natalie put him in his place with a sharp reminder.

"Lyd played tennis, Terrica ran cross-country, I was on the soccer team, and Codi—"

"I'm not an athlete," I cut in, grimacing.

"—Codi's eyes are highly attuned to shapes and colors!" Natalie finished, pointing wildly at my face, and before Cliff could protest any further, she grabbed our arms and pulled us off across the field. We ran away from the boys, howling with laughter, as they shouted a countdown behind us. Their "hunt" would start the moment they reached zero.

"Should I be nervous?" I yelled as we ran toward the cover of the trees.

"Very!" Terrica yelled back. "This shit is serious!"

We disappeared into the trees as darkness fell across the sky. I shone my flashlight ahead of me, panting as I zigzagged around tree roots and plants, my heart throbbing in my chest. Within seconds, I'd separated from the other girls, but Terrica had explained that this was an advantageous strategy. My job now was to find a stealthy place to hide.

I crouched behind a massive oak tree, my breath coming hard and fast. I clicked the flashlight off and waited, listening for the sound of approaching footfalls.

The boys' deep voices boomed across the night: They were calling to each other as they spread out to find us. I crept around the trunk of the tree, peering through the darkness.

Two tall figures were crashing through the brush, the light from their flashlights jumping erratically. I drew back and crept around the other side of the trunk, waiting for them to pass. The moment they'd gone several yards beyond my tree, I dashed out and set off back across the woods, aiming to reach base, where I'd be safe.

A high-pitched yell rang out from the right side of the woods; it was one of the girls, being chased out of her hiding spot. I kept moving forward, the blood rushing through my body, my breath coming in gasps. I hadn't played a game like this in years, but the thrill of it came right back to me, wild and dangerous and raw.

"Whoa!" someone gasped, emerging from the trees and nearly running into me.

It was Lydia. She grabbed my hand and pulled me off to the left, and I barely had time to register the electric buzz of her hand before I heard one of the boys shouting behind us.

We ran wildly, breathlessly, her messy ponytail whipping in front of me. It was a full minute before Lydia stopped, pulling me into a dense cluster of trees. She kept hold of my hand as we crouched behind a massive tree trunk and clicked off our flashlights.

Our panting gradually lessened. Crickets were trilling; a bullfrog croaked in the distance. My eyes adjusted to the pitch darkness, finding Lydia's silhouette mere inches away.

"Sorry," Lydia whispered, grinning apologetically down at our hands. "I grab hold of people when I'm nervous." But she didn't let go.

I swallowed. My heart thumped erratically, and not from Manhunt.

"It's kinda scary out here," Lydia went on. "But peaceful, in a way."

"It makes me feel so awake," I whispered.

She gripped my hand harder. Our eyes met in the darkness.

Crack!

My heart reared at the sound of a snapping twig: Someone was prowling our way. We took off running again, and there was a crash of footfalls as one of the boys chased after us.

"Give it up!" he shouted. It was Cliff, bounding through the woods behind us.

I caught a glimpse of glowing light and raced toward it, Lydia following in my wake. We crashed back across the open field, drawn by the fire, praying that base was only yards away.

"YES!" came Terrica's voice from across the field. "Come on, y'all!"

We were halfway there when another figure emerged from the woods, cutting into our path: It was Samuel, tearing after us with all his might. There was no way we'd both outrun him.

"Keep going!" Lydia shouted behind me, and I pressed on, racing toward Terrica and Natalie. A second later, Lydia let out a war cry, her voice crazy and shrill in the nighttime air as she whipped around and staggered to a halt, her arms held out like a linebacker's. Surprised, Samuel tried to skid to a stop, but his momentum was too forceful: He bowled right into her. They crashed to the dirt, yelling and sputtering, just as I reached the safety of base—and Terrica's and Natalie's outstretched hands.

"YES!" Terrica shouted, pulling me in for a hug. "The majority of us made it—WE WIN!"

I looked around and laughed. Leo was only a few yards away from us, hovering near the firepit. He totally could have chased me down if he'd wanted to, but he seemed more interested in the beers he was pulling from his backpack. The fire crackled and danced in front of him.

Ricky came hustling out of the trees, asking what had happened, as the girls and I jogged over to check on Lydia and Samuel. Cliff had pulled up behind them and was standing with his hands on his hips, shaking his head in defeat. Lydia and Samuel were sprawled on their backs on the ground, coughing and laughing.

"Goddamn, woman," Samuel was whining, his voice strained. "What kinda motherfucking sacrifice—"

"You're the one who rammed into me!" Lydia panted, her hands on her belly. "Fucking freight train—"

"Lyd, as admirable as it was to offer yourself up like that," Natalie said, plopping down on the ground next to her, "I'm pretty sure you could've just kept running."

"I know," Lydia said, still panting, "but I thought some drama would be fun. Either way, we won, right?" She spun her head around until she found me. "And Codi got to be the victory runner."

I laughed, dropping down next to her. "Yeah, I gotta say, it felt pretty heroic."

The others joined us on the ground, all of us coming down off the high of the game. Terrica hovered over Samuel, who wouldn't stop whining about his bleeding knee. Cliff wanted a play-by-play of the game, while Ricky kept lamenting that no one had caught Lydia and Samuel's collision on camera.

"It sounds funnier than it was," Natalie promised him, "but here, it basically looked like this."

She pulled me to my feet and mimicked running into me, just as Samuel had done to Lydia, except she flapped her hands and kicked her feet up like a helpless baby bird. I pretended to topple over in slow motion, exaggerating Lydia's yell. Ricky and the others roared with laughter.

"Offensive," Lydia said as I collapsed next to her.

"It's all good, bro," I teased, wrapping my arm around her neck, but I could feel Natalie's eyes on me again and hastily dropped my arm.

"This is all very sweet and precious," came another voice, and we whipped around to see Leo hovering over the group, "but can we get to the drinking now?"

The fire smelled like only fire can; it crackled and snapped, entrancing all of us. We circled around it, lounging on old beach towels and quilts that Lydia and Natalie had packed, while Leo kept up a steady supply of booze. The beer was lukewarm and fizzy, but it settled comfortably in my stomach, a perfect complement to the flickering fire.

Leo produced his weed next, and the air was soon thick with the smell of campfire and marijuana. I watched as the pipe made its way around the group, with everyone taking a couple of hits. Natalie hadn't smoked last time, when we'd been on the roof, but she did tonight; I wondered if Lydia and Ricky, who were sitting on the other side of me, would do the same. Then I realized it didn't matter who did or did not smoke. It was my choice to decide whether I wanted to try it or not.

Natalie handed the pipe to me, and I stared at it for a long second, making up my mind.

"How do I do it?" I asked, daring to look up at everyone.

I knew them well enough by now to know they wouldn't laugh, and I was right: Not a single person seemed fazed. Only Ricky gave me a relaxed half smirk.

Natalie showed me what to do, leaning into me and flicking the lighter to life. I inhaled as she told me and let the smoke fill my mouth, then breathed it out.

"You'll get a sweet little buzz from this one," Leo said, unusually kind. "Just start with that and see how it feels."

I passed the pipe and lighter off to Lydia, my fingers brushing hers. She took a hit of her own and passed it on.

Our energy was loose and relaxed. There was nothing to do but watch the fire and listen to everyone's voices swinging on the air. The night was warm, infinite, secret, and I had never felt so settled in myself. I lay back on my quilt, gazing up at the star-flecked sky, not bothering to worry that I'd just checked myself out of the group conversation. My phone dinged with texts from Maritza and JaKory, but I silenced it and tossed it to the side. I wasn't in the mood to feel guilty tonight.

Lydia lay down next to me, sighing. I wanted to reach for her, but my limbs were too relaxed. It was enough just to know she was there.

"Stars," Lydia said, giggling. "There are so many of them. Look at that constellation—look—it's like a platypus."

I giggled, too. The idea of millions of stars just hanging out up there was so silly, so absurd. The giggles pealed out of me like hiccups, goofy and unstoppable.

"I think Codi likes the weed," Natalie said, laughing to my right.

"Two thumbs up," I said, extending my arms for them to see, and then I laughed more at the sight of my thumbs.

Time passed in a hazy way; it could have been a few minutes or an hour, but I was comfortable just to lie there and *be*. I knew I was high, and the idea was funny and wondrous. I could only imagine what Maritza and JaKory would think.

Then Lydia was saying my name.

"Yeah?" I asked, leaning up on my elbows.

"We're going to pee," she said, ruffling my hair. Her warm fingers lingered a moment longer than necessary. "Do you wanna come?"

"Yes," I said. I wanted to add more, something funny or silly, but the words were too relaxed to come out.

We stumbled off to the woods, Lydia, Natalie, Terrica, and me, giggling and falling all over each other. Lydia's arm was somehow around me, and I tugged on her hand that lay draped on my shoulder. Her skin was soft and warm and electric.

"Marijuana," I said, giggling without meaning to. "Mary Jane. What a proper name for a drug."

"She's a lady," Natalie said.

"My middle name is Jane," I announced, unsure of why I was sharing this information. "I hate it. My parents had *one* job and they fucked it up."

We spread out beneath the trees, safe from the boys' eyes. Natalie dropped her shorts and peed without fuss.

"Jane's a lovely name," she said thoughtfully, like she wasn't pissing in front of us.

"Yeah, it's a classic," Lydia cut in. "And it's got an amazing legacy. Jane Austen, Jane Goodall—"

"GI Jane," Terrica chimed in, squatting a few feet from Natalie.

"Yeah, see?" Lydia said. Even in the darkness, I could feel her eyes on me. "It's worthy of you."

"Are y'all gonna pee, or what?" Natalie said.

Lydia took her place near where Natalie had just peed. She started to unzip her shorts, and I looked hastily away, my body heating up at the thought of her bare thighs, her bare everything. I stepped several feet to the side and did my business near a protruding tree root, trying to focus enough to get the job done.

"Are we good, ladies?" Terrica asked.

She crunched back toward the field, but Natalie called to stop her.

"Yeah?" Terrica said.

Natalie laughed. Her voice was mischievous in the dark. "Let's go skinny-dipping."

We wrangled the boys into going with us. We doused the fire and left our quilts, empty beer cans, and backpacks in the field. Our party of eight crashed through the woods again, heading toward the river, everyone yelling at Natalie about what a dumbass idea this was, though our abuse was gleeful rather than mad. We were reckless and giddy. The moon was bright and the river had never seemed so enchanting.

We reached it within five minutes, and before any of us could do more than tug off our sneakers, Leo had stripped completely and gone tearing off into the water, hollering like a cowboy. All I could see was a flash of pale, naked skin.

Samuel and Cliff went racing after him, Samuel stripping off everything except his bandana. Terrica and Natalie watched them unabashedly, laughing as they started to tug off their own clothes. Ricky hesitated for only the briefest of seconds before he went tearing in after the guys, his back a wide swath of deep brown skin shining in the moonlight.

I was inebriated enough not to panic, and I knew it was dark enough that nobody would *really* be able to see me, but I couldn't help my pounding heart as I began to pull off my clothes. I'd never been naked in front of any of my peers, at least not since I was little. Maritza had seen me in my bra and underwear, but that was it.

I hastened to pull off my shorts and T-shirt, then hesitated. "Are y'all taking off—*everything*?" I asked the girls.

"Already did!" Natalie yelled, tossing her clothes as she went running off to the water. Terrica followed close behind her, nothing more than a flash of dark, gleaming skin.

And Lydia—oh fuck, Lydia was taking off her bra.

I averted my eyes, then glanced back at her, then averted my eyes again. I couldn't see anything more than a flash of skin, a swing of flesh, but it was enough to make my face sear and my lower belly throb.

"Come on!" she called to me, and beneath her laughter was something else: a high-pitched note of nervousness. I could feel her eyes on me as I fiddled with the clasp of my bra. I tried to say something, but a second later she was gone, rushing off to the water with everyone else.

I followed last, my bare feet slipping over pebbles and dirt, and in some distant, detached part of my brain, a wry voice said, *You're running after a hot, naked girl right now*. I laughed aloud and crashed into the water, crouching low so no one would see my body.

The water was barely deep enough to sit in. It streamed past us, washing over stones, filling our ears with that eternal, moving rush.

"How much bacteria you think we're sitting in?" Samuel asked.

"Just don't drink it, dude," Leo said.

The guys were trying not to look at the girls, and vice versa, and I caught Ricky's eye, wondering if he saw the humor in it. He shook his head subtly and looked away, but I knew he was smirking.

We splashed and yelled and cheered for Leo as he pretended to synchronized swim. Natalie and Cliff ended up closely entwined, and soon enough Terrica and Samuel followed suit, and then it was just Ricky, Leo, Lydia, and me, carrying on the conversation and pretending the other four weren't feeling each other up under the water.

"I feel like I'm in Europe," Ricky muttered, shaking his head at the two couples.

"Or *Deliverance*, but, like, a porno version," Leo said.

Lydia was sitting so close that I could see the water beads clinging to her bare shoulders. She had scooped her hair up into a messy
topknot, but a few flyaways hung around her face, and I had that
familiar urge to reach over and touch them. I couldn't believe she was
right there, completely naked. The top of her chest was just showing
above the water, and every time I noticed, it was like a spring un-
coiled in my stomach.

"I have an idea," she said under her breath.

"Yeah?" the three of us asked.

On her orders, Ricky, Leo, and I followed her out of the water
one at a time, covering ourselves from each other's prying eyes. The
other four were too wrapped up in each other to bother with us. It
wasn't until we were pulling on our sneakers that Samuel popped his
head up and asked, "Hey—what are y'all doing?"

"Nothing," Ricky said innocently.

Cliff looked up, too, his expression just as suspicious. There was a
long, hanging second where all of us were frozen, staring each other
down from the bank to the water. Then Lydia moved.

"Run!" she yelled, plucking up Natalie's clothes.

Ricky, Leo, and I sprinted after her, each of us holding the bun-
dles of Cliff's, Samuel's, and Terrica's clothes. We roared with laughter as we heard them come stomping out of the water behind us,
swearing and shouting death threats. We hustled all the way back
to the open field before we dropped their clothes by the tree line
and collapsed on the quilts by the firepit, heaving with laughter and
exertion.

"Fuck," Leo gasped, clutching his side. "They're so fucked."

"They're so *naked*," Lydia laughed.

Ricky sat upright and tended the fire until it sparked with life again. We moved to crouch in front of it, hoping the warmth would pull the wetness from our clothes. A few minutes later, the other four appeared at the tree line, still shouting swear words at us. Cliff and Samuel scampered out from the trees to gather up the piles of clothes.

"Lookin' good, daddies!" Leo called, waggling his eyebrows.

They rejoined us by the fire, panting and calling us dirty names, but it was clear our little escapade had been the high point of the night. Lydia lay sprawled on her back, still laughing even as Natalie threatened to smother her, and I was awash in the pure energy of her, in her spirit and mischief and spark.

Later, after we'd drunk another round of beers, Natalie suggested we head back to Lydia's house to crash. We loped out of the park and wound our way around a dimly lit road, the smell of river water heavy on our skin. Lydia ushered us in through the basement of her house, where we fell about on couches, sleeping bags, and blankets.

"I'll get us some dry clothes," Lydia said as Cliff started to snore.

"Do you want help?" I offered.

We tiptoed up through the dark, quiet house, not speaking until we reached her room. She switched on the bedside lamp and whispered to me where I stood by the door.

"Did you have fun tonight?"

"I had a blast," I said, grinning.

She smiled back at me, tired but happy, as she rifled through her dresser drawers. "Good," she said, tossing some T-shirts to the floor. "I know you said big groups of people aren't your thing, so I figured a smaller hangout would be."

I stared at her; it almost sounded like she was saying this small hangout was set up *specifically* for me, and I wondered if I'd heard correctly.

"I mean—" she said quickly. Even in the dim light, I could see her cheeks flushing pink. "I just thought, you know, a night out in the woods might be a nice change of pace."

I had this feeling then. It was a feeling like this *was* real, like Lydia did in fact like me as much as I liked her, and yet there was no sense of haste or anticipation about it; instead I felt calm and content, like a fireball could have shot down through the roof and I wouldn't have cared in the slightest.

"Do you know what the best part of tonight was?" I asked.

She glanced hopefully at me. "What?"

I looked at her. I wanted to say something tender, something real, but the smallest talon of fear dug into my side.

"Leo put Samuel's underwear on when we got out of the water," I said, overdoing my smile. "But Samuel hasn't noticed yet."

Lydia blinked, and then she started laughing in the silence, and I scooped up the T-shirts and helped her carry them downstairs.

Early the next morning, before Lydia's family could wake up and realize they had eight teenagers passed out in their basement, we slipped out of the house and trudged back to the park with bleary, half-asleep eyes. We hugged each other quietly and automatically, stifling our yawns behind our hands and muttering that we'd see each other later.

And in the spaces between everyone's goodbyes, Lydia looked at me. I can't describe it any more than that. She didn't smile, she didn't flutter her eyelashes, she didn't do anything that could be read as outright flirtatious, but the truth was she kept finding me.

"Ricky," I rasped when we were tucked inside his truck, "I think Lydia might be for real."

I told him about the conversation in her bedroom as we drove back out to the main road, the faint six -o'clock sun peeking through the clouds. Ricky laughed and dropped his head back, looking like something was obvious.

"Of course," he muttered.

"What?" I asked eagerly.

"This wasn't some random hangout Lydia dreamed up on a whim. She had it *because* she wanted to invite you. That's why she called all our friends first, to make sure we were free so she wouldn't look stupid if you said no." He nodded to himself, thinking. "And Natalie must know. That's why Cliff called to invite me, because Natalie would've told him to."

"Wait . . ." I said, putting the pieces together. "Natalie kept looking at me funny last night!"

"Sizing you up." Ricky nodded. "Trying to see if you like her best friend the same way her best friend likes you."

"Do you think that means Cliff knows, too? Or you think Natalie just told him to check if you were free?"

Ricky seemed to wake up at the idea. "I don't know," he said vaguely. "The idea of Cliff helping Lydia get with a girl is . . . I mean, I wouldn't expect it . . ."

He seemed lost in thought, almost like it was a wondrous possibility.

"Maybe you don't know Cliff as well as you think," I said.

Ricky was still zoning out. "Maybe . . ." he said slowly. Then he snapped back to life, blinking quickly. "Although . . ." he said, a grin inching up his face, "after that skinny-dipping last night, I'd say I know *everyone* pretty well."

12

MY QUIET EUPHORIA TOOK A COUPLE OF DAYS TO GET used to. Every interaction I had with Lydia seemed to confirm more and more that she actually liked me. We were texting regularly now—on a group chat with the others, but also individually between ourselves—and I took to dropping by the café to drink free lattes with her and Natalie after our morning shifts. Ricky was wholly supportive, asking for the latest updates every time we went for a drive, and I was always ecstatic to tell him about it.

It was late June now. The days were hotter, the insects buzzed louder, and the sunlight stretched past nine P.M. Maritza, JaKory, and I went to the movies twice in one week, sneaking grocery store candy and a bottle of Coke into the theater. We didn't feel guilty about it because we still splurged on a large popcorn to share between the three of us, and I thought longingly of Lydia and how much she would have loved it. My brother and I fell into the same late-night routine, staying up until ungodly hours, holing away in our bedrooms but sometimes finding each other in the kitchen at one in the morning. He even offered me the rest of his ravioli one night, gesturing to it in the overlarge pot, and the two of us ate at the counter while our parents slept soundly upstairs. And my portraits, meanwhile, continued to draw fierce interest: First Terrica asked for one, just as Natalie had guessed she would, and then Samuel followed her lead, trying to downplay his excitement about it. I painted them on back-to-back days while they sat there and teased each other, and the looks on their faces when I showed them the finished versions were priceless.

One afternoon, when I popped into the café after the breakfast shift, Natalie surprised me with an invitation.

"Can you come to Lake Lanier with us for the Fourth?"

My stomach skipped. I'd heard them talk about their previous Fourth of July parties like something out of a shimmering dream. Lydia looked up from the booth she was wiping like my answer was the most important thing she would hear that day.

"We're gonna camp again," Natalie went on, "probably just one night . . ."

I tuned her out. Lydia was smiling expectantly at me, and all I could think about was Lydia in a bathing suit, Lydia sleeping next to me in the tent, Lydia stealing me away for a private moment in the dark . . .

"So?" Natalie said. "Are you in?"

I didn't even think twice about it.

"Definitely." I grinned, and Lydia beamed at me.

Maritza asked JaKory and me to come over one afternoon, which was unusual, because we rarely hung out at Maritza's house. Her dad was a big-shot attorney for Coca-Cola, and he had a habit of purchasing expensive gadgets and lavish furniture that he never had the time to enjoy. Her mom, when she wasn't working for Delta, kept their house impeccably clean and perfect, to the point where it was almost sterile. JaKory had taken to calling it "The Museum," especially after Maritza's mom started framing Panamanian art and tagging each piece with the artist's name and date of completion.

We sat on the pristine white carpet in the living room, close to the fish tank Maritza's dad had bought last fall. It was a huge basin of a thing, like one of those gigantic tanks you see in a dentist's office, and it was full of dozens and dozens of tropical fish, swimming past us with bright, colorful movements.

"My mom hates this thing," Maritza said, watching the tank with a challenging expression on her face. "It creeps her out."

"Kinda creeps me out, too," JaKory said. "It's like a prop for a horror movie. Like a deranged murderer breaks in here, kills one of us, and stuffs our body in that tank."

"JaKory, in what fucking universe would that ever happen?"

"It could happen."

I lay back on the carpet, laughing. "'Kory, you have an amazing imagination, but it scares the shit out of me sometimes."

JaKory shrugged. He had a dopey little smile on his face. "Daveon would get it."

Maritza sent me a loaded look. I fixed my eyes on JaKory instead.

"Yeah . . . how's that going?" I asked casually.

"Unbelievably well," he said, still with that dopey smile. "We FaceTimed until five in the morning last night. He said he'd told his friends about me, too."

"Aren't you worried?" Maritza asked. She hesitated, wrinkling her nose. "You're getting so invested in this guy, but you'll never be able to date him for real."

JaKory death-glared her from a few feet away. "Maritza, I know your opinion on this, but it's not going to change anything. My heart's already in this. Either step up and be supportive, or I'll stop telling you about it at all."

Maritza clucked her tongue. "I *am* supportive. I'm just concerned."

"Stop being concerned. I'm fine. I'm *happy*." He leaned against the foot of the couch and crossed his arms like that settled the matter. "Didn't you wanna tell us something?"

That shut Maritza up. She made a show of adjusting her posture and clearing her throat like she was about to drop something huge on us.

"I think I have a crush on Rona," she announced.

I peered closely at her: She seemed triumphant and self-conscious at the same time. I held my breath, unsure whether I wanted to hear more.

JaKory frowned. "From dance?"

"Mm-hm," Maritza hummed, her eyes lighting up. "We've been hanging out after camp a lot, like going to Starbucks or back to her place until traffic dies down, and she's hilarious and energetic and smart and *gorgeous*, and she, like . . ." Maritza paused. "I don't know, I feel like she flirts with me."

I sat up. "Flirts with you how?" I asked, eager to know for reasons beyond Maritza.

"Like . . . the other day she told me I had a good ass," Maritza said, blushing.

JaKory and I looked at each other, our eyebrows raised. Maritza *never* blushed. "Um . . ." he said. "Context?"

"We were standing with the other senior coaches, and we were all trying to figure out how to change one of our steps, so I showed them an idea I had, and Rona just kinda interrupted and said something like, 'Those leggings make your ass look *amazing*.'"

"She just blurted it out like that?" I asked skeptically.

"Yeah. *Very* enthusiastically."

"How did the others react?" JaKory asked.

"Becca just laughed. Vivien seemed annoyed, but what else is new."

JaKory and I traded looks again, holding eye contact this time. I could see he was thinking the same thing I was.

"Isn't Rona the one who said you were overreacting when you were upset about Vivien getting captain?" I asked.

"Well, yeah . . ." Maritza hedged, "but I *was* overreacting." She glanced between JaKory and me. "Why do I get the sense that you two aren't excited about this?"

"We are," JaKory said hastily, "but . . ."

"But what?" she pressed, and when JaKory wouldn't answer, she turned to me.

"But it sounds like you need to go slowly," I said gently. "Rona's . . . *cool* . . . but I always got the impression she would flirt with anyone."

Maritza didn't speak for a long second. Her brows were furrowed, and her mouth hung open like she couldn't believe she was hearing this from us. "Wow," she finally said, widening her eyes, "thanks a lot."

"Come on, Maritza," JaKory said. "Rona's known for being boy crazy."

"So that means she can't like a girl? God, how many times do I have to explain this bisexual concept to you two?"

"That's not what we're saying," I said firmly. "We're saying Rona seems like one of those girls who would flirt with another girl just for the hell of it—like, that she wouldn't really be into it, but she would do it because it's like a game."

Maritza looked so frustrated, I wouldn't have been surprised if she'd chucked a lamp at the fish tank. "Y'all hardly even know her," she said loudly. "And so what if that's what she's doing? Who says I can't enjoy that?"

"You *can*," JaKory said. "We're just telling you the same exact shit you've been telling me: to be careful."

"We don't want to see you get hurt," I added. "Having a crush is fun, but it makes you vulnerable, too."

"Who are you to be advising me on crushes?" Maritza snapped. Her eyes were blazing. "At least I *have* a crush. I'm not wasting my time bopping around a giraffe store all day."

My mouth fell open, but before I could retaliate, JaKory cut in.

"Don't be like that, Maritza," he snapped back. "This isn't a competition. Codi doesn't have to be hitting this at the same pace as us."

He rested a hand on my knee, glancing at me in what he clearly thought was a protective way. It was even more patronizing than the day at the coffee shop when he'd told me to keep an open mind. I could feel the flush creeping up my neck, and my heart pounded like a warning. The old, toxic resentment reared in my blood.

Maritza exhaled, but the blazing look was still in her eyes. "Yeah, well, I'm gonna invite her over when my parents are gone, and then we'll see who's right."

We fell silent. JaKory took his hand off my knee. Maritza picked at the carpet and chanced a look at me, her expression sheepish, but I ignored her. I was sitting there burning up inside, the truth of everything fighting to get out of my mouth, every beautiful and wonderful thing about Lydia and Ricky and all their friends, and yet I couldn't do it. And it wasn't because I was chickening out. The truth was I didn't *want* to share any of it with them. We were sitting there beneath this huge-ass fish tank with the ideas of our desperate crushes flitting around the room, and I didn't want to be a part of it anymore.

"Codi?" Maritza said softly. "I'm sorry I said that. It wasn't fair."

It took me a second to answer. I turned my head slowly to look at her.

"I gotta go. My mom asked me to pick up Grant from a friend's house."

It was a lie, and we all knew it, but neither one of them pushed back on it. They probably thought I wanted to go home and sulk about my small, timid, limited life. I got up from the carpet without saying goodbye and walked out of the house in silence.

On the last Monday of June, my brother asked me to take him to the movies again. He claimed it was because our parents wouldn't want to miss their favorite TV show that night, but I couldn't help wondering if he was meeting up with that girl again.

I looked long and hard at him when he asked me. He shifted uncomfortably on the spot, sighing like my three seconds of staring were unbearable.

"Yeah, I'll take you," I said finally.

For a fraction of a second he looked happily surprised, but then he fixed a stoic expression back on his face. "Cool. It's at seven."

"We'll leave at six forty."

"Yeah."

I wanted to say something to him on the drive to the theater—I was curious and anxious to hear where things stood with that girl—

but something in me held back. Maybe I didn't want to know. Maybe I couldn't bear it in case he'd already beaten me to the punch, or in case things didn't work out with Lydia.

"Thanks," Grant told me when he got out of the car.

"I'll pick you up at nine. Leave your phone on."

"Yeah," he said, stepping away already.

I passed the next two hours reading in my room, figuring I'd better start on the school's summer reading list now that we were inching into July. The novel they'd assigned us was dense and boring, but I knew I could ask JaKory about it later, when I'd gotten over my anger at him. I had always been a slow reader, but tonight I was even slower than usual because I kept stopping to check my phone, hoping Lydia had texted me. Instead I had texts from Maritza and JaKory, exchanging crass thoughts on some celebrity guy they thought was hot, as if our standoff yesterday at Maritza's had never happened.

Finally I gave up and texted Lydia myself.

> *I'm so jealous of you starting college. You don't have to deal with bullshit summer reading anymore.*

She wrote back a few minutes later.

> **Lydia Kaufman aka Jason Waterfalls:** *Yeah haha I know. What are you reading? Is it that bad? Sorry I haven't really texted today, I've kind of had a bad day*

A new, weird feeling came over me then, soft like my stomach had gone all melty but was trying to reach outward at the same time.

Are you okay? Can I do anything?

Lydia Kaufman aka Jason Waterfalls: *Thanks Codi, I wish you could. Just a bad day in math class, we got our midterms back and I didn't do so hot, and we have another test on Wednesday that I have to study for tonight. Sucks*

I thought back to the Lydia I'd seen in the woods: the girl who'd been tackled by Samuel and ended up laughing, the troublemaker who orchestrated our prank to steal everyone's clothes. I remembered what Natalie had told me about Lydia not seeing the good in herself, and I hated to realize that Lydia probably felt like that right now.

I wanted to make her feel better. I wanted to make some grand gesture, something that would surprise her and pull her out of her bad day. I sat there thinking about it, my heart pumping fast, and the answer came to me in a blaze of inspiration. It was perfect, especially because my brother was already at the movies.

I texted Grant with my request, hoping he would see my message before he exited the theater. As I was driving to pick him up, my phone chimed with his response.

Grant: *Ok.*

Grant met me at the car with the huge bucket of popcorn under his arm. "Why'd you want this so bad?" he asked, grunting as he slid into the passenger seat.

"I need it for something. Thank you for getting it."

"It was eight dollars."

"I'll pay you back." I looked around at the people outside the theater. There was no sign of that skinny girl I'd seen him with last month. "Um," I said, hesitating. "Are you waiting on anyone? Or should we go?"

Grant wouldn't look at me. "We can go."

He didn't ask again about the popcorn, and I didn't ask about the girl. When we got home and I made no move to get out of the car, Grant turned back to me.

"Aren't you coming inside?"

"I have to go somewhere real quick."

"Where?" He narrowed his eyes. "Who's that popcorn for?"

I couldn't shut him down, not when he'd been the one to help me buy it, but I didn't want to tell him the whole truth, either. I debated in my head while he watched me carefully.

"It's for . . . someone I'm getting to know," I told him cautiously. "But I'm not ready to talk about it yet."

My brother frowned, but not like he was mad—more like he was processing. After a beat he nodded and said, "Okay."

"Can you tell Mom and Dad I'm dropping something off at Maritza's?"

"Yeah, okay."

"Thanks."

"No problem."

He ambled off to the garage. I considered the popcorn bucket, wondering how to keep it steady now that Grant wouldn't be there to hold it. The only idea that came to me was to buckle it up like a baby, so that's what I did, pulling the passenger-side seat belt snug against it to hold it in place. Then I sat back and looked at it for a moment, and out of nowhere I started laughing, really laughing, just me sitting there in the car by myself and feeling so goddamn good about everything.

I put on a playlist Ricky had shared with me, checked that the popcorn was secure one more time, and backed out of the driveway.

It was after nine thirty by the time I turned onto Lydia's street. For a moment I wondered if I was being an idiot, if she would think I was stupid for showing up at her house this late, but a calm voice inside told me to keep going. I sent a single text after I parked.

Can you come outside? I have something for you.

Lydia opened the door as I was walking up the front steps. Her hair was wet and she wore a big T-shirt that almost covered her pajama shorts. My stomach swooped at the sight.

"What are you doing here?" she asked, grinning as she stepped onto the porch, her floral scent swirling all around me.

I held out the popcorn. "You had a bad day."

Her eyes lit up, and she laughed like she couldn't believe it. "You're kidding. You got this for me?"

"Straight from the movie theater. I thought it would help with studying."

She took the popcorn bucket and placed it on the porch by her bare feet. Then she wrapped me in the surest hug I've ever known.

"Thanks," she said softly, pulling away. "Can you come in for a minute?"

"Don't you have to study?"

"I can take a break," she said, and smiled.

It was only the second time we'd been alone together, unless you counted the few stolen minutes we'd had in her bedroom. I got a better look at her room this time: It was small but homey, with dark wallpaper and a collection of mismatched lamps lighting the space. The overhead light wasn't on; neither was the fan. There was a tennis racket in the corner, a vintage record player on the floor, and an old wooden desk overlooking a window. Her laptop sat open on the desk with a tumbler of water next to it.

"Inspecting my room?" she asked, folding herself onto the bed with the popcorn at her belly.

"I was too drunk to take it in last time. I like how cozy it is." I dropped down into the desk chair, looking over at her. "Do you use the record player?"

"Not really. It's my brother Asher's, but he gave it to me when he left for college. I keep forgetting about it, though. I'd make a horrible hipster."

"My parents had a record player in our old house. Once in a while they'd drink a bottle of wine and put it on, and then they'd just sit there with their eyes closed and listen for, like, half an hour." I bit my lip, remembering. "That's when I'd get my little flip pad and try to draw them."

Lydia laughed brightly. "You drew your parents when they weren't looking? That was your way of being sneaky?"

"I was self-conscious!" I laughed. "My parents were, like, the all-American couple, always socializing and hosting parties, and then they had me, and I just wanted to hide in corners and finger paint. They had *no* idea what to do with me."

Lydia had a tender smile on her face. "I bet you were cuter than you realize."

I ducked my head, laughing softly. "Maybe."

We melted into silence. Then Lydia said, "So . . . this midterm I got back today . . ."

"Yeah?" I prompted.

"I got a sixty-eight."

It was clear, from the way she said it, that she hadn't told anyone else yet.

I wasn't sure what to say. Everything in me wanted to make her feel better, but all the responses in my head felt inadequate. Finally, I opened my mouth and asked, "Do you want to talk about it?"

It was a stupid, cheesy question, but Lydia didn't hold it against me; instead she nodded and let everything spill out.

"I thought I'd studied pretty hard, and when I took it I thought I did okay, like a B-minus maybe, but when I got it back today I felt like someone had punched me. I don't get why math is so impossible for me. My brothers and parents are so good at it, like they can add numbers in their heads so fast, but I've never been able to do that. My parents aren't going to be mad if I tell them, but they'll do this thing where they'll look at me like—like they have to make a special exception because I'm just not smart. It's a look of pity, and I hate it."

"You are smart, though—" I said bracingly.

"Not at math, I'm not."

The distance between us was strained. I could feel the fibers of the chair beneath my legs, buzzing and itching. My muscles were asking to get up, even if my brain was lagging behind them.

I made the decision before I could think about it a second longer, and moved to sit with her on the bed. She scooted to make room for me, but our knees touched the slightest bit, and when I breathed in I could smell her shampoo.

"Do you wanna know something?" I said. "I think school is bullshit in a lot of ways. They have this standard idea of how we're supposed to be, and they hold us to it even if it doesn't fit. Like, this past year in Advanced Art, Mr. Erley had us create portfolios of our work, and I worked on mine like a lunatic, I mean, I even submitted three extra pieces, and I was so proud of everything I'd done. But then we had to do oral presentations about our portfolios, and I get really nervous talking in front of people, so my presentation wasn't very good, and my final grade on the whole project ended up being an eighty-five. An eighty-five because I couldn't explain my paintings to classmates who didn't even care. Mr. Erley wrote all these complimentary things about the paintings themselves, but then he wrote a bunch of insults about my presentation, like 'You need to practice making eye contact' and 'Try to smile sometimes!' And it's like, just because I was scared to present to my classmates, that doesn't mean it should cancel out how good my art was."

Lydia's eyes, so full of desperation a minute before, were now full of fire. "God, Mr. Erley is such an ass."

"You're smart, Lydia. I bet you do fine with math when you're not worrying about it, like with all those checks you have to manage when you're waitressing, but even if you're just flat-out not good at math, I think that's okay and you shouldn't feel ashamed of it. You're good at a million other things, like Manhunt and goofy pranks and making people feel like they matter to you."

Lydia looked straight at me; it was the longest we'd ever held eye contact. "Where did you come from?" she asked, shaking her head. "It feels like you should've been here the whole time."

I could feel myself blushing, and I dropped my gaze to my hands in my lap. "I'm new to the scene."

"Oh yeah?" she laughed. "What scene?"

"The teenage scene."

She smiled at me in a gentle way, the way you can only smile at someone when you've really started to know them and don't have to worry about looking happy all the time. "'The scene,'" she repeated, laughing again. "Only you."

We were quiet again. I glanced at my watch and saw that it was almost ten. My parents would be wondering where I was.

"I should let you get back to studying," I said.

"It doesn't seem as important now," she sighed, scooting off the bed, "but yeah, I guess I should keep trying."

She walked me to the front door and said goodbye. I had just stepped off the porch when she called my name.

"Codi?"

I spun around. "Yeah?"

"I think it's time for you to paint my portrait."

For a moment I couldn't speak. I thought about Ricky telling me to seize the opportunity. Maritza's wise words about the universe rewarding your effort. JaKory's battle of the infinite and intimate.

"I think you're right," I said boldly.

I smiled, and she smiled, and the whole way home I was on fire.

13

I WENT BACK TO LYDIA'S HOUSE ON THURSDAY, RIGHT after we finished our morning shifts. It was my first time being there in the daylight, and I took in the details I hadn't noticed before: the earthy, charming gray color; the navy rocking chairs on the porch; the wind chimes hanging over the front steps. Lydia met me in her driveway, jumping out of her car with her hair swept up in a ponytail and that big, bright smile on her face.

"Ah, the artiste!" she said, pulling me in for a hug. She was still dressed in her work polo, but this time it was a sea-green shade that made her eyes pop.

I laughed and let go of her. "Not an artiste. Just an amateur."

"Psh," she said, handing me an iced coffee she'd brought from the restaurant. "You make art, and it's beautiful. Try and tell me that doesn't count."

We went around to the backyard, where Lydia pointed to a small tree house nestled between the trees. It looked hand built, with mismatched planks and faded, peeling paint on the sides. There was no ladder, but there was a path of crooked two-by-fours scaling up the trunk to the entrance.

"You said to pick a place that makes me feel like myself," Lydia said, glancing sideways at me. She seemed almost self-conscious, like maybe this wasn't what I'd meant.

I grinned. "This'll be perfect."

She climbed up the ladder first, and I followed a beat behind, trying not to stare at the freckles on her thighs. My canvas workbag brushed against my side, and the moment I got to the top, she pulled it off my shoulder.

"What do you think?" she asked, gesturing around the closed interior.

It was a tight fit, obviously meant for little kids. We stood close together, crouching slightly, our heads practically grazing the roof.

"Definitely an intimate setting," I said without thinking.

She laughed and stretched her foot behind her, almost like a nervous tic. "Do you need anything else? I'm gonna fix my hair and change into something that doesn't smell like grease." She paused, her eyes twinkling. "Even though you like that smell."

"Shut up," I laughed, rolling my eyes. "Go make yourself look presentable."

"Are you saying I don't look presentable now?"

I laughed as she scaled down the trunk. Within a minute I'd gotten myself set up, a beautiful blank page and my vibrant set of watercolors in front of me. Now I just had to get in the right headspace.

"Okay," Lydia said, huffing as she reappeared at the hole in the tree house floor, "which shirt do you like better?" She held out two options.

I squinted at them. "Which one do you wear when you wanna feel . . . um . . ."

"Hot?" she laughed.

A faint blush tinged my cheeks. "I was gonna say . . . like the *you* that you wanna be every day."

She poked her tongue out, examining them. "I guess this one." She smoothed her hand over a simple turquoise tank top.

"Great. Let's do it."

There was a pause as she hovered awkwardly, and at first I wasn't sure why. Then I realized she needed to change into the shirt.

"Oh," I said, turning my head away. "Yeah, um . . . yeah."

"Thanks," she said with a loud, fast laugh.

I kept my head tilted down, acutely aware of her tugging the shirt off in my peripheral vision. What did it mean that I had offered to look away, and that she'd expected me to? I mean, this was happening *after* we'd skinny-dipped together. It was broad daylight, sure, but still—this didn't seem like a standard interchange between two friends. I couldn't imagine Lydia and Natalie turning away from each other for something as simple as a shirt change.

"Okay," she said. I looked up as she was pulling her hair out of the shirt collar. "How's it look?"

My stomach was swooping and whirling all over the place. The truth was she looked simply and naturally beautiful, but I didn't know how to tell her that, so I panicked and tried for something low-key instead.

"Dope."

She raised her eyebrows at me, and I mentally slapped myself.

"I mean, *pretty*," I said quickly. "Really pretty."

She seated herself on the floor across from me, her legs crisscross-applesauce style, her hands splayed back to lean on. There was a pocket of silence where neither one of us spoke as I shifted my paper and studied her, and she watched me carefully in return.

"Shit," she said finally. "This really is like *Titanic*."

"Should we call Natalie to come distract you?"

"No." She shook her head. "But you'll have to keep me calm somehow."

"You'll have to keep *me* calm."

"Okay," she laughed. "Let me think about it."

We faded into silence again, and for a while I was able to focus on painting. It was a strange feeling, being so acutely aware of her body and yet feeling detached enough to lose myself in the painting at the same time.

"Can I look at my phone?" Lydia asked, her voice quiet and breathy like she didn't want to disturb me. "I have an idea."

"For a second. I'm about to start on your eyes."

It felt like a naked, intimate thing to say. I smiled at her apologetically, and she bit her lip shyly.

A minute later, she broke the silence again. "All right, I found something," she said, glancing up from her phone. "Questions you ask to know someone better."

I paused my painting. "The artiste has to answer questions right now?"

"Yes. If I'm going to be vulnerable, you're going to be, too."

I snorted. "This *is* vulnerable for me."

"Too bad."

She took me through a list of questions. Most of them were easy, like *What's the story of the day you were born?* ("It was Saint Patrick's

Day," I said, "that's why I'm such a party animal.") Some of them were fun to entertain, like *If you had your own space shuttle, where would you go?* ("Pluto," Lydia said decisively. "I'd apologize for the whole you're-not-a-planet-anymore fiasco.")

Then we got to a question that required a more thoughtful answer.

"'As you walk along the beach on a quiet, breezy day,'" Lydia read, "'you come upon a glass bottle that has washed ashore. Inside, you find a message you've been waiting for. What does it say?'"

She looked up at me. I paused with my paintbrush hovering over the canvas.

"That's a cheesy question," I said.

She raised her eyebrows, unrelenting. "But do you have an answer?"

I tried to think about it, but I was hyperaware of her watching me. I looked at her, and she looked back, and then we both looked away, laughing.

"Okay," I said, "give me a second."

The question settled into me as I focused on painting her eyes. She could obviously tell I'd gotten to them, because she looked directly at me, her eyes bare and bright and steady. It felt more intimate than I'd realized it would—far more intimate than looking into Maritza's or JaKory's eyes, or Ricky's, or even my parents' and brother's eyes; there was something intense but vulnerable about the way she was looking at me, like she wanted to be seen and hidden away at the same time, and the longer I held eye contact with her, the more I felt the same way.

I swallowed, forgetting about my paintbrush. "I have an answer."

"Yeah?" she whispered.

"Well, two answers. A fun one and a serious one."

She smiled like she'd expected nothing less. "What's the fun one?"

"The message would be from a fabulously rich old lady, and she would invite me to her mansion on the French Riviera for a dinner party with a bunch of famous artists."

"I like that. Why does the lady know all these artists?"

"She's just one of those crazy rich people who have lots of talented friends."

"Yeah, and no one even knows where all her money came from."

"Exactly."

A beat passed, and Lydia asked, "Could I hear your serious one?"

I took a breath. I wanted to tell her—to invite her into my scared, insecure, vulnerable self—but it was terrifying as hell. I didn't even know if I could be this honest with Maritza and JaKory.

Her eyes were still on me, searching me, and there was no expectation in them—only wonder.

"Okay," I said. "The message would be from—well, I don't really know, but it would be from someone like God, someone who really knows what they're talking about—and it would say—" I paused. I took another breath. "It would say, *There's nothing wrong with you. You're doing just fine.*"

Silence. I sat there across from her, buffered by the canvas, my face searing with heat, my heart sprinting with panic.

Then Lydia spoke.

"It would be the truth."

She wasn't patronizing or dismissing me. Her voice was clear, and steady, and gentle.

I exhaled. "Could I hear your answer?"

She was quiet, but then she said, "It would be from my gram, who died last year." Her voice wobbled, and she swallowed hard. "And she would say, *There's nothing to be scared of.*"

I was quiet, giving her the moment she needed. Then I asked, "Lydia? What are you scared of?"

She didn't reply right away, and I worried I'd overstepped.

But then she said, in a strained voice, "Going to college. Failing. Not being brave enough. Everything."

I breathed in. A million responses flashed through my brain, but I settled on the one that felt the truest.

"I think saying what you're afraid of makes you brave."

We looked at each other for a long, burning second. I watched her breathe, her chest rising and falling.

"Codi?"

"Lydia?"

She bit her lip, a secret grin on her face. "What's your favorite color?"

I laughed unexpectedly. "*That's* what you want to follow up with?"

"Yes."

I smiled, my hands in my lap now, all thought of the painting abandoned. "It changes all the time. Right now it's violet."

"I love that."

"What's yours?"

"Green," she said right away.

I nodded, unsurprised. "Like your eyes."

She laughed. "Not for that reason."

"Why?"

"The first house my family lived in was green. Like a pastel shade, you know? And anytime a friend's mom would drop me off, we'd turn on my street and I'd say, 'My house is the green one.' I didn't know how to count the mailbox numbers but I knew my house was green, and I loved it."

My heart expanded inside me. In that moment I felt like it was okay to be exactly who I was, because she was being exactly who she was, and that must have meant something. I absorbed it all: her eyes, her secrets, her space in the world.

The only thing I managed to say was, "I like knowing that."

"I like knowing that you know it."

We looked at each other, and I knew what was coming before she could get the words out.

"Hey," she said, her voice shaking the slightest bit, "do you wanna get dinner on Saturday night?"

My insides exploded. I hesitated for a flash of a second, taking it all in, and then I smiled.

"Yeah," I said, my voice ringing through the tree house. "I would really, really love that."

Later, when I was driving home, it felt like Lydia's impression was still stamped into me. It was like coming home from a trip to the beach, when you pull the wrinkled clothes from your suitcase and you can smell sunscreen and sand and ocean not only on your bathing suits, but on your T-shirts and pajama pants, too.

I lowered my car windows and blasted my music, even at the red lights. I let my arm hang out and spread my fingers on the air, feeling the humidity, feeling the air rushing over my skin. I'd never gotten the big deal about teenagers and cars before, the whole freedom and invincibility thing, but now I understood it. When you had a crush and you knew you were going to see her again, especially for something that sounded exactly like a date, suddenly the whole world could never be big enough for you.

14

LYDIA WAS PICKING ME UP AT SEVEN, AND I HAD NO idea what to wear.

It had been raining all day, softening into a gentle sprinkling that I could only hear because I'd opened my bathroom window. I stood in front of the mirror in mismatched socks and an old T-shirt—the interim outfit I'd thrown on after my shower—and lifted the strands of my damp hair, wondering what the hell I was going to do with it.

I was pretty certain this was a date—my first-ever date—but I had a weight in my stomach telling me not to assume, not to get my hopes up, because there was still the possibility that Lydia was just really, *really* nice. I knew Maritza was hanging out with Rona tonight, and her texts to JaKory and me made it clear that she was expecting something to happen. I felt the parallel with my situation and knew I had to protect myself from heartbreak the way I knew Maritza wouldn't.

But maybe Lydia was getting ready like this, too. Maybe she was listening to the record player while she brushed makeup over her cheeks and tried on six different shirt combinations. Maybe she was praying this was a date just like I was.

I dressed in dark shorts with a flowy tank and a long necklace. I never felt very confident about the way I dressed, but this was one of the few outfits I felt good in. I curled my hair, even though it never stayed, and made my eyeliner thicker than usual. For ten minutes I switched back and forth between a pair of wedges that dressed up the outfit and a pair of oxfords that dressed it down. If I'd known for sure whether this was a date, I would have gone with the wedges in a heartbeat.

I wore the oxfords just to be safe.

Right after I'd applied deodorant for the second time, my phone chimed with a text.

Lydia Kaufman aka Jason Waterfalls: *Two min away!*

I hurried down the stairs, my heart sprinting and palms sweating. "I'm going out with my friends!" I called to whoever was listening, and then I skipped out to the garage and pulled the door tight behind me. I hovered on the edge of the driveway, craning my neck to watch for Lydia's car, the rain still drizzling down in a lazy, steady way.

A minute later, Lydia's navy sedan swung into view. She pulled as close to the garage as possible, and I ducked through the rain and into her car, where it was cool and dry and smelled like pine.

"Hey," Lydia said with her usual big smile.

"Hi," I said with my heart in my throat.

I tried not to look at her too long. Her hair was tied over her shoulder in a loose, pretty braid and her skin was showing above the neckline of her shirt. She was achingly beautiful.

We went to a trendy tapas place near our high school. The lights were low and the artwork was funky. The hostess seated us at a two-top near the rain-drizzled window and handed us glasses of sparkling water.

"This place is fancy," I said as the hostess left us alone.

"Have you never been here?" Lydia asked.

"No, but I've heard of it. This girl in my English class said she went on a date here once."

Lydia gave a short laugh and looked hastily down at her menu. I flushed and stared at the cheese list without processing any of the words.

We went through the motions of ordering. Soft drinks, brussels sprouts, vegetable paella to share. It was exactly like going out to eat with Maritza and JaKory, except I never felt breathless when I went out to eat with them.

The tablecloth was a sheet of brown parchment paper, and there was a box of crayons tucked into the salt-and-pepper holder. In between bites of tapas, I grabbed a crayon from the box and sketched out a drawing. I could feel Lydia's eyes on me, and after a minute I heard her laughing.

"The green house," she said, placing her hand over it like she wished it were real. "And is that supposed to be the mailbox?"

"Or a bird feeder. Whatever you prefer."

"Bird feeder, easy."

She had an awed smile on her face, and for one shining, beautiful moment I felt confident that this was definitely a date.

I felt even more confident after she insisted on paying.

After dinner we walked around the shopping plaza, talking and laughing. The rain had let up and the air was cooler than usual. It was Fourth of July weekend and there was a buzz of energy in the air, with people walking about and enjoying the long weekend. I felt like the whole world was as happy as I was.

Lydia mentioned the popcorn I'd brought her on Monday, and I told her how I'd buckled it into the car seat like a child.

"You didn't," she laughed, her eyes bright, her hand brushing my arm.

"I totally did. I would've looked like a freak if I'd gotten pulled over."

"It was worth it, though," she said decisively. "I ate it the whole time I was studying, plus I had some for breakfast the next morning." She bit her lip and looked shyly at me. "Definitely the best study buddy I've ever had."

The drive back to my house seemed much faster than the drive to dinner. I didn't want the night to end, but I wasn't sure how to keep it going. Lucky for me, Lydia didn't seem to want it to end either.

"Does your neighborhood have a clubhouse?" she asked as she turned into the entrance.

"Yeah, if you go to the left."

"Is there a playground?"

"Yeah . . ." I laughed, wondering where this was going.

"Do you like swings?"

My heart drummed. "Yeah, I do."

"Good answer," she said, grinning.

We parked near the swimming pool and wound our way to the playground. The sky was darkening and the air was humming with crickets. We passed a row of bushes with fully bloomed roses, and their scent filled the air, sweet and fresh and aching. I felt like I was in a dream, wandering through a garden with a beautiful girl.

The swings were covered in rainwater, so we tipped them forward until most of the water had run off. Lydia reached over and wiped the last of the water off mine, shaking her hand in the air afterward, and my heart melted at the gesture.

I plopped down on my swing, trying to keep my cool. "I haven't been on a swing in forever."

Lydia sat on the adjacent swing and turned her body toward me. "That's the saddest thing I've heard today."

"Why, when was the last time you were on a swing?"

She scrunched up her face, thinking. "Last summer, in Natalie's neighborhood."

"Just for fun?"

"It was when Natalie and Cliff first started talking, and she wanted me there for backup. We went swimming all day and hung out on the swings afterward."

"Natalie made you play third wheel?" I teased.

"Right?" She paused. "I mean, kind of. Cliff brought his cousin along and I kinda had to hang out with him. I think they were hoping it'd be a double date."

I got a breathless, pinching feeling in my chest. "Oh," I said, forcing a laugh. This was the first time I'd heard her mention a guy, and my stomach soured, worrying I'd gotten her wrong. As nonchalantly as I could, I asked, "Was it?"

Lydia tipped her head to the side, the way people do when they're trying to land on an answer. "A little," she said finally.

My heart plummeted. "Oh."

"It didn't turn into anything, though," she added hastily. "I didn't like him enough."

I nodded. Lydia was looking at me hesitantly, like she was searching for something. I wasn't sure what to say, so I kicked off the ground and started swinging. Lydia followed my lead, and we swung in silence for a minute, facing the sidewalk that wound toward the tennis courts.

"Have you ever dated anyone?" Lydia asked suddenly.

I felt my face get hot. "Um—no," I said quickly. "Not yet."

"You haven't wanted to?"

"I just . . . um . . . haven't found the right person."

She didn't reply. I wanted to look at her, wanted to see what she felt about that, but I was afraid. Our conversation was starting to feel a lot bigger and more meaningful than I could handle.

We pumped our legs faster and faster, kicking high into the air. The streetlamps came on, and over on the tennis courts, some people struck up a night game beneath the overhead lights.

I stopped pumping my legs and let the swing slow to a natural stop. Lydia followed suit, half a minute behind me.

"That was fun," she said breathlessly, as if all thought of our conversation was forgotten. She twisted to look at me and broke into a big, bursting laugh. "Oh my god, your hair . . ."

Before I could process, she reached over and trailed her fingers through the strands. My scalp tingled at the touch.

"The curls are out of control," she laughed.

I could barely breathe. My voice felt lodged in my stomach. "Does it look bad?"

"No, still really pretty."

Her eyes twinkled in the moonlight. I felt myself smiling so hard that my cheeks ached, and her smile grew larger in response. The cicadas' song seemed to swell around us, and my stomach skipped like a dance, and I remembered Maritza and JaKory swooning about roller coasters and poetry.

"You look really pretty, too," I said, my voice shaking.

Lydia looked hard at me. Her expression grew serious, and her hand dropped to my knee. I felt it like a blast of heat.

Neither one of us moved; we just sat there looking at each other. I couldn't stop looking at her mouth, and I knew she was looking at mine, too.

"Codi . . ." she said breathlessly.

It was happening. She liked me and she was going to kiss me. This girl whom I liked so, so much was going to kiss me . . .

And I had no idea what to do.

The realization crashed around me. I wasn't like Natalie or Terrica, confident about making out in a moonlit river; I wasn't even like Ricky, brazen enough to steal a kiss beneath the trees. In this moment, when everything was real, when everything hinged on the brave, reckless confidence of my new self, I realized I'd never become that person at all.

Lydia leaned toward me, her eyes flitting between my eyes and my mouth, but I sat frozen, too paralyzed to close the gap between us.

"Um," I said, shifting my knee out from under her hand.

Lydia jerked back, and just like that, the moment was broken.

Silence.

Terrible, suffocating silence.

I sat there trying to grasp the moment I'd just squandered. My heart was drilling and my palms were soaking with sweat. The tennis court lights were too white and too bright and everything inside me felt like it was struggling to breathe. I'd just thrown away the one thing I'd been waiting for forever.

Finally, Lydia cleared her throat. "It's late, huh?" she said, her voice overly hearty. "Come on, I'll take you home."

Sometime later, I lay on the floor of my bedroom, staring at the ceiling and fighting the tears in my eyes.

My first instinct was to call Ricky and ask if we could go for a drive, but I imagined how he'd look at me when I confessed what had happened, and a dark mass of shame rolled over my chest.

My second instinct was to call Lydia and ask her to come back, but I didn't know what I'd say to her. How do you explain that you like someone so much that it paralyzes you?

Then I got to my third instinct, which was strongest of them all. I wanted Maritza and JaKory. I wanted to lie down between them and sob my heart out and listen to them tell me that it would be okay. For the first time all summer, I desperately missed my best friends. I had been so hurt and angry and resentful, but clearly they had been right about me all along.

Maritza would be practical and scientific about what had happened; she'd use facts to make me feel normal. *You said your heart was beating super fast, right? So your body was in fight-or-flight mode. You thought the situation was dangerous because it was new and unfamiliar, so your instinct was to get out of it, that's all.*

JaKory would be empathetic and rallying. *I'd probably do the same thing, if not worse. It's petrifying to have your feelings out there like that.*

You were feeling intensely vulnerable, but you'll learn how to move past that. You'll get another chance.

I threw my phone on the bed so I wouldn't call them. It wasn't an option—not when I'd been lying to them for weeks. How was I supposed to tell them about Lydia when she was just the tip of the iceberg of everything I'd been keeping from them?

I lay on the floor for ages. My heart was now quiet and dull, almost numb. I closed my eyes and took myself back to the swings, rewriting that moment over and over again to a version where I didn't choke.

Finally, I got up and shuffled out of my room. The house was sleepy and quiet, but there was light beneath my brother's door. I knocked and stepped a foot back, listening to his desk chair swivel on its plastic mat.

He looked guarded when he opened the door. "What?"

"Do you wanna watch something?" I croaked.

He could have said no, the way I'd done to him a million times in the last few years; or he could have asked why, because I knew he could tell I was sad about something; but all he said was, "Yeah, okay," and followed me down to the family room, where we collapsed on the couch and watched *Brooklyn Nine-Nine* until we fell asleep.

15

THE MOMENT I WOKE UP ON SUNDAY MORNING AND remembered what had happened, my stomach roiled. I couldn't bring myself to do anything more than brush my teeth before going to work. My shift passed in a slow haze and I was so irritable that I snapped at some preteen boy who kept badgering me about crocodile bandanas. Tammy suggested I reorganize the stockroom after that.

I managed to send Lydia a single text, and that was after two hours of deliberating in the stockroom.

Thanks for dinner last night. I had a lot of fun.

Her response came an hour later, and it lacked her usual smileys and emojis.

Lydia Kaufman aka Jason Waterfalls: *No problem codi.*

I wanted to take her for coffee and ask if we could try again. I wanted to swing by her restaurant with flowers. I wanted to drive her to the river and kiss her in the back seat of my car, but I did none of those things, because I felt stuck and stupid and ashamed.

By the time I got home from work, it felt like my whole torso was locked up with emotion. I wanted to talk to someone who could soothe me, someone who could tell me everything was okay and that I would get another chance even if I didn't feel I deserved it. I texted Ricky and asked if he wanted to go for a drive.

He pulled into my driveway fifteen minutes later, still in his church clothes and looking preoccupied about something. He barely smiled when I climbed into his truck, and I noticed he wasn't playing any music.

"What's wrong?" I asked him.

He shook his head. "Nothing."

We drove to the river and parked beneath a cluster of trees whose branches reached over the car, draping us in shade. Ricky shut the engine off and tossed his keys into the cup holder, then drew a hand down his eyes like he was utterly exhausted.

"So," he said half-heartedly, "what's up with you?"

I looked at him. The weight on my chest was heavier than ever, but from watching him I could tell that he didn't have the space for my problems right then.

"Maybe we should talk about you," I said gently.

"No, I'm fine."

"Are you sure? You don't seem fine."

"I'm fine."

"Is it Tucker stuff?"

He rubbed his hand over his mouth. "It's nothing you need to hear about." He paused. "Tell me about you and Lydia."

I felt irrationally annoyed all of a sudden. I slumped back in my seat, staring ahead at the river.

"So?" Ricky prompted. "Tell me what happened."

"There's nothing to tell."

He knit his eyebrows together, exasperated. "I thought you said you wanted to talk."

"I did."

He stared me down. "So talk."

Slowly, tentatively, I told him what had happened on the swings the night before. I couldn't look at him; I could barely stand to hear my own voice. I'd thought telling him would make me feel better, but instead I felt like I was handing over something I would have rather kept to myself.

"It's all right, Codi," Ricky said when I was finished. He sighed and rubbed his hand down his face again. "Kissing can be scary."

"Don't patronize me," I snapped.

"I'm not."

"Yeah, you are."

His mouth tightened. We stared at each other, and then he said, "Look, did I ever tell you about my first kiss?"

"You know you didn't."

He ignored my sass and dove into the story. "It was with this girl, Alex Pickens," he said, staring out over the water. "We were in seventh grade, at a service project site our moms made us sign up for, and we were stocking shelves with canned food. She got cold, so I gave her my sweatshirt. Then we kissed."

I'd expected a better story, or at least something with a point. "And . . . did you like her?"

"I thought she was cute, but I didn't want to kiss her in a warehouse."

"But at least you did."

He rolled his eyes, and not in a playful way. "The point is, it was stupid. She wasn't someone I had a major crush on, like you do with Lydia, so it didn't matter."

"Then tell me what it's like to kiss someone you *do* have a major crush on," I pressed. "Tell me what It's like to kiss Tucker."

Ricky went dead silent, glaring at me.

"*Really?*" I said.

He shook his head. "Don't start on this, Codi."

"Fine. We'll just pretend it's not real, like always."

"Did I do something?" he asked, his voice rising. "Or is this just you being pissed off that you fucked up your first kiss?"

I looked away from him, unable to believe he'd said that.

"You know," I said, taking a shaky breath, "the thing about being *friends* with someone is that it's supposed to be a two-way street. That day when I came over to your house, you told me that I wasn't allowed to make you into some kind of project. But you know what, Ricky? You're making *me* into a project. You always jump at the chance to help me because you think I'm this emotionally stunted wallflower who doesn't know what she's doing, but you won't let me do the same for you. Would it be so bad to tell me how you really feel about Tucker? How goddamn upset he makes you?"

Ricky lashed out so quickly that it seemed like he'd had the words prepared for days. "Has it ever occurred to you that maybe you're projecting your own feelings onto me, Codi? Our problems are not the same. I'm not even sure that I'm *gay*! You keep pushing this thing with me and Tucker because you want to have a model for all the things you've been missing out on, but I can't give that to you! I can't act like Tucker and I are in love, like we go on dates and hold hands and kiss each other like we're in some romantic comedy, because that's not the truth! I'm just a guy who's trying to feel his way through everything without getting boxed in by labels!"

"I'm not trying to box you in!" I yelled. "I don't care about labels and identities and—"

"Are you sure about that?" he said harshly. "Are you sure you haven't been sabotaging yourself this entire time with these stupid fucking ideas of how *you're* supposed to be?"

"I don't have a single issue with being gay—"

"But you do have an issue with being shy, and being anxious, and being someone who never went to parties and never went on dates and never kissed anyone before! How much of that stuff is actually you, Codi, and how much of it is you *thinking* that it's you? It's not like you're some defective, half-alive seventeen-year-old who can't make friends or talk to people. You've been doing it all fucking summer! You have an incredible opportunity with Lydia right now, and you're blowing it because you can't get over yourself and stop imagining that you're so different from everyone else!"

His words knocked the breath out of me. For a minute all I could do was sit there and let everything crash over me, my stomach chilled and my throat blocked up.

Ricky was looking straight out the windshield, breathing hard. He was more agitated than I'd ever seen him.

"I'm not trying to tell you who you are and what you want," I said roughly. "Not like you just told me. But something's bothering you, and whatever it might be, I'm your friend and I just want to be here for you."

"I don't need you to be," Ricky said, jamming his key back into the ignition.

That hurt worse than anything; it felt like another way of him saying I wasn't truly his friend. All I wanted was to be there for him like someone he'd known since kindergarten, when every feeling shared was pure and guileless and true. But none of that mattered; the conversation was over.

We drove back to our neighborhood with no music and no apologies. When we pulled up to my house, my brother was in the driveway, shooting hoops by himself. He looked up, his eyes widening at Ricky's truck, but I slammed the car door and stormed into the house before he could ask me any questions.

I was off-balance for the rest of the day. Ricky's words latched on to my skin, scratching away at me until my whole body felt like an exposed nerve. I shut myself in my room and paced around like a crazy person, huge adrenaline rushes surging up through my chest every time I thought of another cutting retort I should have thrown at him.

Then I lay on the floor and stared at the ceiling. I grabbed my phone and turned on some music, closing my eyes and replaying every moment of this summer in my mind, trying to understand how I'd gotten to this place.

My little pity party was interrupted by the sound of a text message.

My heart leapt, hoping for Lydia, hoping for Ricky, but it was neither one of them.

Maritza Vargas: *Can you come over?*

I stared at the message. I hadn't heard from Maritza in days, and the last thing I wanted right now was to try to make sense of where we stood with each other.

What's wrong?

She started typing, stopped, and started again. I waited another two minutes before her message came through.

Maritza Vargas: *You were right about Rona.*

I sighed. I was still upset with Maritza for the way she'd talked to me last week, but I knew something pretty bad must have happened for her to admit to being wrong. For a long minute my anger battled it out with my deep-seated loyalty, and finally the loyalty won out.

Give me 15 minutes.

Maritza's garage doors were shut; the house was all locked up. I wasn't sure why until I remembered that her parents had left for Panama the day before. A stab of guilt dug into my stomach. The old Codi never would have forgotten about Maritza's parents leaving her alone; I would have invited her over in a heartbeat.

I knocked on the back door until Maritza answered, a fleece blanket draped around her shoulders and an exhausted expression on her face.

"Hey," she croaked.

"Hey."

It was strained between us. For a second we hovered there on the threshold, merely looking at each other. Then Maritza stepped back and gestured me inside.

I followed her into her parents' elegant, renovated kitchen with its cold floors and marble counters. There was no sound except for the ticking of a clock. A bowl of her mom's arroz con pollo sat half-eaten on the table.

"Thanks for coming over," Maritza said, not quite catching my eye. "I felt like I was going crazy sitting here by myself."

I studied her; it looked like she might cry at any second, which was something I'd only seen twice in the six years I'd known her.

"What happened?" I asked softly. "Does Rona not feel the same way?"

She swallowed and looked at me, but her response had nothing to do with Rona.

"You're such a good friend," she said shakily. "I don't even deserve to have you here right now. I'm so sorry for how I talked to you last week."

I exhaled. I wasn't prepared for her apology, and I didn't know how to explain that the conversation we needed to have was much bigger than a single instance of "sorry." I barely had the emotional bandwidth to deal with her Rona problem; there was no way I could work on fixing our entire relationship.

"Let's worry about that later," I said, pulling her over to the couch. "Just tell me about Rona."

Maritza sighed and pulled her legs up, tucking herself into the corner of the couch. I spread out across from her, wrapping a cashmere blanket around my legs.

"My parents left yesterday morning," she said, swallowing. "I told Rona she should come spend the night, and she seemed really, really into the idea; we talked about it all week at camp, and she kept saying how much fun we were going to have."

I bit down the weird feeling inside me. It felt wrong that Maritza was telling me about these plans *after* they had happened, when in the past I would have known about them in real time.

"So last night she shows up," Maritza went on, "and I was all spastic and excited, and we ordered Chinese food and watched a movie . . . and then she convinced me that we should drink some of my dad's Puerto Rican rum."

"Uh-oh," I said, knowing how carefully Mr. Vargas guarded that rum.

"So, against my better judgment, we took a couple shots . . . and she started being all touchy-feely . . . and then . . . ." Maritza inhaled. "We started making out."

My stomach plummeted. It was a jarring feeling, watching your best friend beat you to the finish line and remembering that you're not supposed to feel jealous of her for getting there first. All I managed to say was "Wow."

"I can't even explain how it happened, but suddenly she was kissing me and it felt . . . it felt so *good*, dude . . . I mean, I could have done that for hours."

"Wow," I said again.

"But then . . . ." Maritza shook her head like she was trying to make sense of something impossible. There was a distant, defeated look in her eyes. "I don't know, it was like she got bored or something. She stopped kissing me and started talking about how we should invite these guys over."

"*What?*"

"Yeah. I guess she has some friends who live near me, so she texted them and told them to come over. And I was so confused that I didn't even object to the idea. She was like this force of momentum that completely knocked me over. So these guys show up, and Rona was outright flirting with them, *both* of them, and she tells me we should give them some rum, too, and I told her my dad was going to notice that so much of it was gone, and she was like, 'He can get more while he's down there.'"

"Wait—what?"

"She thought Panama and Puerto Rico were the same thing."

"Ugh, Maritza . . ."

"I know. And *then*, she told the guys that she and I had been 'having fun' before they got here."

"No," I groaned, actually covering my eyes with my hands. "Please tell me she didn't—"

"Yes, she did. So of course they started being complete assholes and trying to get us to make out in front of them."

I stared at her, worried about where this was going. I *hoped* Maritza wouldn't be desperate enough to turn her sexuality into a show like that, but with the way she'd been obsessing about hookups lately, I couldn't be so sure.

"Please tell me you didn't . . ."

"Of course I didn't!" Maritza shrieked. "Do you know me at all?

God, Codi, I was *freaking out.* Rona kept telling me to relax, that there was no harm in kissing, but I lost my shit and screamed at the guys to get out of my house."

"Good!" I said, my neck flushing with heat. "Did you kick her out, too?"

"I couldn't; she was too drunk to drive. Neither one of those ass-hole guys offered to take her home, so I got stuck with her. We didn't even speak the rest of the night. She was as pissed at me as I was at her. It's like she thought I was just being a prude and a loser, like she had no idea that making out with her had actually meant something to me."

Her voice cracked on the last word. I reached for her hand and squeezed it.

"I'm sorry," I said gently. "You deserve way better than that."

She swallowed. "You and JaKory were right."

"I wish we hadn't been."

Maritza looked at our hands. Tears were building in her eyes. "I wish I'd never agreed to be a summer coach. I could've just worked a retail gig, like you, and then I could've taken time off to go to Panama." She was really struggling not to cry now, her expression twisted up and her eyes blinking fast. "I can't believe Mom and Dad are down there with everyone and I'm stuck here by myself, crying over some dumb girl."

"She's not some dumb girl. She meant something to you."

Maritza shook her head. "I *made* her mean something. I did the exact same thing I've accused JaKory of doing: told myself something was possible when it was really just wishful thinking. I was an idiot."

"Stop being so hard on yourself," I said, pushing at her shoulder. "You're not an idiot. You're someone who knows what she wants and works hard to get it. It's one of my favorite things about you! So forget stupid Rona. Some other girl or guy is gonna come along and kiss you like it means something, and until then, you just have to keep being the person you are."

Maritza breathed in a slow, steadying breath. "You really think the person I am is okay?"

"I think the person you are is amazing."

She gave me a watery smile. "I believe that, coming from you."

"You should."

She squeezed my hand. For an infinite moment, all was right in the world.

But then she said something else, something that made my insides harden.

"You're an amazing person, too. I shouldn't have judged you for wanting to stay the same. I know you're not the type to throw herself out there and make a million things happen, and that's okay. We can't all be movers and shakers. Some of us have to keep things steady and sure." She paused, smiling at me like we were in on the same joke. "I'm glad you're still the same old Codi. I went out there and got my heart stomped on, but you were here this whole time, waiting in the wings to help me feel better."

She bumped her shoulder against mine, like we'd just shared something tender and heartwarming, but I could only blink at her; an angry flush was creeping up my neck, and suddenly I was hardly breathing.

Was I angry with Maritza, or with myself? She couldn't fathom that I was capable of risk and change and growth, but was that her fault for not believing it, or my fault for not showing her?

"Dude," Maritza said, eyeing me in alarm, "what's wrong?"

I shook my head like a warning.

"I'm sorry," Maritza said, sounding completely bewildered. "I—I meant all that stuff in a good way—"

I stood up and jerked away from her, my face and neck still burning. "I'm gonna go."

"Wait—Codi—I'm really sorry, I was trying to say something nice—"

"Well, you didn't," I said shortly, grabbing my keys off the table.

"I'm sorry," Maritza said again. She sounded very small. "I thought we were having a heart-to-heart—I didn't mean to ruin it—"

"How can we have a heart-to-heart when you don't know anything about me?" I asked bitterly.

She looked like I'd walloped her. "What?"

"Never mind, it doesn't matter."

I was halfway to the door when her voice stopped me.

"But what about tomorrow?"

I stopped, confused. "What about it?"

"Am I still coming over? For the Fourth?"

I had no idea what she was talking about. I couldn't remember making plans with Maritza for the Fourth of July, and although I wasn't planning on going to Lake Lanier anymore now that I'd messed things up with Lydia and Ricky, I wasn't sure I'd be in the mood to do anything else.

"Did we make plans?" I asked, my voice wavering.

Maritza seemed frazzled, unsteady. "My mom called your mom last week to make sure I could come over for it. She wanted to make sure I had somewhere to go, since she and Dad are gone."

The rage burned me up again, threatening to burst out of me and spill across the Vargases' fancy living room. I stood there, paralyzed, too angry to speak.

"I'm lost here," Maritza said in a small voice. "What's going on?"

I didn't answer the question. Instead I turned my back on her and stormed out of her house before she could say anything else.

I didn't go home. Instead I went for a long drive. I followed the path Ricky always took to the river and parked by the water, gripping the steering wheel tightly, trying to squeeze out my toxic energy.

I called my mom, and before she could do more than ask where I was, I started yelling, demanding to know why she'd made Fourth of July plans for me without telling me.

My mom sounded as bewildered as Maritza had been. "Codi," she said, leveling her voice the way she always did when Grant or I got out of hand, "what exactly is the problem here?"

"You just assumed I would want to have Maritza over!" I yelled. "You didn't even ask me! What if I'd made plans to do something else?!"

"What other plans would you have had?" Mom asked, like I had just said the most impossible thing in the world.

A numbness coursed through my body, threatening to swallow me up. "Never mind. I'll be home later," I said shortly, and I hung up.

I sat there shaking, rubbing my hands up and down my thighs. The fact that my mom couldn't fathom my having plans beyond Maritza and JaKory made me feel enraged and pathetic and resentful all at once. I knew it was partly my own fault—that I was hiding whole parts of my life from everyone—but just for *once* I wanted people to believe I was capable of being more than what I'd always been.

Everything was so goddamn stupid. I'd messed things up with Lydia because I was anxious and afraid; my friendship with Ricky was a one-sided joke; and Maritza and JaKory were always going to be there, but instead of that making me feel safe and comforted, it just made me feel *stuck*.

I wanted to grow. I wanted to feel like someone different. I wanted to know that my friends and my weekends and my crushes were things I was choosing for myself. But as I sat there in the hot, quiet night, with the self-righteous rage draining out of me, it seemed I was destined to remain the same limited, lifeless person I'd always been.

That Monday, the Fourth of July, was the worst day of the summer. I woke up with a pit in my stomach, knowing I needed to cancel my plans to go to Lake Lanier with Lydia, Ricky, and the whole crew. I texted Natalie that I'd come down with a freak summer fever and wouldn't be able to make it. It was a stupid lie, but I knew it didn't matter; Lydia would have told her what had happened by now, and Ricky would probably make it clear that he wasn't interested in being my friend anymore.

All morning I tortured myself with visions of how the night could have gone. I pictured Lydia wearing red, white, and blue, her hair tied back like it had been on Saturday night, her eyes reflecting the fireworks. I imagined stealing her away from everyone to kiss her in the dark, and Ricky giving me a knowing grin when we came back holding hands, and the rest of the group embracing us while we ate hot dogs and hamburgers and s'mores.

But instead, I'd be staying home for a playdate my mom had set up for me. A playdate with the two friends who thought I was a loser.

JaKory Green: *Are we still coming over tonight?*
Maritza said y'all had a fight . . .

I sighed. I wanted nothing more than to be alone, but it felt like more trouble than it was worth to cancel plans with them.

Yeah of course. See you around 6.

From the moment they got there, I knew I'd made a mistake. Maritza was still acting tentative around me, and her way of dealing with it was to ingratiate herself with my family more than usual. She made a big show out of helping my mom shuck corn as if it was her penance for how she'd talked to me the night before. Meanwhile, JaKory pretended like nothing was wrong, but he kept studying me when he thought I wasn't looking.

"Stop examining me," I snapped as we sat on the deck, waiting for the fireworks to start.

"Sorry," JaKory said, widening his eyes like I was crazy. "You just seem kinda agitated today."

"I'm not *agitated*. I'm fine."

"Okay. *Sorry.*"

I didn't miss the loaded look he sent Maritza, but I ignored it and poured myself more lemonade.

"So . . . I wanted to ask y'all something," JaKory said a few minutes later. He spread his hands over his knees and hesitated like he was trying to pluck up the nerve for something.

"What?" I prompted.

"Daveon and I have been talking about meeting up . . ." He bit his lip. "Do you love me enough to drive me to Alabama?"

There was a prolonged pause. I felt Maritza shoot me a look, but I ignored her, staring straight at JaKory.

"Are you serious?" I asked warily.

"Not tonight, obviously," JaKory said hastily. "We were thinking two weekends from now, on Saturday the twenty-third. His parents are going on a church retreat, so we'd have the house to ourselves." He paused, his eyes flitting between us. "Please?"

"You're gonna go spend the whole day with a stranger?" Maritza asked. "In Alabama?"

"He's not a stranger—"

"You've never met him before. You have no proof that he is who he says he is. Or that the connection between you is actually real."

"That's why I need y'all to come with me, just in case. You won't have dance that day, and Codi, I was hoping you could ask off from the store—you've worked so much this summer, I'm sure they wouldn't mind. I know it's a lot to ask, but this might be my only shot." He clasped his hands together, his eyes pleading. "Come on. Don't you want this to work? Aren't you happy for me?"

Neither Maritza nor I answered. Silence swelled around us, heavy on the air.

"Wow, okay," JaKory said, his tone deadly quiet. "So, let me spell this out . . . I'm in love with a great guy, but my two best friends don't give a shit?"

"It's not *real*, JaKory!" Maritza said.

"IT IS REAL!" he bellowed. "My feelings are real! God, I'm so tired of you two not listening to me, thinking I'm such a joke all the time!" He rounded on Maritza, his eyes popping. "Is this because it didn't work out with Rona? Is it, like, a jealousy thing? You wanted so badly for things to be different, for us to have romantic prospects, but only if you got to lead the way, right? And fuck it all if I'm the only one who got anywhere?"

"*What?* No—"

"And you, Codi, what's your deal? You've been completely absent all summer, working a million hours at that stupid store and barely spending any time with us—"

"I've spent time with you!" I said hotly, even though I knew it was hardly true.

"Bullshit. You're not *around*, Codi. And when you are, it's like you're only half there, just watching without actually participating—"

"I *am* participating!"

"No, you're not! And I'll bet that's why you're pissed, right, because I have someone, and Maritza kissed someone, and you're just slogging away at that stupid store, afraid to put yourself out there and try something new—"

I stood up in a fierce rush, my anger swelling like a tidal wave. "I *am* trying new things," I snarled, glaring between the two of them. "Maybe I just haven't felt like *sharing* with you guys. And it's because of this! Because you—you—" I thought wildly of Ricky's pointed words, his accusations—"You box me in! You don't let me breathe! You can't even *fathom* the idea that I'd want to try something without you! Well, news flash, I'm not some loser you need to drag behind you like some ball and fucking chain. I've done plenty of stuff without you this summer, and you know what, I haven't missed you at all—"

"What are you talking about?!" JaKory said, springing off his chair.

"I'm talking about outgrowing you! I'm talking about not liking who I am with you! You act like I'm the same exact person I was when we were eleven, but guess what, I'm not! And I'm fucking tired of it!"

The deck door swung open. My parents stood motionless on the threshold, staring between us.

"What's going on?" my mom asked in a scandalized voice.

The three of us stood facing off, breathing fast, unable to hide our anger. I cleared my throat and stared at a spot above my parents.

"What's going on is that I want Maritza and JaKory to leave," I said, struggling to maintain my composure.

"What?" my mom said, as if I had just asked for the moon. "What happened?"

None of us answered. The moment stretched on, heavy and tense and irretrievable.

"Fine," JaKory said finally. "Come on, Maritza, you're taking me home."

"JaKory—" she said.

"Don't," he said, holding up a hand. "Just drive me home, and then none of us have to talk to each other anymore."

Maritza hesitated, but she followed JaKory off the deck and past my bewildered parents. JaKory didn't spare me another glance, but Maritza turned around one more time, the expression on her face something I wouldn't be able to get out of my head later.

My parents were still standing with their mouths hanging open, looking between me on the deck and my friends walking out of the house. I was shaking, trying not to cry, and staring determinedly at the wooden deck panels.

There was the sound of Maritza's car starting in the driveway, and a few moments later they were gone.

"Codi," my mom said softly.

I shook my head and marched past them. My brother stood at the kitchen counter with a shocked expression on his face, but I hurried up the stairs and into my bedroom, where I locked the door and fell onto my bed. I cried until the fireworks started up, blasting and crackling somewhere high above me.

16

THE NEXT FEW DAYS WERE A SLOW, DRAGGING WEIGHT. I felt like I'd been sprinting for weeks, fueled by adrenaline and novelty and giddiness, and now I was crashing hard. For a while there I'd actually thought I was becoming someone new, that I was creating another social and emotional landscape in my small, compressed world, but now I could see that it had all been a short-lived, bound-to-burst dream, and that I was the one who had killed it.

Summer felt markedly different now. It was always different after the Fourth of July, when the new school year loomed much closer, but now it was also emptier, more drawn out, more depressing. I could feel the school year crawling closer and knew it would be exactly the same as it had always been. Being a senior wouldn't make me any different or more real. It might even be worse than the past three years, because now I might be going into it without my two best friends.

"What happened, though, honey?" my mom asked for the millionth time that week. "I've never seen you three fight like that."

"I don't want to talk about it."

"But Codi, they're your best friends," she said gently. "They're practically a part of the family."

I didn't want to tell her the truth: that the three of us hadn't spoken to each other in days, that JaKory had been posting emo poems on Tumblr, that I couldn't help worrying about Maritza going back to face Rona without her parents or JaKory or me by her side.

And, more than anything, that I'd never felt so lonely.

"I guess these things happen," Mom sighed. Then she turned businesslike. "Okay, let's talk about anniversary weekend. Dad and I leave next Saturday morning, which means you're going to be in charge. I need you to make sure your brother gets to wherever he needs to go . . . He mentioned something about Darin's house . . ."

I tuned her out. Grant's social life was the last thing I needed to hear about right then.

A week after my fight with Maritza and JaKory, I woke up early and lay in my bed for a while. The sound of a lawn mower outside made everything feel so mundane and ordinary. I felt like there was no energy in my body, like the muscles and veins and blood flow weren't working properly. It was a feat just to drag myself down to the kitchen for a bagel.

My brother was there, eating ravioli out of a cereal bowl, wearing a faded T-shirt that didn't fit him anymore. I hid my face and set about toasting a bagel. For a moment, it was just the two of us breathing in the empty kitchen.

"Are you trying to burn your bagel?"

I looked up at the sound of Grant's voice. "What?"

"It's been in there too long."

I popped the toasting button up; sure enough, my bagel had started to blacken around the edges.

"Oh," I said dazedly. "Thanks."

Grant's fork clanked against his bowl. "Mom's worried about you," he said with his mouth full.

His tone was casual, matter-of-fact, like he was telling me it might rain that day. I kept my back turned to him, scraping cream cheese onto my bagel. "Why?"

"Because you screamed your head off at Maritza and JaKory, and now you're just moping around doing nothing." He burped and kept talking with his mouth full. "Dad says you're just being a moody teenager."

I tried to say I was fine, that Grant should mind his own business, but the words got stuck in my throat.

"Why'd you get so mad at them, anyway?" Grant asked.

I shook my head. "I don't want to talk about it."

"Are you in a bad mood because you got in that fight with your boyfriend?"

I whipped around as if our parents might be there, even though I knew they were at work. "He's not my boyfriend," I growled. "And it's none of your business."

Grant narrowed his eyes. "I picked up that popcorn for you, remember?"

"So? What, you did me a favor and now I owe you an explanation for everything in my life?"

"No," he huffed, his voice cracking a bit, "but I got that popcorn for you and I didn't tell anyone about it, and I haven't told Mom and Dad any of the times when you've said you were going out with Maritza and JaKory but you're actually going out with that guy in the truck—"

"Why are you always spying on me?" I asked shrilly.

"My window looks out over the driveway!" he said, abandoning his ravioli. "I can't help it if I see you sneaking out all the time!"

"I'm not 'sneaking out'—"

"I haven't ratted you out to anyone, Codi, not even one time."

My brother had a fierce look in his eyes, but there was something deeper coming across, too: He seemed hurt, disappointed, like he was trying to keep himself from wanting something. I stood still, watching him, both of us breathing hard.

What was the harm in telling my brother, really? I'd lost everything already, so what did it matter if I confided those losses in him?

"Fine," I said. "What do you want to know?"

He looked cautious, like I might be pulling a trick on him.

"Grant," I said shortly. "What do you want to know?"

He leaned back on his stool, almost like we were having a casual catch-up session, but I noticed he'd crossed his arms tighter. "Who's that guy?" he asked. "How do you know him?"

"His name is Ricky, he's my friend and nothing more, and I met him at a party."

Grant's eyes widened. "You went to a party?"

I looked away, avoiding the question.

"Maritza and JaKory don't know him, right?"

"No," I admitted, "they don't."

"Why not?"

I shook my head, wondering how to answer something I was still

· 225 ·

trying to articulate for myself. "I just needed something for myself, something they weren't a part of."

Grant was silent for a long moment.

"What?" I asked. "You think I'm a terrible person?"

"No," he said evenly, "I think it makes sense."

"It does?"

"Yeah," he said, like it was obvious. "Maritza and JaKory think they know everything about you, and sometimes about me, but they don't."

I watched my brother curiously. "Yeah."

"Why did you fight with him? Ricky? You both looked pissed when he dropped you off last time. I thought you had broken up."

"I told you, he's not—"

"I know, I know, sorry."

"We had a fight about . . . about him not trusting me. He always wants me to tell him stuff about me, but he won't tell me anything about him."

"That sucks," Grant said, like he was really trying to relate to me. "And it's not fair, 'cause you're probably just asking because you want to know him better."

"Exactly," I said, and the moment I uttered the word, it hit me what Grant was saying. I wasn't even sure he meant for me to read into it, and maybe he wouldn't have wanted me to, but all the same, I was standing there across from my little brother and realizing I had kept him even further away than Ricky tried to keep me.

"You'll fix the fight," Grant said, oblivious to the guilt I was feeling. "Whenever my friends and I fight, we just walk some laps to cool off, say we're sorry, and get back to our game."

"Yeah," I said, still reeling. "Yeah, you're right."

"But why are you mad at Maritza and JaKory? What did they do?"

"I—I don't know."

"Are they your best friends still? Or is Ricky your new best friend?"

"I don't know," I said again, feeling hollow.

"Man. I mean, Maritza and JaKory can be really annoying sometimes, but I can't imagine them not being around anymore. They've been, like, a part of me growing up."

I laughed unexpectedly. "What?"

"They have been," Grant said earnestly. "I've known them since I was in third grade. Maritza helped me with my science fair project, remember?"

"Yeah. I remember." I paused, and now my heart started drumming hard. "Grant? Don't you think Maritza and JaKory and I are kind of—losers?"

"Losers? Who said you were losers?"

I shrugged but didn't elaborate; my heart was still pounding and I knew I was burning red.

Grant averted his eyes. "I don't know, Codi. When I was little it felt like everyone just did what they wanted with the friends they liked to hang out with. But now it feels like there's this pressure to do different stuff." He shrugged. "I always thought maybe you just didn't feel like that. You had your two best friends that you'd known forever, so you were able to keep doing the things that made you happy."

I let that settle into me, feeling out whether it was true. "Yeah . . ." I said slowly, "but maybe I'm trying to figure out other things that make me happy, too."

Grant nodded. "Yeah."

I met his eyes briefly. "I'll ask Ricky what kind of truck he has. Maybe he can give you a ride sometime, if you want."

"Yeah," Grant said casually. "Cool."

We lapsed into silence, finishing our breakfast, until Grant got up and dropped his bowl in the sink.

My heart felt calmer after that conversation with my brother. It was weird, really, because it was a pretty simple conversation, but in the hours and days that followed, it was like a missing piece slid into place.

I texted Ricky to ask if we could meet up and talk, but he said he was at his college orientation. I'd completely forgotten about that, and it was almost jarring to hear it, like a reminder that summer was such a transitory thing. I pictured Ricky walking around the University of Georgia campus with new friends and a new class schedule, and I felt happy and sad at the same time.

Over the next few days, a strange thing happened: I started enjoying my own company more. I'd always spent time by myself, painting and daydreaming, but it was more like punctuation between school or hangouts with Maritza and JaKory. Now it felt like the hours I spent by myself were intentional. I sketched, I painted, I started reading a book on JaKory's list; I drove to the river by myself and journaled about how it felt to be a teenager, and how it felt to not understand yourself, and how it felt to love people without knowing exactly how they fit into your life.

On Wednesday night, I was lying in bed, sketching whatever came to mind, when my phone buzzed with a text.

Ricky Flint: *Can I come over?*

My heart leapt.

I met him in my driveway. Everything was quiet and dark and unfurled, much like the first time I'd met him. Neither one of us spoke as we fell into step together, looping around the back of my house to sneak in through the basement door.

I had assumed he wanted to talk about our fight, but the moment we got inside, it became clear he was upset about something else. He buckled onto the carpet, flopping on his back with his hands grabbing at his head.

"Are you okay?" I asked.

He didn't say anything, just breathed deep with his eyes on the ceiling.

I looked closely at him, taking in his distressed expression. "Can I get you some Tums?"

He rolled his head toward me. "Tums? Why would I want Tums?"

"JaKory's stomach hurts whenever he's upset," I said, shrugging. "I don't know, I was just trying to help."

Ricky looked at me for a while, his eyes boring into mine. "I'm sorry."

I looked back at him. "No, I am."

"No, Codi, really. You were justified in everything you said. I wanted to be your friend but I haven't let you be mine. The past few days, I've been thinking about some shit, and—and you're the only person I've wanted to talk to about it."

I lay down next to him, paralleling his body. "What is it?"

He took a deep breath. "I hooked up with someone at orientation."

The words hung in the space above us. He'd said them matter-of-factly, but I could sense his anxiety.

"Oh, really?" I said, trying to sound steady. "Who was h—I mean, who were they?"

Ricky dragged his hands down his face. "It was a *he*," he said, covering his eyes. Then he went still for a second. It seemed like he was hardly breathing. "Damn it, Codi, it was a *he*."

We were both silent. The air-conditioning hummed in the background. I watched Ricky's eyes, his hands, his chest rising and falling.

"His name was Eric. I went out to the bars with this group of people, and he was with them, and I thought he was a cool guy, but I didn't consider him beyond that. But then we got Chinese food together after the bars closed, and we started talking, and I could just tell he was guarding something. He kept talking about how college was gonna be his fresh start, how he was looking for breathing room, and I said something similar, and then we just . . . I don't know, Codi, the next thing I knew we were making out in the dorm room, and he kept saying, 'I've never done this, have you done this?' and I didn't know what to do."

Ricky was looking imploringly at me, as if I could tell him what it all meant. I knew I couldn't; I also knew it wasn't mine to make sense of anyway.

"Are you scared?" I asked him.

He let out a long breath. I thought he would look away from me, but he didn't.

"Yeah," he said. "Yeah, I'm really scared."

We stared at each other. Then I said, "Tell me."

"It's closing in on me," he said, his eyes getting wet. "This whole time, I've thought maybe I was just this cool, unbound person who was down for anything, girls and guys. But I'm feeling more and more like it's—like it's guys—and what if I don't want that to be true? What if I don't want to be Ricky the gay guy? What if I just want to be Ricky the football player, the business student, the guy who throws parties for his friends? I keep thinking about the night we met, how it must have looked to you, walking along minding your own business and suddenly there's this big football player chasing down another dude 'cause he wants to make out with him, 'cause he can't stop wanting this dude no matter how hard he tries, no matter how much he acts like it's a casual thing . . . Codi, I don't wanna be that guy you saw. I don't want to be that."

"Ricky," I said gently, "you're not that guy. You wanna know how I saw you? I wasn't walking along minding my own business, I was walking along with knots in my stomach, terrified to go to your party but even more terrified that maybe I *wanted* to go. I felt like there was some secret knowledge everyone else had that I didn't have and they would take one look at me and *know*. And then you appeared out of nowhere and you were everything I wanted to be. You were this cool, rebellious senior who threw a party that everybody wanted to come to, and then you ditched your own party to kiss somebody you *really* wanted to kiss. And when he freaked out and ran away, you stayed there, looked me straight in the eye, and asked me who I was. That's the guy you are, Ricky! The guy who goes after things and shows other people how to go after them, too."

His eyes were red and watery. He wiped them and said, "You make me sound a lot cooler than I am."

"Maybe you just have a skewed perception of yourself."

He laughed, still wiping his face. "Who does that sound like?"

I smiled in spite of myself. "Fine. Maybe I've been telling myself a story about who I am, and maybe that story isn't true. But you've been doing the same thing."

"Yeah, I know."

"Do you really like this guy? Eric? Would you be happy if he asked you to hang out?"

Ricky looked off to the side, chewing his lip. He was silent for a full minute, and then he said something very quietly, something that landed pure and vulnerable in the space between us.

"I'd be happier if Tucker asked me."

It was a huge thing, him saying that. We both stayed silent, letting it settle, letting it breathe.

After about thirty seconds, Ricky looked over at me. We locked eyes, and I nodded.

"What do I do?" he asked.

"What do you wanna do?"

"See him. Talk to him." He paused. "Go on a date with him."

"Can you text him and ask him out?"

Ricky shook his head. "That's too much. We've only ever talked in person, when other people have been there. I know this doesn't make sense, but it feels safer that way."

"So if you saw him in a group again, could you ask him out?"

"Maybe if I got to talk to him long enough. I'd definitely feel more confident doing that than just texting and asking."

"Okay," I said, thinking. "When can you see him in a group again?"

"I don't know. Maybe the next time someone has a party?" He sighed. "But the summer is almost over."

We fell quiet. I breathed deep, taking it all in, letting his worries swirl around me.

And then I had a wondrous, terrifying idea.

"Ricky . . ." I said slowly, the idea still taking shape in my mind. "What if . . . I had a party?"

Ricky looked at me like I was crazy. "What?"

"My parents are going out of town this weekend, for their anniversary. I could have people over." I paused, trying to make my intentions clear. "Not a ton of people, but enough that Tucker and his friends coming won't seem like a big deal."

Ricky's eyes were wide. "Are you for real, Codi?"

I laughed, surprising myself. "Yeah, I am. My brother's sleeping at a friend's house Saturday night, so we could do it then."

His face broke into a slow, true smile. "Shit. That could actually work."

"Yeah, it could." I looked hard at him. "You gotta go for it, though."

"I will," he promised.

We grinned at each other, giddy with our own brilliance. Then Ricky asked me something that had been in the back of my mind all along.

"What about Lydia?"

My heart fell as suddenly as it had lifted. "What about her?"

"What do you mean, 'What about her'? Have you talked to her?"

"No, not since that night. I don't know how to explain myself to her."

Ricky narrowed his eyes at me. "Didn't you hear yourself a minute ago? All that stuff you said about telling yourself the wrong story? Okay, so you got spooked on the swings, but so what? That was just a small version of you. It wasn't the real you. The real you wants to be with her, so go be with her."

I wanted so badly to believe him. "But what if I screw it up again? What if I can't handle it?"

"You can handle it, trust me." He paused, then rolled onto his side, looking straight into my eyes. "Look, do you wanna know how I saw *you* the night we met? There I was, thrilled to be making out with this guy, when a girl walks up on us and throws everything for a loop. And then the guy runs away, and the next thing I know, my hand is throbbing and bleeding and it's my own fucking fault. But you know what this girl does? She pulls me out of it, looks me straight in the eye, and tells me that she likes girls like it's the easiest thing in the world to say, like *we're* the normal ones and the guy who abandoned me just hasn't figured it out yet. Then she walks me back to my party so I don't feel so alone. And when I ask her to show me mercy one more time, she goes into the party by herself, even though she's clearly nervous about it, just so she can bring me some bandages."

I hung on his every word, my breath catching in my chest.

"This girl took a bad situation and made it better. She showed up for me, she let me see who she was, and she gave me hope that one day I could let other people see who I was, too. And I swear to you that Lydia sees this same girl, Codi, and she'll be thrilled as hell when you realize that you deserve good things just like everyone else does."

Now there were tears in my eyes. I breathed against them, grateful and awed. Ricky smiled at me, and we lay there on the floor, talking until all the bad stuff drained away.

17

THE NEXT MORNING, I TOOK A LONG SHOWER AND blow-dried my hair. I picked out one of my favorite outfits. I opened my curtains and looked out at the lush green yards on my street. And after I stood there for a minute, taking it all in, I made a phone call.

"Codi?"

Lydia sounded surprised. I tried to keep my voice from shaking.

"Hi. Um . . . I know this is out of nowhere, but . . . could I come see you?"

She was quiet for a long beat. "Right now?"

"Yeah. I wanted to . . . um . . . talk to you. I mean, if you're free. Are you working?"

It sounded like she was walking somewhere. I heard something creak, and then it was quiet again.

"I'm actually not home," Lydia said. "I mean, like, I'm not in Atlanta."

"You're not?"

"No, I'm at my aunt's house in Michigan. The whole family's here." She paused. "My mom made me bring your portrait. She wanted everyone to see."

"You're kidding."

"They all thought it was amazing."

Every other time Lydia had complimented my artwork, she'd sounded joyful and energized; this time, she sounded meek. It made my chest ache.

"Lydia?"

"Yeah?"

"I wanted to talk to you about—you know—the night we went out. I know I was weird, and I know I should have called you before now, and I'm really sorry. I could explain right now, but—but I was hoping to talk to you in person. Are you coming home soon?"

"Yeah," she said tentatively, "we'll be home tomorrow night."

"Could I come see you?"

I didn't even think before I asked; I felt such a rush to see her that the question just poured out of me.

Lydia sounded breathless. "Yeah, okay."

"Great," I said, my voice steadier now. "And hey, um . . . I'm having some people over on Saturday night. Will you come?"

"Okay. Maybe."

"Great. Okay. Um, well, I'll see you tomorrow. Have fun in Michigan. I hope you get to play Manhunt with everyone, and I hope you win."

There was a hint of a smile in her voice now. "Thanks, Codi. I'll see you soon."

"Bye, Lydia."

We hung up, and I looked out over the green yards, and I knew with a bone-deep conviction how tomorrow night was going to go.

Friday was full of sweet anticipation. I drove along the river with Ricky by my side, listening to one of his early 2000s playlists and finalizing our plans for Saturday night. This party felt like the culmination of everything I wanted to become that summer: a newer, braver, more alive person. The kind of girl who could throw a party where people would shotgun beers and invent new drinking games and make out with someone in the laundry room. I felt grown-up like never before.

There was only one thing missing.

"I was thinking," Ricky said as I pulled up to the riverbank, "maybe you should invite Maritza and JaKory tomorrow night."

It was like he'd read my mind. I parked and took the key out of the ignition, looking over at him.

"It's your house. Your party," Ricky went on. "They're your best friends."

"I know, but I don't know how I'd explain any of this," I said, gesturing between us. "They'd be pissed at me."

Ricky took a deep breath and looked out over the water. "That's why I thought I should talk to you. Maybe you should . . . should tell them the truth. Right back to the beginning. This all started with me, so you should tell them about me. Tell them how you walked up on me kissing Tucker that night, and how I begged you not to tell anyone—"

"You didn't beg me—"

"I asked you, though. And I'm the one who brought you to Taco Mac and introduced you to Lydia. How were you supposed to explain that to Maritza and JaKory if you couldn't actually explain being friends with me? It's my fault, and I feel like I should own it. You should tell them."

I shook my head, staring at the keys in my hand. "It's not your fault. I could have found a way around it if I wanted to, but I didn't want to. I wanted to keep this all for myself."

"Do you still want to?"

I looked away from him, staring out over the river. "No. I want to be honest with them."

Ricky's tone was soft. "You miss them."

"Yeah. I do."

"And they've got to be missing you, too. I know I did, and I've only known you a couple of months."

I looked down at my phone. I imagined calling Maritza, conferencing JaKory in, and confessing everything about the last two months. The silence that would follow. The hurt they would feel. The pathetic explanation I would try to give.

I would have to come clean sooner or later, but I wasn't ready for it yet.

"I just want one more day," I told Ricky. "I want tomorrow night for Lydia and me, and for you and Tucker, and for all the people who have made this summer so meaningful. And then I'll tell Maritza and JaKory everything."

Ricky pulled his lips into his mouth. I could tell he was doubtful, but all he said was "It's your story, Codi. Tell it however you want to."

Lydia's text came late on Friday evening.

> **Lydia Kaufman aka Jason Waterfalls:** *I just got home, did you still want to come over?*

> *Definitely. I'll be there faster than you can say Jason Waterfalls.*

My heart pounded like crazy on the drive over. I felt vaguely like I was in one of those movies Maritza, JaKory, and I had watched a million times, right at the end where the girl gets the girl.

It was dark by the time I pulled onto her street. I turned off my AC and stuck my hand out the window, hoping the rushing air would clean the nervous sweat off my palm.

And there was her house, quietly beautiful, with the expansive front porch and the wind chimes tinkling beneath the lights. She was sitting in one of the rocking chairs, legs crossed, waiting for me. When I got out of the car, she stood up and lingered at the top of the steps.

"Hey," I said shakily, crossing the yard, the crickets buzzing all around me.

She was fidgeting as I walked toward her. "Hey."

"How was your trip back?"

She watched me carefully. In the glow of the porch lights, her flyaway hairs danced like gold. "Is that really what you were dying to talk to me about?"

I reached her and looked up into her nervous face. "No," I said softly. "Can we sit?"

We sat side by side on the front steps, her hands wrapped around her legs, my hands fumbling with my car keys.

"Are you feeling better?" she asked after a minute. "Natalie said you canceled on the Fourth because you were sick."

"I wasn't sick," I said, looking straight at her. "I said that because I was afraid to see you."

Her eyes moved between mine. "I know. Why?"

I cleared my throat and stared ahead of me, at the dark road and window-lit houses.

"That night on the swings . . ." I began. "I didn't . . . I mean, I wasn't sure how to . . ."

I could sense her body language; she was so careful, so taut.

"I thought . . . maybe . . . that you were going to kiss me."

I took a deep breath and looked at her. She looked back with scared, searching eyes.

"Were you going to kiss me?" I asked.

She swallowed. "Did you want me to?"

My heart was pounding. I couldn't look away from her clear, vulnerable eyes.

"Yes," I whispered. "It's just . . . um . . . I've never kissed anyone before."

It was one of the hardest things I'd ever said, yanked straight from the shame pit inside me. I checked her expression, but she didn't flinch or widen her eyes the way I'd worried she would. I steadied myself and kept going.

"I've never done *anything* with *anyone*," I said, trying to make her understand. "And you'd been asking me about dating, and . . . and I panicked. I'm sorry."

Lydia's entire body relaxed. She exhaled and wiped a hand down her face. "Shit," she said, laughing with relief. "I thought you were going to say something bad."

I blinked at her, surprised. I thought my lack of experience *was* something bad.

"I thought you were going to be like, 'I don't like you like that,'" Lydia went on. "I thought that's why you pulled away and why you haven't talked to me since. I worried I was reading you wrong this whole time."

"No," I said, eager to make myself clear. "No, you were reading me right. I'm just—I don't know. Scared."

Lydia looked steadily at me. "Does it scare you to know that I like you?"

"Um, yeah," I said, blushing. "But it also makes me really happy."

"And you like me, too?"

My whole face was on fire, but I breathed past it and kept looking at her. "Yeah. Yeah, I do."

She smiled at me in a calm, anchoring way, like she understood exactly where I was coming from. "I'm scared, too, Codi. It's like I told you that day in the tree house . . . sometimes I feel scared of everything. But I like being around you. I like knowing you. I would love to spend the rest of the summer just hanging out with you."

I let that settle into me. The way we were sitting, the way we were talking, it seemed like we had all the time in the world. Like I could try something new and there would be enough room to breathe in it.

Slowly, carefully, I scooted closer to her on the steps. I laid my hand over her knee, the way she'd done on the swings. "I wanna hang out with you, too. And not just as your friend."

She stared at my hand for a moment. Then she raised her own hand and laid it over mine, touching my fingers gently.

"You said you've never kissed anyone?"

"Yeah," I said.

"Does that bother you?"

"Yes," I said, laughing self-consciously.

"Okay . . ." She nodded, searching me again. "Does it bother you that I have?"

"No," I said, surprised to find it was the truth.

"Okay . . . so then . . ." She breathed and settled her eyes on me. "Would it be okay if I was your first kiss? Not tonight, but at some point?"

In the strangest, most wondrous way, as we sat there with our hands intertwined on her knee, I was suddenly calm. Not outwardly—my arms were shaking—but in my heart, in my stomach, in the places where I knew myself best.

"Yeah," I said breathlessly. "And actually, I would love to kiss you right now."

Lydia broke into a grin. "Really?"

"Really."

She sat there, her eyes dancing back and forth between mine, and in a crazy twist I never would have believed of myself, I was the one who leaned forward. There was one infinite split second where I almost froze again, but I pressed my way forward, and then I kissed her, softly and carefully, right there on the front porch steps.

It was poetry. It was the top of a roller coaster. It was electric, sweet-toothed magic.

"Okay?" Lydia asked, checking my expression.

"Better than okay," I said, looking at her mouth. "That was . . . that was . . ." I couldn't stop nodding. "Um, yes. Wow."

She laughed and tugged me toward her again, and this time, she kissed me. I watched her eyelashes flutter when she pulled away.

"Yep," she whispered, with her eyes still closed, "yep, that was definitely a wow."

18

MY PARENTS LEFT EARLY SATURDAY MORNING, THEIR car loaded up with suitcases and bottles of wine. Grant and I stood sleepily in the driveway, watching them pack the car, both of us murmuring our agreement when they told us to keep the house clean, to be nice to each other, and to call them if anything went wrong.

"And Codi, don't forget to pick Grant up tomorrow morning," my mom said for the fifth time. "Grant, be good at Darin's house, and keep your phone on for your sister."

"Yeah," Grant and I said together.

The moment our parents were gone, Grant and I went back inside to sleep. We didn't talk again until I was driving him to his friend Darin's house to spend the night. It was late afternoon by this point, and I was itching to drop him off so I could head home and get things ready for the party.

"Are you friends with Ricky again?" Grant asked as we cruised down suburban roads.

"Oh," I said, surprised by the sudden question. "Yeah, I am. We made up and everything's cool now."

"Cool," Grant said. "What about Maritza and JaKory?"

"Um . . ." I breathed out, switching the radio for something to do. "I still haven't talked to them, but I'm gonna call them tomorrow."

"Good," he said matter-of-factly. "You don't want this drama to get out of control."

I burst out laughing. My little brother sounded like a friendship consultant, determined to keep me in check. Grant frowned at me, confused by the laughter, but then a smile stole over his face. He changed the radio station back to the previous one and kicked up his feet like his work here was done.

Saturday night arrived, dark and hot and deceptively humble. I cleared space in the garage refrigerator while waiting for Ricky's truck to come rumbling up the street, my hair still warm from the curling iron and my cotton dress sticking at my hips. Lydia had already texted that she'd be coming with the rest of our friends, and I was bursting with the need to see her, to touch her, to steal a few secret moments in the heat of the party.

Ricky looked handsome when he got out of his truck. His short-sleeve button-up was fitted against his muscles and he wore an impressive watch I'd never seen before. There was a nervous energy about him, but he grinned and pulled me into a hug.

"Cute dress," he said, wrinkling his nose. "Who you trying to show off for?"

"Look who's talking. I could smell your aftershave before you even opened the door."

He laughed, but there was hesitation in his eyes. "Is it too much?"

"No," I said, hugging him again. "Tucker will love it."

We stocked the refrigerator with cases of beer supplied by Leo; our other friends had promised they were bringing more. I closed off the bedrooms upstairs, making a mental note to tell Leo to keep people out of them. We queued up Ricky's playlist—he said there was no way he was letting me pick the music—and synced up his phone to my parents' sound system. Then we had nothing to do but wait.

They arrived slowly. Samuel and Terrica got there first, bounding in with another case of beer; Leo and his cousin ambled in after that, scanning the house for the best hookup spots; then some baseball players rolled in, hugging me and clasping hands with Ricky; and before I knew it, the kitchen had swelled with more people than Ricky and I had anticipated. It was a wild juxtaposition: the counter where my brother ate ravioli, now the scene of Samuel and some other guys chugging Bud Light; the table where Maritza and JaKory and I had built our Egyptian pyramids for sixth-grade history class, now the spot where Terrica had corralled some girls into beer pong; the foot of the stairs where my mom pulled her work flats on in the mornings, now the place where Ricky stood waiting for Tucker.

And then suddenly Lydia was there.

I hadn't seen her come in, but I heard a swell of voices and turned to find everyone greeting Lydia, Natalie, and Cliff. I stood frozen, watching her, the surreal thrill of having her in my house washing over me.

She met my eyes and blinked really fast, and she smiled so big that I thought everyone must have noticed. She hugged me tightly, and over her shoulder, I caught Natalie grinning at us.

Lydia looked like she wanted to say something, but there were people everywhere. Julie Nguyen was baking cheese fries in the oven and Aliza Saylor was already on her second Lime-A-Rita. I took Lydia's hand and led her out to the garage, where it was empty and quiet.

"You look beautiful," she told me, her eyes sweeping over my dress.

I was so giddy I started to laugh, and Lydia laughed, too, and we couldn't stop looking at each other, holding each other's sweaty hands in the humid, dimly lit garage.

"Here," I said, pulling two striped lawn chairs over to the driveway, "sit and have a beer with me."

"You're ditching your own party?"

"Small get-togethers are more my thing," I said, raising my eyebrows.

"I noticed," she said, "and look how that worked out for me."

We sat there for a while, side by side with a cold beer each, looking out on the dark summer night. Lydia took my hand and ran her fingers along my skin, and when I looked at her, neither one of us could stop smiling.

We finished our beers and stood up to go back inside, but I took her hand before she could open the door. We looked at each other for a beat, and then I leaned forward and kissed her. It felt as scary and wonderful as it had the night before.

She kissed me back, and it went on longer this time, until suddenly we heard—

"Whoa!"

It was Tucker, frozen in the driveway, the floodlights too bright on his face.

"I'm sorry," he said, backing away, his hand extended like he was trying to push himself as far back as possible.

I was still holding Lydia's arm. We looked at each other, and I knew she wasn't afraid.

"It's fine, Tucker," I said. "Do you want a beer?"

He remained frozen as I moved toward him with the beer in my hand. He took it but didn't open it. There was a long, awkward pause.

"It's really okay," Lydia said from behind us. "Here, one second, Codi and I need a refill, too."

She brought me a new beer. I opened it, and Tucker opened his. The three of us stood in a loose circle, drinking under the floodlights in my driveway.

"I didn't mean to walk up on you," Tucker mumbled, not looking at either one of us. "Sorry I'm late for your party."

I looked at Lydia again, and she had this look in her eyes I'd never seen before—like she trusted I knew how to handle it, and like she believed there was something wonderful in me.

"I'm glad you came," I told Tucker, tapping my beer can against his. "Everyone will be happy to see you."

There are many things I could say about that night. It was the third party I'd been to that summer—or fourth, if you counted Ricky's—and I understood the flow of the ritual by then. I was at once electrified and at ease to be the one hosting it. I looked around my kitchen at all these other kids my age, laughing and beaming with that late-summer glow, their bare skin catching the light and their summer hair long and shaggy and shining. We told stories, we took turns getting drinks, we squabbled over the music and made fun of Cliff's dance moves. I talked to new people, but also to people I'd gotten to know over the last two months. And all the while, Lydia kept finding me, sometimes with a look from across the room, sometimes with a hug right at my side.

We eventually migrated down to the basement, where everyone became louder and crazier. Samuel, Terrica, Leo, and Leo's cousin were playing with my brother's old miniature air hockey table, except they were using beer bottle caps instead of a puck; Cliff and Natalie were practically humping in the corner, a few feet away from another couple I barely even knew; Magic Dan was shuffling playing cards to impress Aliza Saylor, who had lost her underwear somewhere on the stairs; and the baseball team had started a game of Kings with a few girls who didn't even go to our school. Lydia and I stayed by each other's sides, talking with Ricky and Tucker until they announced they were going outside for a cigarette. Ricky gave me a meaningful look, and I nodded, and they slipped out the door without anyone noticing.

Things didn't die down until after two o'clock. By that point, everyone had left except for my friends, who were spread in a circle on the basement floor, playing another round of Don't Judge Me, But that was mostly just sex jokes. They were obviously too drunk to drive, so Lydia and I got them blankets and pillows and tumblers of water that they knocked over onto each other's legs. We tried coaxing Natalie and Terrica to sleep on the couches, but they were busy having "a moment of connection" and insisted they needed to cuddle on the floor.

"What about Ricky and Tucker?" Lydia whispered, after we'd

pulled Natalie's and Terrica's dead-weight selves onto separate couches. "Are they still outside?"

I hesitated. I knew Lydia wouldn't say anything if we found Ricky and Tucker making out, but I didn't want to make that decision for them.

"I'll check," I said, squeezing her hand, "and then I'll show you where you can sleep. You can have my bed."

Ricky's and Tucker's voices were muted when I opened the basement door. I shone my phone to the right and found them sitting beneath the deck, frozen in place.

"It's just me," I said, and their bodies relaxed.

"Come chill with us," Tucker said.

"Can I bring Lydia?"

"Yeah, bring your girlfriend," Ricky said, smirking.

And that's how we ended the night, with Lydia, Ricky, Tucker, and me sitting beneath the deck, talking with soft, sleepy voices. The moon was out and the earth was quiet, and I felt more real than I ever had before.

"Feels like time doesn't exist right now," Lydia said.

"Feels like there's more space for everything," Tucker said.

Ricky shot me an easy, peaceful smile, and I held his eyes in the glow of the moon.

"I don't want to kick you out of your bed," Lydia said as we drank water in the quiet, humming kitchen. "You take it, and I'll sleep on the couch."

"No, it's yours," I insisted. "I want you to be comfortable."

Lydia took a long sip of water. She hesitated, and then she asked,

"Is it big enough for both of us? Just for sleeping, I mean. I would love to hold your hand while we sleep, but only if you're okay with that."

I looked at her, and she had that same look in her eyes she'd had in the driveway earlier.

"That would be really, really nice," I said.

We left Ricky and Tucker to figure out their own sleeping arrangements. Lydia took my hand, and together we trudged sleepily up the stairs. Only then did I realize how fuzzy the alcohol had made me. I wasn't even sure where my phone was, but I was too tired to care.

Lydia stepped slowly into my room, taking it all in. She lingered over my desk, touching my sketchpad and watercolor palette with the tips of her fingers. She ran her hand over the fuzzy maroon blanket at the foot of my bed, her eyes flicking up toward the pillows. She picked up the lone picture on my nightstand and smiled at it for a long moment.

"This must be Maritza and JaKory."

My stomach clenched. "Yeah."

"Still trying to figure things out with them? Is that why they weren't here tonight?"

I felt the sudden need to confess to her. "I didn't exactly invite them. Ricky said I should, but I didn't feel ready to."

She searched my expression. "Well, whenever you feel good about things with them again, I'll be really excited to meet them."

She wrapped her arms around me, burying her face in my neck. I hugged her back, but my stomach was still clenched.

"Are you okay, Codi?"

"Yeah," I said, hugging her tighter.

She rubbed her hands up and down my back. "It was a great party."

I swallowed against the sudden swelling in my throat. "You think so?"

"People like being around you. You know who you are and what you feel."

I couldn't answer. She kissed the side of my head and asked, "Ready for sleep?"

I gave her an old art camp T-shirt and a pair of lounging shorts. She washed her face at my sink and I sat on the bed, watching her, my heart settled and aching at the same time.

We crawled into bed and lay facing each other. She played with my hair, smoothing it back from my face. I didn't want to close my eyes, but I couldn't fight the exhaustion coming over me.

"Will you tell me about the green house?" I mumbled. "The one you first lived in?"

She whispered to me, her words sweet and comforting, and I fell asleep with her hand in my hair.

It was the last nice thing I remembered before I woke up, hours later, to the sound of Maritza and JaKory screaming at me.

19

"WHAT THE FUCK, CODI?!"

My head was throbbing, my limbs felt like lead, and everything was far too bright. I pulled myself up in bed and was disoriented to find Lydia sitting next to me.

"What the fuck?!" Maritza shouted again, and all my senses caught up to me.

Maritza and JaKory were standing at the foot of my bed, their expressions wild with shock. In the doorway behind them, my brother stood stock-still, his mouth hanging open.

I didn't know what time it was. I didn't know how Maritza and JaKory had come to be there. I didn't even know if Ricky and the others were still in the house.

"What's going on, Codi?" JaKory asked, his voice shaking. "There are people from school downstairs. They look like they just woke up here. Did you throw a *party*?"

There was a pressing silence. I could feel Lydia's eyes on me, but I couldn't look back.

"Do we know you?" Maritza said loudly. She was staring hard at Lydia, and my stomach plummeted so fast I thought I might be sick.

Lydia took a sharp breath next to me. Her arm moved against mine. "I'm Lydia," she said in a small voice. "It's nice to meet you both. Codi's told me a lot about you."

Maritza and JaKory looked back to me. Their glares, their looks of betrayal and hurt, burned right through me.

"That's funny," Maritza said in a low voice, "because Codi hasn't told us *anything* about you or anyone else here."

The silence that followed was unbearable. My heart was pounding so hard it hurt.

JaKory shook his head. There were angry tears in his eyes. "Come on, Maritza," he said, turning away, "we're obviously not supposed to be here."

They tore out of my room, and I stumbled out of bed after them.

"Lydia, I'm so sorry, I'll be back in a minute," I said, and then I pushed past my brother and chased Maritza and JaKory down the stairs, begging them to listen to me. In my peripheral vision I could see the kitchen was full of my other friends, frozen in the middle of breakfast, watching everything with their mouths open.

"Codi!" Natalie called. "Should we leave?"

"No," I said, hurtling out the door, "no, everything's fine!"

I ran down the driveway and into the street, where Maritza's car was, my bare feet burning on the hot asphalt.

"Maritza! JaKory! Hold on!"

They turned around. I waited for them to start yelling again, to curse me out, to call me names, but they just looked at me like they'd never seen me before.

"I'm sorry," I said, trying to catch my breath. "I—there's a whole story behind this—"

"Okay," JaKory cut in, voice full of acid. "What is it?"

I opened my mouth, but no words came out.

"So you have a whole new set of friends we don't know about," Maritza said, tears spilling out of her eyes. "Is that why you've been so weird this summer? You went off and became this whole new person who throws parties and has girls sleep in her bed, but you couldn't bring us along for the ride?"

I still couldn't answer. I stared at the asphalt, wondering if it was real, wondering if any of this was real.

"They looked at us like we were aliens," JaKory said.

"They just don't know you yet—"

"Right," Maritza said, wiping her face. "They think we're *strangers* bursting in on your party. Just a couple of nobodies. They don't know that we've been to your house more times than we can count, that we know the code to your garage, that your brother knew to call us when he couldn't get ahold of you this morning—"

"I know, I know, I'm sorry—"

"And you had someone in your *bed*," Maritza said, her voice cracking. "You're dating someone and we've never even heard her *name*."

"It just happened recently," I said, wiping my own eyes. "Literally just the other day."

"Have you kissed her?" JaKory asked.

My stomach contracted, and my face flushed with heat. I could only stare at him and Maritza, the answer obvious on my face.

JaKory nodded very slowly, his jaw set. "Right," he said, his voice unnervingly calm.

"I was going to tell you, I promise, I just needed a few days to get used to it—"

"I'm really happy for you, Codi," Maritza cut in, her voice shaking. "But I guess you were right. I don't know you anymore."

I didn't know what to say to that. And before I could think of anything, they had taken off in Maritza's car.

I sat in the driveway for I don't know how long. The sun was brutal on my neck, but I didn't move.

Lydia found me. She folded herself down next to me, laying a hand across my leg, but I was too embarrassed to look at her. A long moment passed before she reached for my hand.

"Are you okay?"

I started crying. Not hard, but enough to need a tissue. I wiped my nose on my shoulder and hoped she didn't notice.

"What happened?" Lydia whispered. "I thought they were your best friends. I knew you were having issues with them, but I didn't realize it was this bad."

I looked at her. There was no judgment in her eyes, only compassion and concern.

"I was trying to be different this summer," I told her, wiping my nose again. "It's like I told you that night at Samuel's party . . . I didn't like who I was with them. I wanted to try something new. But I never meant to hurt them."

Lydia brushed my hair back, her hand gentle on my face. "Why didn't you like who you were with them?"

I swallowed. "It's hard to explain."

"Try."

"Okay, like . . . do you know how I became friends with them? It was the first week of sixth grade, during recess. I'd gone to this really small elementary school and didn't know how to make new friends. I spent all of recess standing alone by the door waiting for it to be over. And JaKory had just moved here because his parents split up, and during recess he would just walk around the field aimlessly. Maritza was trying to hang around the popular girls, but you could tell she was trying too hard and was always the odd one out."

"Mm-hm," Lydia said, rubbing my back, her eyes intent on mine.

"So one day, this teacher called JaKory and me over to organize the recess crate. I think she was tired of seeing us standing alone and wanted to give us something to do. So JaKory and I started organizing it, and a minute later, Maritza ended up with us. She'd insulted one of the popular girls, and they'd all ditched her, and the teacher had seen it and brought her over before she could start crying. We started talking, and I remember feeling like—like I was safe, because they were as nervous and awkward as me. When the bell rang, we walked back into the building together, and we've been friends ever since."

Lydia's eyes were steady. "And you don't like that story."

I shook my head. "I didn't even choose them, Lydia. A teacher whose name I can't remember put the three of us together because we were weird and lonely and didn't fit anywhere else."

"But does it matter?"

"Yes, it matters! I don't want to be that person anymore."

"I don't think you are."

"But I feel like I am when I'm with them."

Lydia trailed her hand down my hair again. "I'm gonna get everyone out of here," she said quietly. "Give you some space to figure this out."

"I don't need space," I said quickly.

Her hand stilled. "Well, you need *something*, and I'm not sure what it is."

I looked at her. "I'm sorry."

We were silent for a minute, and then she said, "Codi, just so you know, I like who you are. Not just the you who wears pretty dresses to parties, but the you who was a painfully shy kid and who freaked out on the swings when I tried to kiss her. You don't have to be just one version of yourself. You're far more dynamic than that."

I wiped my eyes again. "Thank you."

She kissed me very carefully. "I gotta tell you," she said, "if I was that fancy old rich lady who sent you a message in a bottle, I'd tell you so many beautiful things about yourself, you'd never have to worry again."

She kissed my forehead and led me back into the house.

Ricky stayed with me for most of the day. He cooked omelets with peppers and cheese, all the while telling me that everything would be okay. He was more settled in himself, more open and tender than he'd been with me before. Beyond the terrible weight of my fight with Maritza and JaKory, I was happy for him.

"What happens with you and Tucker now?" I asked.

He shrugged, but it was a more peaceful shrug than I'd seen before. "We'll take it one step at a time. First things first, I'm taking him to dinner on Wednesday."

We smiled across the counter. Nothing more needed to be said. Then together we cleaned the house from top to bottom, just as we'd done that afternoon in May, until there was no sign of partying to be found.

It didn't matter; my parents found out anyway. Grant had called them when he couldn't get ahold of me to pick him up, and when my mom had called Mrs. Stinch, our neighbor, to check on me, Mrs. Stinch had told her about the line of cars and pulsing music. "I never took Codi for a partier, Jen," she'd told my mom, which was just about the most passive-aggressive line I could think of.

My parents were at a loss for what to do with me. It seemed beyond their conception of possibility that I had enough friends to throw a party in the first place. When they asked me straight up if I had in fact thrown a party and I responded with a calm and matter-of-fact "Yes," they simply stared at me in bewilderment.

"I was very responsible about it, if that helps anything," I told them. "Nothing got broken or stained, and nobody threw up anywhere."

They exchanged a look; it was clear they had no idea how to handle this. Finally, my mom held her hand out and said, "Give us your keys. You're grounded for a week. Totes-n-Goats and this house, those are the only two places you're allowed." She looked at my dad, as if to check that that's how it was done. He merely shrugged and raised his eyebrows.

I stayed quiet, grateful that my punishment wasn't worse. It crossed my mind that I would be losing a full weekend—and there were only three left before school started—but one weekend of being grounded didn't seem like a bad trade-off for the first party I'd ever thrown.

"And go apologize to your brother," my mom said. "You left him hanging, and that wasn't right."

Grant was in his room, the door shut, muffled music playing from his laptop. I knocked and heard the swivel of his desk chair.

"What?" he said when he opened the door.

"Can I talk to you?"

He looked suspicious. "About what?"

"I don't know, Grant, just let me in."

He stepped back but left the door only narrowly open, so that I had to squeeze through the doorframe while he watched me. I walked toward his desk and leaned against the window, looking out on the driveway below. He really could see everything from here.

"So?" he said.

I turned around to look at him.

"Sorry I forgot to pick you up from your friend's house."

Grant's eyes burned into mine. "It was really shitty."

"I'm sorry."

"Darin's parents were pissed. They wanted everyone out by nine thirty so they could go to church. You said you would be there by nine fifteen."

"And I forgot, and I'm *sorry*. It's not like I've ever done this to you before. How many times have I picked you up from basketball camp or the movies or your other friends' houses? And I'm always on time, and I never complain if you're late."

"Don't act like you do that to be nice or something. You only do it because Mom and Dad make you."

I ignored this and launched an attack of my own. "You didn't have to call Maritza and JaKory. I told you in the car that I wasn't talking to them yet."

"Who else was I supposed to call? They almost couldn't get me either. Maritza's grounded and her parents took her phone *and* her car. JaKory had to call their house and tell them that I was stranded and no one knew where you were. Mrs. Vargas almost came and got me herself."

"Maritza's grounded?" I asked, momentarily distracted.

"Her dad caught her drinking his rum. It was the only thing JaKory asked her about. He didn't seem like he wanted to talk to her. Probably because of that night you screamed at them on the deck."

I turned away from him and stared out the window again. My stomach was in knots. "You don't get it."

"Don't act all dramatic just because you've been a shitty friend," Grant said, his voice acidic. "You probably think you're cool now because you threw a party, but guess what, that doesn't make you cool. You were cooler before, when you cared about people."

"I still care about people!" I said, stung.

"Yeah, your *new* friends," he said patronizingly. "You obviously don't care about Maritza or JaKory or anyone in your family."

"You don't know how I feel," I said, my voice shaking. "Everything's been so easy for you. You're athletic and outgoing and Mom and Dad's pride and joy, and you're—"

I caught myself; I'd been about to say he was straight. The word died on my tongue.

"Yeah, you've got me all figured out, Codi," he snarled. "Get out of my room. You suck at apologizing."

He threw himself into his desk chair, and I stormed out of the room.

It was a long week.

I went to work, helped uppity suburban moms find peacock-print bags, and came home to a quiet house, where my brother ignored me and my parents watched me like they still weren't sure who I was. I tried to call JaKory, who screened my calls, and even talked myself into calling Maritza's house phone. It was Mr. Vargas who answered, and he told me firmly that Maritza was grounded, and that he needed to get back to cleaning his fish tank.

Lydia came by a couple of afternoons to check on me. She brought me iced coffee from the café, and we talked over the kitchen counter about her math class, our work shifts, and the morning after the party over and over again.

"Have you talked to them yet?" she'd say, with her hand on the small of my back, and when I'd explain I hadn't been able to reach them, she'd rub circles over my shirt and promise I'd figure it out.

Ricky and I texted back and forth, and on Thursday, after he got off work, he came over to tell me about his date. We went down to the basement with sodas and ham-and-cheese sandwiches, and he gushed about the jokes Tucker had told, and the liberating anonymity they'd enjoyed at the restaurant down in the city, and even the fact that Tucker had said his name.

"He never used to say it before—he'd just avoid calling me anything—but now he says 'Ricky' when he's talking to me, and I'm just like . . ." He shook his head and pointed quickly to his torso. "It hits me right here."

"Who knew you were such a romantic?"

"Shut up. You're the only person I can tell, so you have to deal with all the mushy stuff."

I looked at him. "Still don't want to tell the friends you feel like you've known since kindergarten? Not even Cliff?"

He rubbed the crumbs off his fingers. "Feels like I've known you since kindergarten, too, and that's enough for now."

If my brother saw Lydia or Ricky coming and going, he didn't say anything about it. He stayed shut up in his room, playing music and watching TV shows, or otherwise went out to hang with his friends in the neighborhood and didn't come back until dinnertime. We didn't speak to each other and generally pretended like the other one didn't exist. It wasn't until Friday night, four days after my failed apology attempt, that he acknowledged me at all.

"Did you ever ask your friend Ricky what kind of truck he drives?"

I looked up from my phone, where I'd been hovering over another unanswered text to JaKory. Grant wasn't looking at me, but he had paused between bites of SpaghettiOs.

"No," I said quietly. "I forgot to."

My brother shook his head, not like a pissed-off fourteen-year-old boy, but like a tired, disappointed old man. He picked up his bowl and shuffled out of the kitchen without another word.

Saturday, the day before my grounding was over, went on forever. I worked from noon until close, one of the longest shifts I'd had all summer, and one of the most boring, too. Tammy stood at the open storefront, holding her wrists together behind her back and shifting from one foot to the other while she stared across the shopping plaza.

I dragged myself around the store, spraying Windex on every glass surface and rearranging the zebra pencils so they all faced the same direction, and contemplated crashing Maritza's dance camp on Monday just so I could talk to her.

"Codi," Tammy said, turning half around, "what's today's date?"

"The twenty-third."

"Aw, shoot. CuppyCakes has that promotion up for half off their muffin tops, but it says 'Now through 7/22.' I meant to get one yesterday. Shoot, shoot, shoot."

July 23 was ringing something in my brain, but I couldn't place it. I trailed around the store again, trying to remember, but nothing came to me.

It wasn't until I was home, sitting on the deck with a glass of ice water pressed to my forehead, that I remembered with a sick, plunging feeling why today's date was resonating.

Saturday, July 23. The day JaKory was supposed to meet Daveon. The day he'd asked Maritza and me to drive him to Alabama.

I checked my watch: It was almost ten o'clock—long past the hour I could have driven him there. Maybe, I hoped, Maritza had wrangled her way out of being grounded to drive JaKory there in time; or maybe Daveon had found a way to haul himself here instead, and he and JaKory were now nestled comfortably under some blankets, watching *Doctor Who*. I couldn't bear the thought of JaKory sitting alone in his room, texting Daveon about how they'd find some other way to see each other, bitterly explaining that he'd never expected his two best friends to leave him hanging like this.

I called him before I could think twice about it. He didn't answer.

I called again. He ignored me again.

I texted him, sending up a prayer to the universe.

Did you make it to meet Daveon?

He answered after a long delay. I could almost feel him glowering down at his phone, hating me for asking.

JaKory Green: *What do you think?*

The plunging in my stomach intensified. My entire body was prickly and hot.

JaKory Green: *To clarify, no, I did not get to meet the boy I'm so deeply in love with. But thanks for caring.*

I felt sick with myself. Of all the things I'd messed up over the last week, this one was by far the worst.

I sat there on the deck, the insects loud, the air still warm, the summer swelling with its last untouchable days. I thought of my parents, who were inside watching *NCIS* reruns and would no doubt be heading up to bed by eleven, and of my brother, who was shut up in his room, hating me, thinking I didn't care. I wondered if he was right.

Time stopped measuring itself as I sat there, unmoving, the water glass gradually warming in my hand. Suddenly I was reliving the entire summer in my head. I saw the beginning, with Maritza and JaKory and my brother, and I saw the night everything changed, with Ricky by the trees. I looked down at my feet, my stomach, my hands, and wondered if they were really mine. I wondered if they were the same now as they had been in May, before everything began.

I didn't figure anything out, not like Lydia had promised I would;

instead I just got to this point, after sitting out there for a while, where I knew what I wanted and needed to do.

Ricky screened my first call, but when I tried him again, he picked up on the second ring.

"Everything cool, Codi? I'm out with Tucker."

"I need a really, really huge favor," I said, springing up from my chair. "How do you feel about driving to Alabama?"

20

The text came at a quarter to midnight.

> **Ricky Flint:** *On your street. Two houses down. My lights are off.*

I was already down in the basement, waiting to sneak out the back door, and I didn't wait a second longer. My heart lurched as I crept up the back walk toward the driveway. It was after I'd stepped onto the street, my head already turned to search for Ricky's truck, when an idea tugged at my brain. I stood there for a long second, fighting an internal battle, wondering what the consequences might be if my parents found out.

Then I turned around and crept back into the house, up through the basement, and onto the second floor.

My brother's light was on. I knocked very softly, hoping my parents were already asleep.

"Go away," Grant said.

I knocked again, and then again, until he finally opened the door.

"*What?*"

I almost felt stupid, now that I was standing here in front of him, but I took a short breath and plowed ahead. "I'm trying to fix things with JaKory and Maritza. I'm sneaking out, and Ricky and I are driving to Alabama. In his truck. Do you want to come?"

My brother looked hard at me. He seemed confused, and after a second he went to the window.

"I don't see him," he said, his voice doubtful.

"He parked down the street so Mom and Dad wouldn't notice." I felt my phone vibrate and knew it was Ricky, wondering why I was taking so long. "You don't have to come, but I just wanted you to know you were invited."

My brother paused with his hand on the window. After a second, he asked, "Can I ride shotgun?"

Ricky and Grant took to each other immediately. Ricky loved all the questions Grant asked about his truck, and Grant loved all the questions Ricky asked about basketball, and they agreed that my taste in music was nothing short of deplorable.

"Oh, 'cause your music taste is so much better, Mr. Nickelback?" I asked.

"Don't listen to her," Ricky told Grant. "She's making shit up."

"Oh, yeah, no question," Grant said, sitting taller in his seat.

There were very few cars on the road, and we reached JaKory's neighborhood within minutes. "Turn up here," I told Ricky. "Grant, show him where to go."

Grant proudly guided Ricky to JaKory's house. Ricky shut his lights off immediately, and I left the two of them sitting in the front while I crept out and snuck up JaKory's driveway. It was after midnight now, and the only sound was the sprinklers in the front yard.

I'm in your driveway. I have a car. Let's get you to Alabama.

JaKory slipped out the front door a minute later. He squinted through the dark at the truck in front of his house, then looked back to me with his eyes practically bugging out of his head. "What in god's name did you smoke tonight?"

"I don't have time to apologize like I want to," I said hastily. "Especially because you deserve a very eloquent apology that I wish I had the words to say. But I know you want to meet Daveon, and I know today was the day you'd planned on, and Ricky and I are totally game to drive you there, if you still want to. Can we make it happen?"

JaKory stood rigid for a long beat. Then he snapped out of it and made a phone call.

I stood a few feet away from him, listening to the *spritz spritz spritz* of the sprinklers, my mind still filing through the logistics of this plan.

"He can do it," JaKory said, his voice urgent now. "Give me five minutes."

He dashed back inside, and when he reappeared at the door of Ricky's truck a full seven minutes later, he was dressed in a linen button-down shirt and that goddamn fedora.

* * *

JaKory directed us out of his neighborhood and down the roads that led to the interstate, but there was one more thing we needed to do first. I told Ricky to make a left, and JaKory sat back and shrugged like he already knew what I was planning.

It didn't feel right to go without Maritza. Somehow I knew that if we went to Alabama without her, our friendship would never recover. She would want to be a part of this, and she deserved to be.

The lights were off in her house. I didn't bother texting since her parents still had her phone; instead, I slipped to the back door, felt in the birdhouse next to the overhang, and pulled out the Vargases' spare key. I thought I must have been crazy—after all, I was technically breaking and entering—but I turned the key in the lock anyway.

The house was dark and silent. Mr. Vargas's fish tank was illuminated in the family room, the electric pink and orange fish darting around in the blue light. I crept past it and up the stairs to Maritza's room, my heart thudding. When I reached her door, there were TV noises coming from behind it, and I breathed: Maritza watching Netflix was something I knew how to handle.

My knock was too soft. If I tried any louder, I might wake up her parents. I nudged the door open slowly, sticking my head out so she'd see it was me right away.

Maritza was sitting on her bed, frozen with her hands around her laptop, her expression freaked out and pissed off at the same time.

"What the fuck?"

I closed the door and moved to stand in front of her bed. She kept looking at me like I'd gone crazy, like I was scaring her a little bit.

"JaKory's meeting Daveon tonight," I whispered.

She didn't say anything. We looked at each other, waiting for something to happen.

"So?" she asked finally.

"So I'm going with him . . . and we want you to come, too."

Her eyes narrowed. "You're driving JaKory to Alabama? Right now?"

I tried to bite down on the answer, knowing she would hate it, but it rushed out of me anyway. "Technically, Ricky's driving us."

For a fraction of a second, she seemed to wilt—but then her eyes flashed and she snapped her laptop closed.

"*Ricky*," she said, snorting meanly. "Of course. Your new best friend."

"He's not my best friend."

"Oh, are you reserving that spot for your girlfriend now?"

"Maritza . . ." I began.

"You're deluded if you think I'm about to go on this little adventure with you after you lied to me all summer."

I was trying really, really hard to look at her, but at this point I had to turn away. I wasn't sure what to say next. For about the millionth time that summer, I saw myself as if from far away, standing pathetically in the middle of my old friend's room, wondering how things had gotten to this point.

"I know I messed up," I said finally.

"Understatement."

I took a deep breath. "Look. This isn't about you and me right now, it's about JaKory. He has one chance to meet Daveon, and we haven't taken him seriously about it, and I think that's really shitty of us. You can go back to hating me when we get back from Alabama, but for tonight, I think we should help him."

Maritza stared me down for a long moment. Then her eyes flitted away. "I'm grounded right now."

"So am I."

"I have Mass in the morning."

"I have a nine-o'clock shift."

She looked away again, but I could see her calculating in her head, weighing the correct answer.

My phone started buzzing in my pocket. It was JaKory, yelling at me to hurry up.

"I know, I know, we're coming," I told him. "We'll be right down."

Maritza's eyes were narrowed when I hung up.

"'We,'" she said. "That's presumptuous."

I merely looked at her, waiting.

Finally, after a long pause, she rolled her eyes and threw the covers back.

"This is so dramatic," she said, hopping in place as she pulled on her sneakers. "Leave it to JaKory to get his first kiss this way."

It might have been the strangest car ride of my life.

Maritza and JaKory sat next to me in the back seat, neither one of them talking, JaKory fidgeting and checking his phone every minute. Ricky and Grant had gone quiet, sitting up front with the GPS illuminated between them. Grant kept his elbow on the console like Ricky did, and every few minutes he turned around and scanned our faces. He never once asked what we were going to Alabama for.

We took the downtown connector through the heart of Atlanta, past Georgia Tech and The Varsity, past the exit for Martin Luther King Jr. Drive, around the curving skyscrapers and golden-domed capitol building, the city lights real and beautiful and bright. There were cars speeding past us in either direction and I wondered where all these people were going, and what they would say about five teenagers sneaking off to Alabama so one of them could kiss the boy he'd been dreaming about all summer.

The interstate took us south of the city, past the airport, onto dark highway lanes with fewer cars and streetlights. We were somewhere between western Georgia and eastern Alabama, and there was nothing but trees and exit signs. I lowered my window and let the air brush my face, breezy and soft, still warm. I waited for the others to ask me to put the window back up, but they simply lowered theirs, too, and that's how we drove for a whole rolling hour, no talking, no music, just the air rushing past our open windows.

After a while, JaKory checked his phone and leaned forward into the center of the truck. "He says they're almost there. They hit some late-night construction, but it only added five minutes."

"Aren't we going to his house?" I asked.

"Different house," Ricky answered. "Waffle House."

Maritza snorted next to me.

I'd only been to Waffle House twice before: Once on a family road trip to Virginia, when we couldn't find any other breakfast places off the interstate, and once with Maritza and JaKory, on our way home from a varsity basketball game where Maritza had danced at halftime. Both times I'd eaten greasy hash browns with ketchup and accidentally stuck my elbow in the syrup stains on the table. But I could see why JaKory and Daveon would pick Waffle House as their meet-up point: It was the kind of place where people were always coming and going, even in the middle of the night. You could be anyone you wanted to be, and no one would look twice at you.

We pulled off the interstate near a place called Opelika, Alabama. It was a dimly lit exit with a few streetlamps and a 24-7 service station. Ricky drove slowly, carefully, he and my brother leaning forward to scout the area. JaKory was silent as a mouse, but his fingers drummed manically against his leg. I caught Maritza's eye and looked pointedly at him. She hesitated, then grabbed his fingers and squeezed.

"There!" Grant said, pointing up ahead.

The bright yellow roof loomed into view. We stared at it like we'd never seen such a place before. Ricky rolled quietly into the parking lot, where a handful of cars were scattered unevenly. He took the long way around the building, doing a loop of the whole lot.

"He's in there," JaKory rasped, ducking in his seat. "Oh my god, oh shit, he's really in there."

"Where?" Maritza and I said.

"In the left corner, by the window!"

Maritza and I craned our necks, trying to see. I could just make out a red shirt and the top of a boy's head.

If my brother had caught on to what was going on, he didn't acknowledge it. He glanced at JaKory, and then at Maritza and me next to him, but said nothing.

Ricky parked in the second row of spaces—far enough away that JaKory and Daveon would have some semblance of privacy, but still close enough that we could make a quick getaway if anything went wrong. He shut the engine off, and suddenly there was no sound at all.

You would have thought that Maritza or I would speak first, prompting JaKory to get out of the car, but it was Ricky who turned around and spoke to him.

"Are you ready?"

JaKory nodded. He got out of the truck without looking at anyone, but then he hovered by the door, smoothing down his shirt.

"Do I look okay?" he asked.

He wasn't looking at us, but it was clear who he was asking.

"You look awesome," I said.

"Like Prince Charming," Maritza said earnestly.

"What if . . ." he asked in a small voice. "What if it doesn't work out?"

I met his eyes. "What if it does?"

JaKory took a long, deep breath. "I don't know what to say to him."

Maritza reached forward and straightened his fedora. "Say hi," she said. "Quote some poetry if you want to. Just get in there."

It was after two A.M. now, but everything felt timeless and still. Ricky and I sat on the curb together, with Maritza a few feet down from us. Grant was walking back and forth on the curb perpendicular to us, his hands in his pockets and his eyes straining to see the various kinds of cars in the lot.

Ricky was watching Maritza, whose tenderness had evaporated the moment JaKory had gone inside. She now sat with her arms hooked around her knees, her face turned resolutely away from me.

"Do something," Ricky whispered, knocking my elbow.

I looked at Maritza again. She was still turned away, but I stared at her long enough for her to feel it.

"What?" she snapped, glaring at me.

I stood up and went over to her. "Can I sit?"

"I'm not in the mood, Codi."

I stepped over the curb and onto the grass behind her. There was scattered litter here and there, a paper fast food cup and a dirty napkin, but the spot where I stood was clean. I plopped down onto it and rubbed a blade of grass between my fingers.

"So your dad noticed the missing rum?" I asked.

She ignored me.

"How long are you grounded for?"

Still nothing.

"Are they at least letting you work at dance camp?"

This time she answered.

"I'm quitting dance."

I stared at her. "What?"

She pulled her knees tighter but said nothing else.

"Maritza, you can't quit dance, it would be such a waste! Is this because of Rona?" She stayed silent. "Come on, dude, I'm sorry for lying to you, but you have to talk to me."

She turned halfway around. "Something happened and I really *want* to talk to you about it, but I don't trust you anymore."

I fell silent. Maritza was the type of person to lord that over somebody, but that wasn't what she was doing. She was hurt.

"I'm sorry," I said softly. "I'm really, really sorry. I can't imagine how you felt walking into my house last weekend."

"Like someone had punched me in the stomach and then told me I should've expected it."

"I'm sorry," I said again.

"Yeah, you keep saying that, but it doesn't mean anything anymore. You made me feel like I was the stupidest, smallest person in the world, like I could never compare to all those people standing in your kitchen. You must've had so much fun with them this summer, drinking and partying and all kinds of stuff you never did with JaKory and me." She paused, and her voice quivered. "Are you ashamed of us?"

Now I felt like someone was punching me in the stomach. "No, Maritza, of course not."

"Then *why?*" she asked, her voice breaking. "Why did you do that?"

I was silent for a long, long moment. Then I asked, "Can I tell you the whole story?"

She neither nodded nor shook her head. I started talking before she could decide.

I told her about the night I'd come upon Ricky in the trees, and how he'd been upset, though I didn't explain why. I told her about everything that grew from there: the night at Taco Mac when I'd first met Ricky's friends, the conversation in Lydia's room when I'd first suspected she liked me, the moment on the swings when I'd missed my chance, and the moment on the front steps when I'd gotten it back.

"But why couldn't you tell me all this before?" Maritza asked, looking pained.

I hung my head. "I just—I wanted it for myself. You know how much I love you and JaKory, but sometimes it feels like you try to tell me who I am based on what *you* see. I met Ricky that night, and suddenly it felt like I could be whomever I wanted to be because he wouldn't know the difference. I needed to know I could do that. And I needed to know I could do it without you and JaKory. I wanted to feel like I was becoming *my*self, not *our*selves."

Maritza was quiet. She breathed in, slow and deep.

"I'm sorry," I said again. "It was selfish."

Maritza swallowed. She shifted on the curb so her feet were now in the grass with mine. "It wasn't selfish."

"It wasn't?"

She sighed. "Remember last year when you asked if you and JaKory could come to Panama sometime?"

"Yeah. I was serious."

"I know." She paused. "A few months ago, Mom and Dad told me I could invite you guys this year. They said I could bring you for a whole week, even two if you wanted. They'd already cleared it with my grandmother and everything. Mom was so excited; she kept saying, 'Aren't you going to call your friends and share the wonderful news?'"

I looked at her. "But you had the dance job lined up."

She shook her head. "No, not at that point, I didn't. It's just—Panama's always been *my* thing, you know? It's the one time a year I feel like someone different, like an alternate-universe version of myself, if I had been a regular Panamanian girl who grew up with her whole family around her. You and JaKory won't ever understand that because your whole family is here, in the States. And I adore my family, but I think what I love even more is who I am when I'm with them. I don't have to be the girl who's trying to prove something *all the time*. When I'm with my cousins and everyone, I get to blend in, and—and I feel like they love me just for the sake of loving me."

I smiled sadly. "And it would've been hard to share that with Ja-Kory and me, because then you would've felt pressure to act like the version of yourself that you are around us."

She winced apologetically. "Yeah. So I guess I understand where you're coming from."

"Thanks."

She busied herself with the grass for a moment, plucking up

blades and laying them vertically across her palm. "Codi?" she said. "Just so you know, I think you're one of the best people I've ever met. And I think being friends with someone should be like the concept of infinity—like you truly believe that person has no limits, and you just want to keep counting upward with them to see where they go." She paused. "I'm sorry I haven't made you feel like that lately."

My throat was too tight to speak; all I could do was nod in gratitude.

"It still stings that you lied to me," Maritza went on, "but the selfless part of me is happy for you. If you've grown closer to Ricky and your other new friends, that's okay. I don't have to be your best friend in the entire world. I just want to be in your life."

I picked myself up and went to sit next to her on the curb. She let me.

"You are my best friend, Maritza. There's no replacing you."

I reached for her hand, squeezing it tight. She swallowed and blinked very fast.

"Do you think Ricky's becoming a best friend, too?" she asked thickly.

I hesitated, but there was no trace of jealousy or insecurity in her expression. She was asking me the way she asked about my paintings: like it mattered to her because it mattered to me.

"I think he's becoming one," I said, and I told her about that moment Ricky and I had looked at each other in the trees, how it felt like we understood each other intuitively.

"I love that feeling. It's how I felt when I met you and JaKory."

I paused; the expansive feeling in my chest deflated a little. "Yeah. The recess crate."

"No, the next day," Maritza said.

"Wait—what?"

"Don't you remember the next day? That teacher, Ms. Hillgrove, asked us to carry the recess crate to the gym, and on the way we found that flower garden on the side of the school?"

"I don't—"

"We were reading 'Rikki-Tikki-Tavi' in English class, so you and I got down in the bushes and pretended to be the cobras, and JaKory started yelling at us in a British accent? It was so weird, so random, but all three of us just went with it. I still remember going home and telling my parents I'd made friends."

I had no recollection of the moment, but a grin was spreading across my face. Maritza laughed and wrapped an arm around my shoulders.

"We were weirdos, Codi."

"We're still weirdos."

"Even you?"

"God, more than ever."

She laughed again, and there was a trace of relief in it. "Well, as long as Ricky and Lydia and these other people didn't take that from you, I guess I can live with them."

"Thanks," I laughed, squeezing her arm. The air between us had changed; it felt light, spacious, like I could truly breathe in it. "Now tell me what happened with dance."

"Oh, lord," she sighed. "It's dramatic."

"Tell me anyway."

It was a long story, starting with the tension between Maritza and Rona after the night they'd made out on Maritza's couch. The animosity between them had escalated in the last three weeks, but the other dance girls hadn't known why.

"Then we had a team sleepover last night," Maritza said. "My parents temporarily ungrounded me so I could go, because I lied and told them it was mandatory. We were playing Truth or Dare, and it was stupid stuff, you know, like Maggie had to answer which dance team dad she'd have sex with, and Brenna had to text this guy a picture of her bra. Then Rona was dared to kiss one of us, and the team picked *me*."

I gasped. "Oh god. Did you do it?"

"Of course not, that's the problem. Everyone was chanting *Kiss her, kiss her*, and I freaked and started yelling that I wasn't gonna do it. All the girls got really quiet, and they were looking at me funny, and Mary Glenn was like, 'It's not a big deal, Maritza, we're all a little on the spectrum.' They thought I was some kind of conservative, homophobic freak."

She paused; her expression was wounded.

"What'd you do?" I asked.

"Tried to tell them they had gotten it all wrong, that I just didn't like making a joke out of something that wasn't actually a joke, but no one would listen. They just kinda migrated away from me and started talking about what movie we should watch. So I grabbed my bag and got the hell out of that stupid-ass basement, and I ran out the front door so Mary's parents wouldn't see me, but then—well—"

"What?"

"Well—Vivien followed me out."

"Vivien *Chen?*"

"The one and only," Maritza said with a wry smile. "I was sitting there crying in my car, trying to calm down enough to drive, and all of a sudden she's tapping on my window. She gave me a really big hug and asked if I wanted to talk. I told her the truth about what had happened with Rona, and you know what she said? She said, 'Rona has no idea who she is or what she wants, but you do, and you can't let her take that from you.'"

"Wow," I breathed.

"And then . . ." Maritza's eyes grew bright. "She told me that a few months ago, she kissed a girl from her church. And that she was always here if I needed to talk."

"Hold on," I said. "Are you saying—Vivien Chen likes *girls*?!"

"I think she does," Maritza said, and the way she laughed was shy, almost blushing.

I stared at her. "Do you have a crush on Vivien Chen?"

She shook her head, but there was no denying her smile.

"Maritza!" I said, giddy with shock.

"She was texting me all day, asking how I was feeling. She kept sending me GIFs of *The Sandlot*."

I laughed, remembering the GIFs Lydia had sent in the beginning. "Oh yeah, this is definitely a thing."

Maritza shook her head. "Doesn't matter. I can't deal with those dance girls again."

"Of course you can. Vivien's right, you can't let Rona or anyone else take something you love away from you. You know that."

Maritza was quiet. "You know . . . this whole time, I thought that if I didn't make a constant effort to put myself out there, nothing would ever happen for me. For *any* of us. I was so worried about forcing things into existence that I didn't realize what was happening on its own." She took a deep breath. "I never should have forced things with Rona. I could feel in my gut that it wasn't right. And I shouldn't have tried to tell you and JaKory who you were or what you needed. You guys did a much better job figuring it out on your own."

We swiveled around to watch JaKory through the Waffle House

windows. He was talking animatedly, and I could see his smile even from here. Daveon was wearing his fedora.

"That damn fedora," Maritza said, clucking her tongue. "Anyway, I'm tired of all this emo bullshit. Are you in the mood for a coffee?"

She went inside to get us a cup while I wandered back over to Ricky and my brother. They were both sitting on the curb now, and I sat down next to them and let their conversation wash over me. When Maritza came back, she was carrying four coffees on a tray, and she handed them around to each of us.

"You'll get used to it," I told Grant, who had taken a sip and failed to hide his grimace. "It grows on you."

For a while we sat there in the humid night, watching cars pull in and out of the lot, counting the tired, grimy people who walked in through the doors and back out sometime later. There was one car that remained on the opposite side of the parking lot the whole time, which Maritza surmised must be Daveon's friends waiting for him.

At last, JaKory stepped out of the Waffle House with a boy about his size who wore glasses and a red flannel shirt, despite the peak July temperature. We watched as they walked over to the long-parked car, from which two people, a guy and a girl around our age, stepped out to shake JaKory's hand. It was obvious that JaKory and Daveon were wildly happy, that their giddy energy was spilling over into every gesture and grin.

"Our turn," Maritza whispered, as the four of them loped our way.

JaKory's smile was even happier up close. "Y'all, this is Daveon," he said, brushing his shoulder against the other boy's, "and his friends Kara and Julian."

We introduced ourselves to each other, everyone smiling and gripping hands almost like we had accompanied JaKory and Daveon to their wedding. Even my brother seemed excited.

"I'm so happy we got to meet you," I told Daveon, looking him square in the eye.

I could tell he was shy, but he looked right at me through his thick-framed glasses. "Me too," he said. "This whole night has been a dream."

Maritza was conferencing with JaKory. Based on their gestures, it looked like they were trying to work out some kind of plan. I was about to ask what was going on when JaKory took Daveon's hand and led him toward the back side of the truck.

"So," Maritza said, snapping the rest of us to attention, "how about we move over this way?"

The remaining six of us moved farther into the parking lot, forming a kind of protective barrier between the truck and the rest of the world. When I glanced around the truck bed, I could just see JaKory standing in the grass, his head close to Daveon's.

Leave it to Maritza to make sure JaKory got his kiss.

It was another ten minutes before Kara checked her watch and said they should get going. Reluctantly, we backed toward the car, none of us eager to make JaKory and Daveon say goodbye. Ricky stepped up and knocked gently on the hood of the truck.

JaKory lumbered back toward us, pulling Daveon behind him, their expressions sad and resistant.

Everyone said their goodbyes. I hugged Kara and Julian and gave an extra-long hug to Daveon. Finally, it was just JaKory and Daveon who had to say goodbye. They hugged each other hard while the rest of us examined the asphalt.

Our cars left the parking lot together, ours in the lead and the others' right behind it. JaKory kept his eyes on their car until it disappeared onto the opposite interstate. We were all very quiet.

"Well?" Maritza said finally.

"Well what?" JaKory said.

My brother whipped his head around. "Well, *how was it?*" he asked, and we all laughed.

JaKory shook his head and leaned against the window. He was smiling like I'd never seen before.

"Perfect," he said. "He was perfect."

We drove east into the gradually lightening sky, with only a handful of other cars on the interstate. The windows were down and the air rushed over my hair, strands of it catching on my eyelashes. The music was playing just loud enough to know it was there, but too softly to know the song.

We got back to our northern corner of Atlanta just as the sun was creeping up. We dropped JaKory off first, waving him out of Ricky's car in a daze. He stood in his driveway with the early-morning light coming over his face, and I didn't know whether it was my perception or not, but he looked like he was holding himself taller.

Maritza hesitated when we got to her house. She opened the door to get out but pulled back at the last minute and put her hand on Ricky's arm.

"Thanks for everything," she told him. "You're almost as good a driver as me."

Ricky laughed and squeezed her hand. "Bye, Maritza. I'll come watch you dance sometime!"

I followed her out of the car. We lingered in the driveway,

exchanging a knowing look, and then I hugged her. She hugged me back, and when she pulled away, her eyes were wet. Neither one of us said anything about it.

Then it was only Ricky, Grant, and me on the quiet drive back to our neighborhood, with the light growing stronger and the birds waking up. Ricky rolled his truck to a gentle stop in front of our house just as the sprinklers began to *spritz spritz spritz* on the neighbors' lawn. Grant made a show of shaking Ricky's hand, then got out of the truck and waited for me in the driveway.

"Will you be able to catch any sleep before church?" I asked Ricky.

"Not much," he said tiredly. "But it was worth it."

I wanted to say many things to him then—things that had grown inside me over the last two months as I'd gotten to know him and his world better—but I knew those things weren't necessary to say aloud. Instead I looked at my friend and gave him a tired smile.

"Feel like a dumbass teenager?" he said.

"Something like that."

"'Night, Codi."

"'Night, Ricky."

I followed my brother down the driveway and around to the basement. We slipped into the house and up to our rooms, and he gave me a single wave before he shut himself behind his door.

I put on my pajamas, crawled into bed, and fell asleep to the birds singing.

21

THE LAST DAY OF SUMMER BURNED HOT LIKE ONLY August can. By ten A.M., it was scorching outside, the sun so fierce that even walking to the mailbox was a chore. The trees and flowers were past the point of bloom and had crossed over to the first stages of wilting and withering.

Thank god we had the pool. There were hardly any kids there that day, probably because they were being yanked around on last-minute trips for school clothes, binders, and mechanical pencils. There was an old couple I'd never seen before who looked unapologetically pleased about the start of the school year, a group of middle-school boys who had no doubt ditched their moms for one last day of dunking each other's heads in the deep end, and one family whose toddler was obviously too young for kindergarten. And then there was us.

Maritza and JaKory weren't there yet, but they were on their way and had promised us snacks and a fruit tray from Publix. Maritza had texted that she was letting JaKory drive her car. He wanted to practice now that he was applying for his license, but there was one major downside Maritza hadn't anticipated:

Maritza Vargas: *He claims the driver gets to control the music, and this punk won't stop playing emo Troye Sivan songs*

For now, it was just the four of us: Ricky, Cliff, Lydia, and me. Ricky had finally told Cliff about his liking boys—and Tucker—and Cliff was making a show of embracing it.

"I always thought Leo DiCaprio was a handsome motherfucker," he told Ricky, as if they were sizing up football recruits. "I probably wouldn't say no if he tried to kiss me. I mean, if he tried to go beyond that, I don't think I'd—"

"Dude," Ricky said, cutting him off. "You don't have to go there."

"I'm just saying, we're all a little gay, aren't we?" Cliff asked. "I can see the appeal of Tucker. Dude has some serious throwing arms."

"Yeah, it's his 'throwing arms' that really do it for me," Ricky muttered. He rolled his eyes, but I could tell that he loved being able to talk freely in front of his best friend.

"Whatever, bro," Cliff yawned, lying back in his lounge chair. "Just make sure you don't go out with any dickheads at UGA. Whatever guys you choose to date, they'd better be able to hang."

"Aren't you and Tucker gonna keep dating?" Lydia interrupted, rubbing sunscreen onto my shoulders.

"I don't know," Ricky said, biting his lip. "Clemson's only an hour-and-a-half drive from Athens, but I'm worried we'll get caught up in our own stuff . . ."

Lydia turned quiet, rubbing more sunscreen into my neck. She and I hadn't talked about what would happen when she left for GCSU in ten days' time.

Maritza and JaKory got there then, and to my surprise, Maritza had brought someone with her. Vivien Chen was prettier than I remembered, or maybe I had just never paid attention to her before. Today, as she walked over to us carrying the fruit tray in her hands, she was smiling generously. She was also, I noticed, wearing one of Maritza's favorite shirts.

"Does everyone know Vivien?" Maritza asked, trying to play it cool.

Lydia caught my eye. I'd told her everything about the drive to Alabama, including Maritza's surprising development with Vivien, and she'd quickly become a big fan of "Vivitza," as she called them. She winked at me and sprung up from our chair to welcome Vivien with a hug. She couldn't have been any cuter.

It had taken a little while to get to this point. Maritza and JaKory weren't exactly gunning to be buddy-buddy with my new friends, but they had warmed up to Ricky and Lydia over the last two weeks. Ricky had even come out to them, which was a grander gesture than any I could have expected from him.

The seven of us stayed there all afternoon, swimming and tanning and picking at the snacks. We played Categories in the pool and Never Have I Ever on the lounge chairs. When an ice-cream truck came by, I used my surplus money from Totes-n-Goats to buy ice cream for all of us.

"God bless those dancing-pig cocktail napkins," Ricky said, taking a bite of his Drumstick cone. "They really came through for you."

We stayed until we could no longer deny it was dinnertime. Ricky and Cliff left first, clasping each other's hands by Cliff's truck. Cliff scooped the rest of us into hugs, even Maritza and JaKory, who startled before they hugged him back. Ricky followed suit with his own round of hugs, and the sight of him squeezing my two best friends made my throat ache in the best way.

"Hope your first day is awesome," Ricky said as he let me go. "Are you still coming by to paint my portrait afterward?"

"Only if Cliff's there to talk about gay stuff," I teased.

"Shut up. Don't waste the first day of senior year, Codi, all right? Or any of it."

"I hear you."

"And tell Grant I said hi."

"I will."

We loitered by the cars after they left. JaKory walked off when he got a call from Daveon, a grin on his face before he'd even answered, and then it was just Lydia, Maritza, Vivien, and me.

"I'm staying on dance team," Maritza told me, rolling her eyes but smiling. She gave Vivien a look.

"What?" I asked.

Vivien grinned. "I had a little chat with Rona. Apparently she's terrified of me? Yeah, I don't know, I've been told I come off as intimidating. Anyway, I told her to leave Maritza alone."

Maritza smiled the same way JaKory was smiling these days. "Turns out dating the captain has its perks."

"Have you told your team?" Lydia asked.

"Hell no," Maritza said. "We're trying to fuck with them, see how long it takes them to catch on."

"Most likely the entire year," Vivien said, and Maritza laughed and kissed her on the cheek, which was the most un-Maritza-ish thing I'd ever seen.

"*Vivitza*," Lydia cheered under her breath, raising her fist in a victory pump, and Maritza rolled her eyes and smiled bigger than ever.

"I'll see you tomorrow," I said as JaKory came back over to the group. "Meet at my locker?"

"Yeah," JaKory said hastily. "I'm bringing copies of my curated summer reading list. I laminated them and everything. Mrs. Barley's going to hate me. But Daveon—"

"Daveon loves you," I finished. "We know."

"I was going to say Daveon added a couple of suggestions," Ja-Kory said. "But yeah, same thing."

We split off between the cars, the other three jumping into Maritza's—she didn't let JaKory drive this time—and Lydia and me into hers. It was baked with heat, and for a minute we sat with the doors open and the AC blasting, coughing and wiping the sweat off our faces.

"Precious Vivitza," Lydia said wistfully. "Reminds me of when we first met."

"No way, we're cuter than them," I said, grabbing her hand.

She pretended to think about it, her face screwed up comically. "You know what?" she said, turning to me. "You're right, we are."

We didn't talk on the short drive back to my house. We were that summer-sun kind of exhausted, and I was content just to sit there holding her hand. I'd held her hand for almost two hours the night before, when I'd taken her to the movies. We'd done all the classic date-night things: the popcorn, the shared soda straw, the making out in the car afterward. It had been like something out of a teen dating PSA, and as I'd lain there in the back seat of my car, making out with Lydia on top of me, I thought of how Mrs. Wexler, my seventh-grade sex ed teacher, had never been able to describe to the girls what would happen to our bodies when we were turned on. If I had known Lydia then, I wouldn't have found the whole thing so mysterious.

The garage doors were up and both my parents' cars were in their spaces. When we sat down to dinner tonight, they would launch into their usual start-of-the-school-year speech, emphasizing good grades, good behavior, and trying new things. I was pretty sure I'd have that last part covered.

"I hope you have the best first day," Lydia said, idling her car in my driveway. "I can't wait to hear all about it."

"I'll come see you tomorrow night," I said, kissing her goodbye. "We can go for a drive."

We were putting off the conversation we needed to have about whether we'd keep dating, and I knew that; but in that moment, with the thrill of a new school year fresh in my stomach, I was too hopeful to be afraid. Whatever happened with Lydia and me over the coming year, I knew I'd be able to handle it, and so would she. We were braver than we'd been two months ago.

Lydia kissed me long and slow, her hand on my face, her hair still wet from the pool. I squeezed her hand and got out of the car, waving as she backed out of the driveway.

My parents were lounging in the family room, watching their favorite news program. They told me dinner would be on the table in twenty minutes. I hurried up to my room, keen on taking a hot shower, but before I could do more than shrug off my pool towel, there was a knock on my bedroom door.

Grant was standing there, looking perplexed. He crossed his arms and opened his mouth to speak, but no words came out.

"What's up?" I asked. "What's wrong?"

He shuffled into my room. "I didn't mean to see, but my window looks over the driveway—"

"Oh god . . ." I said, rolling my head back and covering my eyes. "You and that damn window."

"Is that the girl who was in your bed? Is she the person you took the popcorn to?"

I hesitated. This was supposed to be a big moment for my brother and me, and part of me still wasn't ready for it.

Grant searched my expression, waiting for an explanation—not just about Lydia, but about me. I was probably never going to be ready for this conversation, but after everything that had happened between Grant and me this summer, I knew he'd earned a bit of faith.

"Yeah," I said finally. "Her name's Lydia."

"And you're dating her?" Grant asked.

I tried to keep my expression cool. "Yeah, I am."

"Do Mom and Dad know?"

"No. Just us."

My brother considered this. He nodded, and I knew what question was coming next.

"How did you—?"

I expected any variation of *How did you know, How did you come to terms with it, How did you hide it this whole time*, but I guess that goes to show that I still had a lot to learn about my brother, because the question that came out was "How did you know she liked you?"

I blinked. "What?"

"What if—you know, what if you can't tell if a girl likes you?"

He asked it cavalierly, his eyes on my wallpaper like it didn't matter—but I remembered that night at the movies, and the skinny girl he'd nearly kissed.

"She does like you," I said.

"What?"

"The girl from the movie theater, with the long brown hair and the braces, right? She likes you, I could tell."

My brother blushed. The corners of his mouth twitched. "Uh, actually . . . I'm talking about a different girl. I met her at orientation on Thursday, and Darin and Ryan and I hung out with her and her friends yesterday."

I laughed in surprise. "Damn, Grant, you've got all the prospects."

He glanced away, trying to hide his grin. "So how do I know if she likes me?"

"You just do. Hang out with her long enough, get to know her as a friend, and you'll know it in your gut if she likes you. Or bring her around Maritza, JaKory, and me, and we'll figure it out for you."

He shook his head. "No, no, that's okay. I'll just . . . yeah, I'll just keep hanging out with her. Thanks."

He shuffled back out of my room, closing the door behind him.

I stood there in wonder for a moment, shaking my head at all of it, until a laugh bubbled out of my throat. Then I went to take a shower before I ran out of time.

ACKNOWLEDGMENTS

FIRST: NONE OF THIS COULD HAVE HAPPENED WITH-out my fearless agent, Marietta Zacker. Your heart for Codi, Ricky, Maritza, and JaKory has driven this entire thing from October 2017 through today. Thank you for your fierce advocacy and steady faith. Additional thanks to Erin Casey and the team at GZLA.

I prayed for an editor who would understand the heart of this book while knowing how to make it better, and I received just that. Mekisha Telfer, you are literally a godsend. You took a heartfelt but anemic manuscript and knew exactly where it needed lifeblood. I'm so grateful for your brilliance, your vision, your instincts, and your kindness.

Annie Quindlen and Kim Quindlen (Ruane or whatever), thanks for being so game to read my drafts and offer feedback. I'm grate-ful to my other early readers: Debbie Savino, Sean Ruane, Meaghan "Fashion Secrets" Quindlen, Haley Neer (who wants people to know she's single), Adrienne Tooley, Marquise Thomas, and Sana

"The Dark Lord" Saiyed. Ruqayyah Strozier, your critique was especially helpful. Hurry up and finish your book. And Sarah Cropley, I couldn't have gotten inside Codi's artist brain without you. Thank you for sharing your talents.

I'm lucky to have an amazing hometown community. My deepest thanks to my FFF ATL family, especially Kathy Farrell, who always knows the way forward, and Casey Long, fairy gaymother extraordinaire. Julia B. and Dr. C., thank you for helping me be the healthiest version of myself while I wrote this novel. Decatur Writers Studio, I wish you had more parking, but I'm thankful for your classes and community-building. Thanks to Joshilyn Jackson, whose writing class I took at DWS in winter 2018, and to my critique partners, Kimberly Hays de Muga, Kay Heath, and Cassie Gonzalez.

I've wanted to write books my whole life. Thank you to three special teachers who nurtured and sharpened my writing talents: Mrs. Judy Miller, St. Louis School in Pittsford, New York; Mrs. Sandy Bensky, Singapore American School; and Professor Teresa Goddu, Vanderbilt University.

The beating heart of this story is friendship, so I'd be remiss if I didn't thank my amazing friends. To my HR girls, QTCs, Spewies, Vandy gang, Keops krew, Louisiana loves, and Atlanta fam (even you, Thomas), thank you for being you. Special shout-out to my siblings, Kim, Michael, and Annie, for being my Day One best friends.

Melissa Correa, thank you for being my ride-or-die through this whole thing. The teenage version of me would have been ecstatic to know you'd walk into my life someday. You are Maritza's roller-coaster drop, JaKory's poetry, Ricky's kindergarten friend, and Lydia's green house. You are Codi's renewed belief that she deserves good things. I couldn't love you more.

More than anything, thank you to my family. Aunt Tish and Uncle Stephen kept me well fed and laughing while I worked on revisions down the Shore; Aunt Meggie and Uncle Bobby did the same while I worked on the second round of revisions over Christmas. To all the Quindlens and Kearneys, especially Grandmom, Grandpop, Mom-Mom, and Pop-Pop, I wouldn't be who I am or where I am without you. A special note of gratitude to my godmother, Aunt Patty, to whom this book is dedicated.

Mom and Dad, you encouraged my writing passion from the time I was six years old. Thanks for acting like it was totally normal that I spent the majority of my high school years writing Harry Potter fanfic in the basement. I couldn't have done this without you. Love you so much.

Finally: Maryse Alexandre was there the day I got the call that this book would be published. I wish you could be here to see it in print. I miss you all the time.